# Lightscape

A novel by

Emily K. Karlewicz

To Evan, with all my love.

"Every good and perfect gift is from above, coming down from the Father of the heavenly lights, who does not change like the shifting shadows."

**James 1:17**

## Preface

**The wind was blowing hard the night I left.** I remember because the grass on the hills swayed violently, with each fragile blade bending and screaming in total chaos. It wasn't the grass that was in anguish, although it might have looked that way. No, the only living thing I knew that felt such absolute despair and confusion...was me.

I willingly turned my back and drove away from him; the one person who had ever truly loved me and wanted me. As if it was nothing...as if he *meant* nothing. Yeah sure, he had told me to go. He had begged me to go, but I shouldn't have listened.

I should have been strong enough to stand up and face it. I should have been strong enough to stay, for him. But I was a coward, and I did the only thing I knew, the only thing I was good at. I ran.

# Chapter 1

**It was late April, and the sky reflecting off the white-capped waves of the bay was a beautiful clear blue**. Not a single cloud was present in the vast space above my head, and the sun glistened off of every dew dropped flower...the perfect day. I should have known that this day would be different. Special.

I was sitting on my favorite bench beside the beach, doodling in my sketchbook when it hit me. Who would have thought that a Frisbee to the head could hurt so badly, but it did. The collision knocked me out of my reverie, and knocked my sketchbook out of my hands. After a few unpleasant words escaped my mouth I reached down to retrieve my book, and that's when I realized I wasn't alone.

There he was, kneeling in front of me with a sheepish smile on his face, and my sketchbook in his hands. Usually I hated it when people tried to look at my private sketches, but I wasn't thinking about that just then. I was thinking of his smile.

It was confident and beautiful, and probably the most symmetrical mouth I had ever seen. He had two perfectly plump lips with a set of just as perfect dazzling white teeth. It was intoxicatingly flawless, and I would have been happy to continue staring at it all day, except that I was diverted by the peculiar emotion visible on his face.  He looked guilty, apologetic, but why?

What did he have to be sorry for?

I crinkled my forehead in contemplation, but I couldn't think properly.  My head was hurting too much from the...

"That was your Frisbee?" I asked the handsome stranger, lifting my hand to rub the sore spot on my head.

"Yeah, sorry about that," he apologized.  "I thought I had it.  Are you okay?"

"Yeah," I shrugged, dropping my hand to my lap and fiddling with my pencil. "It... you just startled me, but I don't think there's any permanent damage."

With a rueful grin he slowly stood, giving me the opportunity to check out the rest of his appearance, which had gone completely unnoticed until then due to his rather distracting mouth.

Tall and slender in his long sleeve polo and jeans, he towered over my small frame.  His muscular arms were visible beneath the fabric of his shirt.  He was strong.  Although it was just barely spring, his olive complexion was nicely tanned, unlike my pale, freckled skin, and the highlights in his short sandy blonde hair glinted brightly in the light of the sunny day.

"I think you dropped this before," he said, holding out my

drawings and distracting me from the perusal of his gorgeous body.

"My sketchbook! Thanks," I said, taking it from him and shoving it under my arm.

"Don't mention it."

There it was again, that smile. It automatically made me feel at ease and it made me smile too. I was all of a sudden very brave.

"So, do you spend most of your time hitting girls with Frisbees when they're not looking?"

Where did that come from?

He half smiled, half smirked at my comment, and then answered, "Only the pretty ones."

That definitely shocked me, and I blushed. Something I didn't do often since talking to boys was a very uncommon occurrence for me. I must have done it wrong too, because his face changed suddenly. It became hard, and he was no longer smiling. I knew that I had blown it. I was always messing things up.

"Maybe we started this all wrong," he said. "Let's pretend like this never happened."

I knew it.

Then out of nowhere he took a step forward, and asked, "Can we try it again?" and for the third time in less than a few minutes he captivated me with a smile so strong and warm that I blushed for the second time.

What was wrong with me?

I had no idea how to handle this type of situation, so I just stood up, extended my hand to him, and said, "Hi, I'm Selkie."

"Hi, Selkie. It's nice to meet you. I'm Aidan."

He extended his own hand, gently grasping mine in his, and what happened next was so surprising that I actually gasped. His hand touching mine sent tingles down my spine and made my heart race. I even thought I felt sweat beading behind my neck. It was as if I had received an electric shock...and then it was gone. Although my arm was still outstretched toward him, he no longer held my hand. I lowered my arm and looked at his face. For a mere second I could have sworn his face looked almost feverish, but then it was gone as quickly as it had appeared and only his smile remained.

This was so strange.

I was glad when he started to speak again. It helped take my mind off what had just occurred between us.

"So, Selkie, that's an interesting name."

Interesting. Yeah, I'd heard that before, along with weird,

strange, funny, and stupid.  I mean, let's face it, *most* girls grew up with normal names like Mary or Susan, with parents that loved them and wanted them...but I wasn't like most girls.

My parents, who obviously never cared a lick about me, left me alone to grow up with a name that everyone else loved to make fun of.  At the age of nine, tired of being tormented everyday by other children, I went to the library to research my interesting name, and discovered that it was derived from some ancient Irish myth about a female seal that could shed its pelt and become human.  At first, I thought that the story was kind of creepy, but then I put it all together.  My pale skin, my red hair, and my unusual yet authentic Irish name.  I had finally found a piece of my past that for so long had been empty and uncertain.  I was Irish.  I wasn't just an orphan with no connections or things of her own anymore.  I had a true bond to something or somewhere on this earth that no one could ever take away from me.

I lifted my chin and looked Aidan straight in the eye. "You say interesting...I say different."

Aidan smiled and leaned forward slightly. "Different is good."

On impulse I leaned away from him and hugged my sketchbook tight against my chest.  He noticed my retreat and quickly changed the subject.

"So...you're an artist then."

It wasn't a question.

"No, not really," I replied. "It's just something that makes me happy. I'm not very good at it."

"Mind if I take a look?"

I automatically grimaced and closed myself off. I wasn't used to letting people in, to showing people my feelings. My sketches were a part of me somehow. It was hard to explain, but whenever bad things happened in my life, and there had been a few, I could always open my sketchbook and draw a world that was full of joy and beauty and hope.

Whenever I set my pencil to the page, it felt like I was home. Safe. No one could touch me, or hurt me, or leave me. It was just me inside a dream world.

Now this stranger was asking to be admitted into this fantasy of mine. To enter into the one place that only one other person in my life had ever traversed. He wouldn't have known it, but it was like he had asked me to rip open my chest and give him my beating heart.

Almost every part of me wanted to leave, just turn around and walk away. It would be easier. I had done it before. Countless times. Almost every part of me wanted that...but there was another part, small and uncertain, hidden far away where I didn't even know where it was, that was yearning to show him; to give him just a glimpse of the real me. It was the same place that still trembled from that first electric touch.

So I gave in. I released the tension that had built up inside of me from his request and slowly opened up my chest, retrieving my most valuable and fragile treasure. As I freed my inner self I felt a rush of fear, but pushed it aside. For some reason I trusted him.

Be gentle with me, I thought, before I handed him my soul. As he took the book, it was as if he understood completely. He held it tenderly in his large hands, and then he opened to the picture I had just finished sketching prior to the Frisbee attack.

The picture showed a large magnolia tree in full bloom. Tiny pink petals lay scattered around the base of the trunk. Vibrant green grass surrounded the tree and small patches of yellow daffodils and purple wild flowers were dispersed through the field. The sky was clear and untainted by clouds.

While he examined my picture I closed my eyes, imagining the world I had created in my book. A sense of peace and calmness filled me. I slowly opened my eyes and looked around. The picture I had drawn was very similar to the world outside of my sketchbook. It really was the perfect day.

I turned to Aidan expecting him to be engrossed in the book still. Instead he was staring at me. I returned his gaze ready for whatever would come next.

"It's beautiful," he said.

And I knew he meant it.

"You're a very talented artist. What a beautiful vision of the world you have. I haven't seen anything like it before."

"Are you a fan of art?" I asked.

"You might say that."

"Well, in that case. Thank you."

"You're welcome."

Aidan beamed at me, and then cautiously took a step forward. This time I didn't cower, but just smiled back at him, unable to hide my newfound confidence.

"Hey Aidan, what's taking you so long?" inquired a voice from behind me.

I quickly turned my head to discover three sweaty guys striding briskly toward us with looks of impatience. Though they were clearly friends of Aidan their faces were strange to me, and I found myself slowly retreating back inside myself, fleeing from the onslaught of unwelcome fears and emotions.

I also found myself again with my sketchbook. Had I taken it back, or had Aidan given it to me? I quickly glanced in his direction and his face said it all. A moment of understanding flickered between us, and I felt even more attuned to him.

How strange to feel so close to a person I had barely met.

As his friends came near, Aidan's smile faltered. "I guess...I should be going," he said uncertainly. "But it was very nice to meet you...Selkie."

The way he said my name was as if he was singing it, a tune that only reverberated in the short space between our two bodies.

He was leaving.

"Wait," I said before I even knew what I was doing. "Is that it? I mean, what I meant to say was...well...you did just hit me with a Frisbee!"

What a stupid thing to say.

That smile that I had grown to love in such a brief time began to appear once more. "Your right, I did."

"Well aren't you going to make it up to me?"

"What would you suggest?"

"Well, I come here often...and it does get pretty lonely sometimes. I wouldn't mind some company. Maybe some company that happens to like art."

I was vaguely aware I was blushing, and that Aidan was not the only one watching this exchange, but I didn't care. I was being reckless with my thoughts and my heart, and I felt alive for the first time in my life.

As I spoke my request, Aidan's face was almost unreadable. So many emotions seemed to play off it in such a short time. I recognized a few. Excitement. Curiosity. Anticipation. And one that was confusing to me, because I thought the last few minutes had been the best of my life. The feeling was pain, or sadness, or something that had no name, but then it was gone and his smile was once again his most admirable and prominent feature.

Finally he took a deep breath, and said, "How about tomorrow?"

When he spoke, it could have been my imagination, but it seemed as if his friends all seemed to react all at once, and I swear the looks on their faces were filled with disapproval. As if they found me unworthy of his attention. I even thought I heard one of them grunt his displeasure, but none of them actually spoke or took a step in our direction. Aidan didn't seem to notice, so I guess it was nothing.

We quickly said our goodbyes, agreeing to meet again at the park the next day, and then his friends, who didn't give me another glance, whisked him in the direction of the parking lot. I stood beside my bench, my arms wrapped tightly around my sketchbook, and watched as Aidan piled into the car with the others.

As they drove away, I was overwhelmed by a strange tinge of sudden loneliness, as if all the warmth from our electric encounter had burned a hole through me leaving me empty, and only he could fill it up again.

## Chapter 2

**As I walked home, I found myself almost in a trance.** I had a strange feeling in my chest that I had never experienced, which seemed to tickle my ribs and cause me to laugh out loud without my permission. I was lightheaded; yet I felt as if I could run miles with the amount of energy that was stirring inside of me. To think that in a few short minutes my very being had utterly transformed—My old self gone in the blink of an eye. I was happy to send it on its way; to make room for all the joy and peace his mere presence bestowed on me.

Could this be what love feels like?

It couldn't be. I barely knew him. I didn't even know his last name, and even if it was—love—he couldn't feel the same.

Could he?

Well it wasn't just my feelings that had sent me into this daze. If it had been, I doubt I'd have the courage to admit them even to myself. No, it was his every word and action that made me confident he felt it too. There was no way he could deny the riveting shock that pulsed between us.

As I stood at the main intersection of town, my eyes began to take in more of my surroundings. The sun lay low in the sky, and various shades of pink and orange streaked the horizon.

Spring was beginning to be visible in all the plants and trees that grew strong, regardless of the buildings that smothered them.

Although the town of Belfast, Maine was considered small, I always felt like it was growing too fast. Every year a new business was built, slowly deteriorating the beautiful landscape that I called home.

A light breeze suddenly blew past, filling my nose with the familiar smell of the Penobscot Bay. I loved living near the ocean. Another thing I guess I could thank my parents for, if only they hadn't left me here alone.

I crossed the street and headed in the direction of my apartment. It was a short walk from the park to my home, one that I did almost every day. As I turned the corner at Main Street and Cedar, I was surprised to find the entire road and both sidewalks blocked. There appeared to be some kind of accident involving a telephone pole and several cars farther up the street. The police weren't letting anyone through, which meant I would have to find a new route home. I decided to walk a few more blocks up before cutting over and getting back on the right road.

As I walked on, I continued to daydream of Aidan. His smile...his voice...the feel of his soft hand. I could have been lost in my head for hours, but if I wanted to make it home before dark I would have to start paying attention to where I was going.

I had wandered off from the part of town I was familiar

with and found myself on a rather neglected side street. The buildings were older and made of a red brick, which once might have been vibrant, but now were worn and weather-beaten. It looked like the establishments that had once occupied those now ragged walls were no longer in business.

The streetlamps for the next few blocks were out, unfortunately, giving me more proof of the street's lack of activity. The path was eerie and unwelcoming. I decided to cut my losses and head back the way I came. It wouldn't add much time to my trip, and it was better to be safe than sorry. I had probably gone too far down the street already.

I had just begun to turn around when out of the corner of my eye something stirred within the shadows. A quick gasp escaped my lips and my whole body tensed. As I stood there frozen in place, a curiosity began to form inside my head, and it urged me to move closer.

With trepidation I slowly stepped forward, and as I stared into the darkness, I wasn't sure, but I thought I could make out the figure of a man. A strong gust of wind blew past me, knocking me to the side, and that's when the thing within the shadows took a step forward.

I might have been overreacting, but I suddenly found myself running. Running faster than I had ever thought was possible. My heart began to work harder and my breath became labored. I was vaguely aware that whatever I had left behind was running too, and gaining on me. It was very close. I had at least a few more blocks to go before I would hit civilization, and whatever energy I had left was dwindling.

Suddenly, a bright light obscured my vision and I stumbled. Before I could correct myself my knees slammed into the pavement. My hands were next, meeting the hard concrete with such impact that my eyes instantly started to water. There was a second of uncomfortable pain, and then I was up again, running even faster than before. The light was still blindingly bright, but I staggered on.

Then out of nowhere a car sped past me, honking its horn in protest, and at the same moment the light was gone. I skidded to a stop nearly falling over again. My heart was pounding out of my chest and my hands and knees were burning from the fall. I couldn't go any farther. I slammed my back against a nearby building, nearly knocking the wind out of me and collapsed to the ground. I knew I only had seconds before whatever was chasing me finally caught up.

But nothing ever came.

I sat there slumped against the wall and listened as my heart began to slow and my breathing returned to normal. The seconds ticked on and still nothing came. My body relaxed, but my mind was still racing.

What had happened? Just a minute ago I was running for

my life. Wasn't I? It felt so real, so raw, could I have only imagined it?

I started to process in my head what had happened. It was dark, and I saw something move in the shadows. It was shaped like a man, I thought, but seemed too large, too oddly formed. The shadows seemed to move and change, never settling on a definite figure. I couldn't quite make it out, but what I thought was some big, scary monster out to get me could have also just been a deception of the night; my imagination playing tricks on me. Which one was more logical?

Then there was that strange light, but again I thought of what was more plausible and remembered the car. As it drove by me the light had vanished instantly, and so it must have just been the car's headlights that I saw. Perhaps I had let my imagination run wild, and what did I have to show for it but a banged-up knee, bleeding hands, and a ridiculous story to tell once I got home.

I sat there for a few more seconds wondering how I could have been so stupid, then finally pushed myself up and continued home. The rest of the trip was surprisingly uneventful, and I managed to make it to my door without another incident.

Leaning down I retrieved the hidden key from beneath the grimy doormat and slid the key into the lock. As usual it was jammed. So I had to give it a few jiggles before it would unlatch.

As I pushed the door open, suddenly very aware of how tired I was, a strong smell of incense and smoke wafted toward me. I had always hated the stuff, but my roommate and best friend Tabitha swore it helped her think clearly. She must have been trying to write the next *War and Peace* because the room was filled with so much smoke and fragrance I could barely breathe. I immediately walked to the kitchen window and propped it open, taking in a deep breath of fresh air, before turning to find Tabitha lounging on the couch in her pajamas, reading a trashy tabloid.

Looking very comfortable in her oversized sweatpants and hoodie, she had propped herself up using lots of pillows, and her long legs were sprawled out in front of her. With her face resting in her hands, she leaned toward her magazine, balancing her weight on her elbows, while her smooth caramel brown hair fell forward covering her lightly bronzed face.

I glanced over at the clock. It was after eight already. I was exhausted. Then I remembered that it was Sunday, and my mind quickly changed from thoughts of sleep, to thoughts of irritation.

"Tabitha, I thought you were supposed to be at work?"

"Well, hello to you too," she said without even looking up.

I frowned. She was always doing this. "Oh, I'm sorry. Hello Tabitha, how are you? Have you been sitting here all day, because I thought you were supposed to be at work?"

"I wasn't feeling well earlier," she half spat at me. "So I decided to call in sick."

"But you're feeling better now?"

She rolled her eyes at my question. "Obviously."

I was starting to get really upset, just like every other time we had this conversation, which lately seemed to be very often. "Honestly Tabitha, how do you expect us to pay our rent if you can't even get your lazy butt off the couch and go to work?"

She finally removed her gaze from the page she was reading and looked me square in the face. "You know how much I hate working there," she retorted.

That was almost an understatement. From the moment we both applied to work at the local grocery store, Tabitha made it clear that she hated the idea. However, when you're an eighteen-year-old orphan newly emancipated from the state, with no money and no degree, you take whatever you can get.

We were both instantly hired. I guess no one else wanted to work there either. Ever since then all she ever did was complain and find ways to ditch, but that's the kind of person she was, when things got tough, or in this case boring, she did all she could to get out of it. It was a defense mechanism. It was one reason we got along so well, we were both good at running.

I met Tabitha almost seven years ago when we were placed with the same foster family. We were both exceedingly shy, neither one of us good at making friends, and so we kept each other at a distance for a while. That is until the day Tabitha came across my sketches and realized we had a common bond.

Tabitha had always loved music. When she was nine she got a guitar through a Christmas charity event, and for the next few years she spent all her time teaching herself how to play. By the age of eleven she could read any kind of music you put in front of her, and had even written a few of her own songs. She was a true artist, and the day she found my drawings she knew I was an artist too. From then on there was no getting away from her.

After two years together, most of it spent hiding away in our rooms, we were removed from our foster family after they realized we weren't the kind of kids they wanted to adopt. They said we were too detached, that we would never open up and be comfortable. But who could be comfortable in a house that wasn't theirs? How could you get to know someone when you knew they wouldn't be there for long?

Tabitha and I were sent to different houses, and spent the next few years hopping from home to home. We kept in touch over the phone, and swore to each other regularly that we would remain friends no matter what. On my eighteenth birthday, I left my foster family and asked Tabitha to move in with me, and by the end of the day we had the lease to our apartment, and a new chance at life. In the end, after all the instability, our friendship was our only constant; it was the one thing that we had to hold on to.

We could have sat there all night, each trying to convince the other that we were right, but neither one of us would budge. I loved Tabitha like she was my real sister, but sometimes she really annoyed me. If I had to choose between working at a place I despised or having money for my next meal, well the choice was simple. She didn't agree with me. Sometimes she could be a real brat.

Much too tired to argue I decided to leave the fight for another day and go to bed, but as I turned to leave the living room Tabitha noticed the scrapes on my hands. I had almost forgotten about the bizarre story I had to tell her.

"Wait. A. Minute." she said as I finished describing my encounter with Aidan. "Are you telling me you talked to a boy?"

She was as astounded by that fact as I was. I simply nodded my head and smiled. She returned the smile, but said nothing else.

I quickly moved on to the incident in the street, but when I spoke about the "monster" in the shadows she just laughed at me, and said, "I always knew you were crazy," before standing up and heading to the kitchen for a snack.

Practically asleep on my feet, all I wanted to do was climb under my covers and go to sleep, but instead I followed Tabitha into the kitchen. There was still one more thing I had to do before passing out, and I was certain Tabitha wasn't going to like it.

"I need to ask you for a favor," I told her, leaning on the counter for support.

She looked at me with her kind eyes and had no idea what I was about to ask her, or else she wouldn't have looked at me so nicely.

"Okay, so here's the thing," I said nervously. "I promised Aidan we would meet tomorrow afternoon. Only I'm suppose to work from…"

"Oh, *Hell* no," Tabitha interrupted, already fully aware of what I wanted.

"Oh come on! Please Tabs, just this once," I begged. "I wouldn't ask you to do it if it wasn't important."

"Important to who?" she countered. "I know your love life sucks, but working your shift tomorrow would suck even more." She paused for a moment, considering something, and then said with a smile, "Unless there was something in it for me."

I should have known she would make this difficult.

Frustrated, I gazed around the room to try and find

something to bribe her with, and that's when my eyes landed on the perfect bargaining chip.

"How about some new strings for your guitar?"

Two of the strings had broken last week, and she didn't have money to replace them. I knew she was dying to get new ones so she could play again.

"I've been saving up for some new pencils," I said, walking over to her guitar and strumming the four remaining strings, "but the money is all yours if you would do this one thing for me."

I knew I had her. I could see it in her eyes as I lazily strummed my hand against the strings, but I knew she wouldn't show defeat so easy. She was incredibly stubborn.

Tabitha stood there pretending to reflect over my offer as I continued to pluck at the strings, until finally she gave in, and sighed, "Fine. I guess I can fill in tomorrow, but this is going to be the only time."

"I promise, the only time," I said, giving her a hug. "And hey, who knows, maybe he won't even show up, and then you won't have to worry about it at all," I added jokingly.

She looked at me more seriously for a moment. "Why do you always do that?"

"Do what?"

"You know what. As soon as something good starts happening to you, you start thinking about all the bad that could happen too."

"Well that's because it usually does," I shrugged.

"Selkie, just relax and enjoy this, for once," she said, placing her hands on my shoulders. "It will be so much better if you do."

I took a deep breath and instantly relaxed. Sure, Tabitha could be selfish and obnoxious sometimes, but she also had a huge heart. She knew just what to say to calm me down.

She wasn't lying to me either. She didn't say those things just to relax me. She meant them. What's more, I knew she was right. Something told me that this time would be different. I wasn't going to let my fears of the past dictate my future any longer.

Giving Tabitha another quick squeeze, I wished her goodnight for the second time, and then stumbled to my room to put on my pajamas. Ignoring the need to brush my teeth, I peeled back my covers and hopped into bed, and by the time my head hit the pillow I was already drooling.

Everything started as a blur, bright colors swirling beneath my eyelids. Then the blur began to transform and undistinguishable shapes began to appear. Slowly a picture came into view. I was sitting on the bench in the park. My sketchbook lay beside me, unopened. Sunbeams danced across my face, and I was smiling.

I stood and began to walk forward. Colors whirled again and the picture changed. I was in a field. My hands lightly grazing the tall grass as I walked through. Off in the distance stood a man. He lifted his arms in my direction, beckoning me to him. As the sun touched his face, I saw his smile, and my heart began to melt. Aidan was waiting for me. I began to run, and as I reached him I launched myself into his strong arms. He pulled me close and lightly brushed his perfect lips against my forehead. I felt at home in his warm embrace.

Then without warning the sun was gone, and fog rose from beneath the ground, surrounding us. The darkness engulfed me and I was alone. The heat that radiated from Aidan's touch was gone. The air was cold now, sending shivers down my spine. I looked around and found myself on the deserted street. I was looking once again into the shadows.

The darkness began to rush forward as if to swallow me up. I turned to run, but it was everywhere. I was trapped. I frantically began to fight against the darkness, flailing my arms and legs. I struggled to break free, but as my body encountered the shadows I was filled with fear, and then a face appeared within them, and I screamed.

## Chapter 3

**I awoke to Tabitha's gentle hands violently shaking my shoulders.**

"Selkie, wake up!" she yelled.

"Wh-what's wrong?" I slurred. "Why are you shaking me?"

"Because you were screaming so loud, I thought you would wake up the whole building."

"I was screaming?"

That didn't make sense. Why would I be screaming? Then as if my mind were answering me, the dream and all of its terrible pictures came flooding back to my memory, filling me with terror.

I decided I didn't want to sleep any longer. I quickly sat up, but instantly collapsed back onto my pillow. My head was light-headed and I felt like I might be sick. I also realized that my face and neck were covered in a thick layer of sweat.

"Selkie, what happened?" Tabitha asked, sitting down beside me. "Did you have a bad dream or something?"

"More like a nightmare!"

I took a deep breath to calm myself and closed my eyes. The face in the shadows appeared behind my eyelids and I shivered. I vigorously rubbed at my eyes, trying to wipe the scary vision from my head.

"Do you want to talk about it?" Tabitha asked.

"No…I'm okay," I said, shaking my head. "I just want to forget about it."

I glanced over at the clock on my nightstand. It was only five thirty in the morning. I was sure that I wouldn't be able to sleep anymore, not when I knew what would be waiting for me when I closed my eyes, so I just decided to get up. Tabitha helped me stand, just in case my legs decided to misbehave, and I managed to get up without falling over.

"I'm sorry I woke you up," I told her through a yawn. "You can go back to bed. I'm just going to go make some tea, and watch some TV."

"How about I go make some tea, and you go take a shower," she said, pointing to my clothes. "'Cuz girl, you smell."

I glanced down at myself and noticed that my pajamas were soaked in sweat too.

"Gross."

"You said it, not me," and then squeezing her nostrils together with her thumb and finger, she added, "Now go shower, stinky."

Laughing, I playfully punched Tabitha's arm and then headed to the bathroom while she went to the kitchen to make our favorite chamomile tea.

I turned the shower on as hot as it would go, and then went to the sink to brush my teeth. As I grabbed my toothbrush from the cup on the counter, I glanced at the mirror and was surprised by my reflection in it. I looked terrible. The ponytail I had worn to bed was loose and untidy, and the hairs that framed my face were plastered to my skin from all the sweat. My skin was paler than usual, if that was possible, and I had dark circles under my eyes. Thankfully, as I finished brushing my teeth the mirror began to fog up from all the steam in the room, hiding my appalling appearance from me. I quickly replaced my toothbrush back into its cup and hopped into the shower.

As the hot water rolled over my body, I began to feel more like myself. I placed my face directly under the stream, relishing every droplet that fell upon it, and then grabbed my luffa, smothering it in my lavender scented body wash.

After I had finished washing every bit of sweat from my body, I thought of my plans to meet Aidan later and decided I'd better shave too. I stayed in the shower, meticulously shaving all the hair from my body, until the water ran cold.

When I finally made it to the kitchen, my tea was waiting

for me on the counter, next to a note.

*Selkie,*

*You were taking too damn long, so I went back to bed. And don't think about waking me up before my alarm goes off. Try not to scream too loud.*

*Tabs*

*p.s. Enjoy the tea!*

With a smile I grabbed my mug and headed to the couch. I had several hours to kill before I could even think about getting ready to meet Aidan. So I decided to surf the seven free channels we had. It was still too early for any good shows to be on yet, and so I ended up just watching stupid infomercials about smoothies that could make you lose a hundred pounds in a month, and a magical knife that could cut through shoes.

A little later, the local morning news came on, which I only ever watched when there was absolutely nothing else on. I always found it boring or extremely depressing, but luckily for me, most of the morning's stories were upbeat.

The weatherman presented his forecast for the week, each day consisting of partly sunny skies and moderate warm temperatures for the time of year. Then the sports guy gave a run down on the wins and losses of the weekend, but anything to do with sports or athletics I normally tuned out, so I didn't catch much.

All in all, the news was positive and I enjoyed sipping my tea with honey and watching the absurdly happy reporters with big hair and bad makeup. However, just before the end of the hour they had to ruin it.

The head anchor started to give more details about the accident that I had passed the night before. The reporter calmly spoke the details of the story, "In other news, several people are in the hospital this morning and three others are dead, after a telephone pole broke in half and fell into oncoming traffic yesterday evening. Police say they are still investigating the reasons behind this strange incident. A witness at the scene said that it looked like the pole had been sawed in half, but at no time during the day did anyone see any unusual activity. For more information on this tragic accident let's go out to Tamara live on location..." That's when I turned the TV off.

It was hard enough living in a world where parents abandoned their children and poor innocent people were killed in freak accidents. I didn't need a constant video stream reminding me of how miserable life could be.

As I lay on the couch, curled up in my favorite fleece blanket, the sun began to rise outside my living room window. The sun's radiant beams blanketed the land and I was in awe of its majestic beauty.

I had never been the religious type. I certainly didn't go to church every Sunday. I had been dealt a difficult life, one that should have made me the biggest cynic. However when you could open your eyes each morning and see such a magnificent view as the one that was before me, how could anyone doubt that God existed?

I immediately grabbed my sketchbook. Usually I liked to sketch with pencils; they were inexpensive and easy to carry. Other times, mostly when I was alone and really inspired, I liked to use watercolors. I ran to the desk in my room and found the cheap watercolors and brushes I kept in the second drawer, then went to the kitchen and filled a cup with warm water. I brought them back to the living room and laid all the supplies on the coffee table facing the window. I opened my book to a clean page.

I dipped my brush in the water, and then gently rubbed the brush in the green paint. I began with an outline, defining the structures in the landscape, illustrating depth and length, creating a surface for the sun to penetrate with its light. When I was satisfied, I cleaned my brush and immersed it again in color. This time in a light blue, washing the upper portion of the paper in it to construct the sky.

Once that was complete, I began to add more detail and color, first pink, then yellow and finally red. The colors blended well, uniting together and making colors of their own. As I traced the horizon, the paper responded, creating a misty yet honest resemblance of the landscape.

When the painting was finished, I felt like a part of me had broken free and been smeared amidst the paint on the page. It was a wonderful feeling. Feeling calmer, I curled up on the couch again, and rested my head against a pillow. I continued to stare out the window for a while, enjoying the view, until my eyes grew heavy and finally closed.

When I awoke it was several hours later. The sun was high in the sky, and the sound of birds chirping rang through the open window. I guess I had forgotten to close it the night before. It was another glorious day. Soon I would be outside enjoying it with Aidan. My stomach churned with excitement.

I went to the kitchen and placed my mug in the sink. On the counter lay Tabitha's note. She had scribbled out the original message and wrote a new one in its place.

*Selkie,*

*I didn't want to wake you. I left for work (YUCK) and will be back around seven. Wear the shirt and pants on your bed, they're my favorite. Have Fun!*

*Tabs*

I went to my room and lying on my bed was a white spaghetti strap and my forest green cardigan. She had picked out a pair of khaki capris to go with them. I was glad she had figured this out for me, because I would have spent hours just trying to find the right outfit.

What she had chosen was cute but casual, and perfect for a first date. Or least I thought so. I didn't really know what I was doing, and Tabitha knew that too. This was not just my first date with Aidan; this was going to be my first date with a boy, period.

I glanced at the clock and saw that I only had less than an hour until our date. I was going to have to hurry. I quickly threw on the clothes and grabbed my brown flats from the closet. I went to the bathroom then to fix my hair and face. Thanks to my impromptu nap my hair was matted down at random spots. I wet it with water and quickly blow-dried it, flipping out the ends with a curly brush, then parted my hair to the side and pulled it out of my face with a brown headband.

Then I got to work on my face. I applied some foundation and blush to my ghostly complexion and used extra concealer under my eyes to help hide the dark circles that still remained. I finished my primping with a little touch of mascara, and then a spritz of hairspray to calm all the fly aways.

Once I was pleased with my appearance, I moved into the living room to grab my sketchbook and purse. I checked the clock on the microwave and realized I was out of time. I hadn't eaten anything yet, but I couldn't afford to be late. I took an apple from the fridge, grabbed my coat from the closet, and then made my way to the door.

As I stepped outside I was consumed with anticipation. When I first laid eyes on Aidan he captivated me with his smile, and when we spoke, I trusted him without even knowing why. Then we touched, and it was as if a part of me had been dead and he had shocked me back to life. Every part of myself yearned to see him again.

Yet even with all those feelings I was uncertain of what to do. This was so unfamiliar to me, I didn't know how to respond. I didn't want to mess it up. Not this time.

I took a deep breath to relax my nerves. In only a few minutes I would be with Aidan again. The thought of him near me sent a thrill through my body, erasing all my previous fears. I didn't know what was going to happen, but I couldn't wait any longer to find out. I took another deep breath and then urged myself forward, heading in the direction of the park.

# Chapter 4

**It took me less time to get to the park than I had thought.** Probably because I practically jogged the entire way out of pure excitement. I threw what was left of my apple in the trash and made my way to my favorite bench. I thought Aidan might have beaten me, but when I reached the bench he wasn't there. It was just as well. I was so nervous I needed a few minutes to collect myself. I started to pace back and forth as a way to release some pent-up tension.

I decided I should keep my mind off of what was about to happen, because it would only drive me crazy. So I chose to concern myself with my appearance instead. I noticed that my lips were dry. I had a bad habit of biting them when I was anxious about something, leaving them parched and red. Not the most attractive thing to reveal on a first date. I pulled out my lip-gloss and applied several layers to my chapped lips.

My hair was also a mess. The wind had tousled it during the walk over, so I ran my hands through it a few times trying to tame the tangles. It didn't do much good, but I hadn't thought to bring a brush. I wanted to inspect my face as well, but I hadn't brought a mirror either, so I just hoped my face looked better than my hair. This whole analysis of myself took only a few moments, and there was still no sign of Aidan.

My legs were achy from all the activity from the previous night, and pacing back and forth wasn't helping. So I went and positioned myself underneath the magnolia tree, leaning my back against its strong trunk, and perused the rest of my surroundings.

Across the lawn near the playground was a family. I watched as the mother and father busied themselves with arranging blankets on the grass and preparing the food for their picnic. Their two children, both under the age of six, were sitting close by pulling the grass from its roots and throwing it at each other. They laughed happily, finding their game extremely amusing.

The father, finished with his tasks came to sit next to his children. Seeing them covered in grass made him chuckle, and he gently ruffled their hair before grabbing a blade of grass and placing it between his two thumbs. Raising them to his mouth he began to blow on the piece of grass. His children watched with amazement as a high-pitched sound emanated from his hands. Their faces lit up with excitement as their tiny hands searched the ground for instruments of their own.

Patiently, he showed them how to replicate the sound and encouraged them when they struggled. Finally after several minutes they both managed to produce some type of noise, and the father beamed with pride. When lunch was ready, they each squeaked one more note, and then brushed themselves off and walked hand in hand back to the blankets.

I stared with envious eyes at the happy family. Their love for each other was palpable, hovering over them like a shelter, protecting them from the harsh world. I wanted to just reach out and take a little for myself.

As they laughed and ate together my heart wrenched with jealousy. If only I had been born into that family my life could have been so different. Unfortunately, my life had taken another path, and I had no love or safe refuge to guard me.

I couldn't watch anymore. It only made me feel depressed, and I hated feeling sorry for myself. It never changed anything.

I moved over to the bench and sat down, turning my back on the family and their fortunate existence. Their life would never be mine, and it was time I accepted it. My life was a hollow shell with nothing meaningful to fill it, but I was hoping that today might change all that.

If only Aidan would get here.

Several minutes had elapsed during my observations and with Aidan nowhere to be seen, he was now definitely running late. I was starting to worry.

My mind was instantly bombarded with ramblings that tried to explain his absence and calm my uncertainty. Perhaps he'd lost track of time, or was stuck at work. Maybe he locked his keys in his house, or misplaced his wallet. He could even be on his way right now, but had gotten stuck in traffic. Those all made very good sense.

That's when my thoughts took a turn for the worse.

What if he wasn't running late?

What if he had been in an accident?

What if he had been hurt or even worse, what if he was...?

I stopped myself right there. This was crazy.

I was crazy.

There was no reason I should jump to such conclusions. He had probably just thought we had said a different time and was going to be here later. That was fine. I could wait.

I pulled out my sketchbook and decided to pass the time doodling instead of creating senseless scenarios in my head. I didn't think I would be waiting too much longer, so instead of drawing a full picture I decided to try and perfect my technique with flowers.

I began with my favorites—daffodils, lilacs, roses and lilies. I had always been a perfectionist, and could spend hours working on a single bud until I was satisfied. Every flower required special dedication, but I loved spending time with each leaf and blossom.  It was never tedious.  It was always the highlight of my day—until now.

I had covered at least seven whole pages with flowers when I finally got the courage to glance at my watch.  I quickly did the math and realized I had been sitting there for over two hours.  Aidan still hadn't shown up.  How long could I wait?

As if my body was answering my question, my stomach rumbled and I suddenly realized I was starving.  I guess the apple I had earlier was not going to cut it.  I grabbed my purse and rummaged through the pockets for anything that could subside my hunger.  On the bottom of my purse, next to some loose change and a few bobby pins, I found a single piece of gum.  It wasn't even the good sugary kind, but a small square of sugar free spearmint.  It would have to do.

When I unwrapped it, I found that most of the gum had melted and was rebelliously sticking to the wrapper.  I was desperate.  I pulled off whatever I could manage and then used my teeth to scrape off the rest.  The gum made my mouth salivate, and that's when I discovered how dry my mouth had become.  Too bad I didn't pack myself a drink.  What I would have given for some water, but I couldn't chance leaving to find a fountain, just in case Aidan arrived.  I was just going to have to hold out a little bit longer.

I continued to sit and wait, vigorously chewing that small stick of gum until it was as hard as a rock and had lost all of its flavor. When I couldn't take it any longer, I found the wrapper and placed the gum in it, sticking the remains of my miserable meal in my purse.

Suddenly a light breeze began to blow, cutting right through my coat and sweater, chilling me. Tiny goose bumps emerged on my skin. I briskly rubbed my hands up and down my arms trying to keep them warm. It was getting colder as the daylight was beginning to dim, and when I glanced up at the sky the first star of the night was visible. I hadn't checked the time in a while and I was afraid to see how late it had gotten.

I nervously looked at my watch and my fears were instantly confirmed. It was almost evening. I had been sitting at the park for over three hours now, and Aidan still hadn't arrived. It was obvious to me then that he wasn't ever going to show up.

The moment that thought registered in my mind, a heavy weight like a ton of bricks began to press against my chest. The pressure intensified as each second slowly ticked by and every breath became excruciating. As the weight increased, it felt as if my torso was collapsing in on itself, making it harder and harder to breathe. Eventually, my lungs refused to respond. My whole body began to shake, and I found tears welling up threatening to spill over and consume me. I had to calm down.

I quickly opened my sketchbook and turned to my favorite page. It was the picture of the park I had drawn yesterday, just before meeting Aidan. I closed my eyes and tried to visualize the peace it had brought me when creating it. Slowly the pressure on my chest eased and air began to circulate through my lungs. Once again, I was grateful for the gift I had been given. It was the only thing in my life I could rely on.

I thought Aidan was going to change that. I had convinced myself that he was special. I took a chance and exposed my heart. How could I have been so stupid? I had promised myself a long time ago that I would never let another person get close enough to hurt me, but then a cute guy smiles at me and I feel a few tingles, and I'm dumb enough to allow myself to hope; to think that things could be different; to think that I could trust him. So finally, after all this time I decide to let myself go—just to be let down again. Figures.

The pressure in my chest had settled, but I could no longer hold back the flood of tears. They rolled down my cheeks and continued down my neck, falling upon the page of my sketchbook that was open on my lap. As the tears continued to flow, I looked down at the beautiful day I had drawn. It was completely soaked. I closed my eyes, unable to see the picture in such a state, and that's when the clouds rolled in and the rain began.

## Chapter 5

**I remained frozen on the bench, unable to even open my eyes, while the rain pelted my face and drenched my clothes.** My entire sketchbook was wet as well—all my pictures—ruined. If I were smart I would have left when the first droplet of rain had fallen, or at least concealed my sketchbook from the storm. Instead I sat there looking like a statue, while a battle raged within me.

Part of me knew that I should leave, forget about Aidan and release the hold he had on my heart. But another part still hungered to see him, and it was killing me. The place in my heart that had once smoldered from Aidan's touch and filled me with joy was now revolting against me, spreading through my whole chest like a wildfire.

There was not one part of my heart that was not ablaze from the inferno. I wished that the cold water assailing my skin would find passage to my heart and extinguish the flame before all that was left of me was worthless ash. Yet no relief came. My soul continued to burn, as my body remained unmovable.

Eventually, the wind and rain became too much for my body to withstand, and I found myself shivering so much that my teeth were chattering. I was freezing. Some natural survival instinct took over then and I regained control of my body. The heat still remained deep in my chest, but I could endure the pain, as long as I concentrated on something else.

I focused on my body that was miserable with cold and realized that the most important thing should be getting home, and getting out of the wet clothes clinging to my body. The rest could wait. So I devoted my every thought to the task at hand, and faster than expected I found myself staring at my apartment complex.

When I approached the door, I just stood there, terrified to enter my own home. I couldn't face Tabitha, not like that, but I also couldn't stay outside all night. So I took a deep breath and opened the door, but quickly discovered my fears were unnecessary. Tabitha's door was shut and I had a clear path to my room. I silently closed the door and locked it, and then tip toed to my room, throwing my soggy sketchbook in the trash as I went.

Once safely in my room I stripped off my clothes, plopping them in a wet heap in front of my closet, and then picked up the towel that was still lying on my bed and dried myself off. Wrapping the towel around my head I went to my dresser to find some pajamas and a pair of fleece socks for my frozen feet, and when I was finally warm and dry I headed straight to my bed and curled up under the comforter.

I had figured out how to get home and avoid Tabitha without too much difficulty, but now I had to figure out how I was going to forget about Aidan and move on with my life. It couldn't be that hard, I thought.

I was wrong.

The week that followed was by far the worst week of my entire life. I woke each morning to the sound of rain pounding on my roof, and it filled me with dread knowing I would have to trudge through it to get to work. Once at work, I had to act as if I cared about the customers and their ridiculous coupons. I had to contain my frustrations when they asked for assistance to locate items that were "impossible to find," even though they were clearly labeled on the signs right above their heads. I found every job I was given to be tedious, and I was on the verge of quitting every other minute.

Still, work wasn't even the worst part. Whenever I got home Tabitha was always there, waiting to cheer me up. I had to pretend to laugh at her jokes or smile at her stories, when all I really wanted to do was curl up in a ball and cry. I couldn't let my best friend know how I really felt. I was afraid if I did, she wouldn't understand. Truthfully, I didn't understand it myself.

None of that compared, however, to the terrible things that awaited me when I closed my eyes each night. In my dreams two faces continued to haunt me. The first one, with its handsome features and dazzling smile, was sweet and inviting. It enticed me forward and every step filled me with happiness. But when I was finally close enough to reach out and touch it, the face would disappear, leaving me heartbroken. No matter what I did he was always out of reach, always unattainable.

The second face was far more terrifying. It was a face of shadows and darkness. It danced before my vision, ensnaring me with its vicious and violent gaze. It consumed me with fear and drained me of all feeling. I wanted to run, but couldn't make my body move. So I just stood there, frozen in place, powerless to do anything. That's when the shadows would overwhelm me and I would wake up screaming.

*   *   *

Every evening the dream became more excruciating, and the face in the shadows began to linger for what felt like eternity. One night early in the week, I was so terrified I screamed louder than I had ever screamed before. When my eyes opened, Tabitha was there once again, anxiously calling my name. She hovered over me like a protective mother until I acknowledged her presence. Then she commenced with the questioning.

"Selkie, are you okay?"

"I'm fine."

"Bullshit! You're not fine. Now tell me what's up."

When she spoke she tried to stay calm, but I could see how concerned she was. Her forehead was creased with worry and the skin under her eyes was almost as dark as mine from all the sleepless nights.

"It's not that big of a deal," I told her, brushing it off.

"Not that big of a deal? This is the third night in a row I've been woken up by your screaming, and you still won't tell me what's wrong."

"It was just a bad dream. I told you…I don't want to talk about it." It was bad enough I had to relive it every single night. I was tired of having this conversation.

"Well if you won't tell me what's going on, then what the hell am I supposed to do?"

The lack of sleep and my frustration over the dream finally got the best of me, and I snapped back, "I don't care what you do, just leave me alone!"

She instantly recoiled from me, as if I had slapped her across the face. "Well forgive me for caring! I just wanted to help, but if you're going to be a jerk, forget it."

"Tabs."

"No, it's fine." She stood and moved angrily toward the door. "I mean it's not like you don't have anyone else you could talk to about this. Oh wait…you don't!"

Ouch.

"Tabs, I'm sorry if I hurt your feelings, but…"

"You know what Selkie…save it. I'm tired, and unless you're going to be honest with me I don't want to hear it." She opened the door and stood there waiting for my answer.

When I didn't speak she just shrugged, and said, "Whatever," and with the cruelest tone possible, she added, "sweet dreams," before walking out of the room and slamming the door behind her.

After that night, I didn't have to worry about Tabitha's worried glances, or her eagerness to protect me, not even her ridiculous chatter after work each evening. The following morning she made it very clear, unless I was willing to open up and let her help, she wasn't going to talk to me.

Tabitha was really hurt, and I couldn't blame her. I was a terrible friend. I wanted so badly to tell her everything, but I was a coward. So we spent the rest of the week avoiding each other's eyes, and silently co-existing.

\*    \*    \*

Everything was a meaningless blur that week. I couldn't even bring myself to purchase a new sketchbook. I had no desire to draw. Why should I create a beautiful picture of the world that would never exist outside my imagination? It was pointless. So I miserably drifted through the haze, without a purpose or destination.

Within the blur, however, were a few short bursts of

clarity that kept my heart beating. They were the moments I lived for. They were the moments I saw Aidan.

The first time I saw him I was in aisle 12, stocking bags of frozen broccoli next to the bags of frozen peas. I heard a sound behind me, and at first I thought it was another annoying customer in need of assistance. I quickly stood and closed the door to the freezer, and that's when my eyes froze on the reflection in the glass. There he was, smiling at me. I took a deep breath to prepare myself, and then turned around, but he wasn't there. I searched the entire store, but it was like he had vanished into thin air.

The next time I saw him I was walking downtown. The rain was falling in sheets all around my umbrella and there was a thick fog hovering close to the ground. I was getting drenched, so I decided to duck into the pharmacy until the rain let up. I was looking out the window when he came striding into view. Our eyes met for only a second and then he had passed. I quickly ran to the door, abandoning my umbrella, but when I got outside he was nowhere to be seen.

The last time I saw him I was in the food court at the mall. I had gone there to get a gift for Tabitha. I couldn't stand not talking, and I knew a few trashy magazines would weaken her defenses and we would be able to make up and move on.

I had just bought a pretzel and was stepping on the escalator, when I noticed four burly guys leaving the music store.

As I slowly descended, one of the guys in the group turned around and stared directly at me.

When he smiled, I almost fainted.

I ran down the rest of the moving steps and when I reached the bottom I found the normal stairs and sprinted up them. When I landed on the second floor I spun around, but just like both times before, he was gone.

Could I have only imagined him? I couldn't be sure. He looked real...but just like in my dreams he would always disappear before I could reach him. Maybe I was hallucinating...or maybe I was just plain crazy.

The truth is...I didn't really care. Whether he was real or not didn't matter to me. What mattered was the way I felt when I thought of him. Yeah, he had hurt me, but the pain could not compare with the joy that overflowed when I saw him...or when I thought I saw him.

When a few days went by without catching a glimpse of him, I became desperate; so desperate that I found myself buying a new sketchbook and walking in the direction of the park. I decided that if I couldn't see him in person, my memory would have to suffice. He was going to be the first person to reside in my sketchbook, just as he was the first person to reside in my heart.

It was still drizzling when I entered the park, but the

worst of the storm had passed, and it had poured so much during the last week that a little light rain didn't bother me. When I got to my usual bench, it was silly, but I felt more alive than I had in days. It had been exactly a week since I had been stood up. I should have felt depressed or angry. Instead I felt exhilarated. I don't know why I hadn't thought of it before. I could see Aidan whenever I wanted. I just had to open up my sketchbook and create him.

I sat down and opened my book with shaking hands. I had never gone this long without drawing, and I was a little nervous. Still, my excitement overcame the nervousness and I quickly sketched out my backdrop. I wanted this picture to be perfect. I made the sky a light blue, filling it with fluffy white clouds, and then placed my favorite tree under a brilliant shining sun, bathing the grass underneath the tree in gentle shadows; a picturesque landscape.

Now came the hard part, drawing Aidan. I had never attempted to sketch a portrait before, and I had no idea where to start. I decided to begin with his dimensions and go on from there. I visualized in my mind what he looked like on the day we first met.

I began with his head, replicating his well-groomed hair, prominent cheekbones and strong jaw. I moved down his body then, tracing his neck that lead to his muscular shoulders and wide chest. I completed his torso with a polo shirt and continued to his lean and sturdy legs.  Once I had the basic outline, I went back to add the fine details like his almond shaped eyes, his gentle hands, and his perfectly plump lips.

I stared at the finished portrait, and was not surprised to find Aidan's resemblance unlike anyone I had ever seen.  He truly was a gorgeous human being.  What I hadn't anticipated, however, was the emotion that arose in me once the picture was complete.  I thought drawing him would bring me comfort and strength, but all it brought was more fire and pain.  My chest was ablaze with a deep yearning that no likeness of him could tame.  I was overcome with hopelessness, and as I closed my eyes and wished for the aching in my heart to cease, all I could see was Aidan's face.

"Selkie?"

When he spoke, my heart began to beat so fast that I thought it might jump out of my chest.  He sounded so real, so close.  I slowly opened my eyes, and there he was just like I had pictured him.  Our eyes met, and it was as if we had never been apart.  He closed the distance between us in less than a second, and as he gently placed his hand on mine, the fire in my heart spread through my entire body.  He felt it too, but this time he didn't pull away.  Instead he just smiled that amazing smile as he tightened his grasp, and said, "Sorry I'm late."

## Chapter 6

**I kept my hand in his for one sweet moment, relishing the softness of his touch, and soaking in every part of his gorgeous face.** But soon the blissful emotions that his appearance had conjured began to fade, and were replaced by thoughts of mistrust and sadness. I reluctantly removed my hand from his and swiftly slid to the other side of the bench, turning my back on him. My mind was reeling with confusion, and all the emotions I had kept locked up deep within me were beginning to rise, threatening to erupt out of me at any second. I tried to calm myself down by taking deep breaths, but it didn't work. Finally I couldn't contain it anymore, and a steady stream of tears began to flow down my cheeks.

It was then that Aidan moved closer, and placing a hand on my shoulder, he said, "Selkie, please don't cry."

"I'm not crying," I squeaked as I shrugged his hand off. "I mean, why would I be crying over a guy I just met once and know nothing about? That's ridiculous!"

"Selkie, I know you're upset, and you have every right to be, but please, let me explain."

"What's there to explain?" I cried. "I thought we had a connection, but obviously I was wrong. I was just stupid to think a guy like you could be interested in someone like me."

"Selkie, would you just stop and look at me!"

He gently placed both hands on either side of my face, and then turned my head so that I could look directly into his smoldering gray eyes.

"Please believe me when I say that I am so sorry I hurt you," he said tenderly, and then releasing his hold on my face he softly wiped away my tears, before lowering his hands and placing them on my own. "You were right about feeling something between us, because I did too, and I can't even describe how amazing it felt. And since that day, all I've been able to think about...is you."

Afraid to get hurt again I started to pull my hand away, but he held it so securely it wouldn't budge.

"Selkie, I know it sounds crazy, because like you said...I don't know you," and then with a smile he squeezed my hand, and said, "but I really want to."

"But if that's true, why didn't you show up that day?"

He released his hold on me, running his hands through his hair as he said, "It's kind of hard to explain."

"Try me."

I was still unsure and confused about our situation, but I was eager to hear his reasons for standing me up and making me miserable all week.

"I wanted to see you, more than anything, and believe me I tried but…well… my life is…complicated."

"How complicated?"

He released a frustrated sigh and quickly stood. "I don't even know where to start," he said pacing back and forth in front of the bench. "I mean my life has basically been planned out since I was born, and it's really hard to deviate from what I'm expected to do."

"What are you expected to do?"

He instantly stopped pacing, and turned to look at me. His face was filled with tension, and he appeared to be struggling with something. But then he just shrugged it off, and said, "It doesn't even matter, it's not that exciting…it just makes it almost impossible to have a life outside of…my life."

Now I was really confused.

Trying hard not to cry again, I asked, "So are you saying that we can't…see each other?"

In a flash he was by my side again, this time so close that I could smell his sweet intoxicating breath. He cupped one hand around my face and smirked. "I said it was almost impossible to have a life…not… completely impossible."

He still wasn't making much sense, and his hand on my face was not helping me think. So I placed my hand on his and gently pulled it away.  Knowing it would be easier to concentrate if he wasn't sitting so close to me, I stood and stepped away from the bench.  When he didn't follow me, I knew he understood.

"So where does that leave us then?" I asked awkwardly.

"I'm not sure," he shrugged. "But I know we can figure it out." Then sheepishly he added, "It won't be easy, so I understand if you don't want to try."

It was me that moved this time, and I was so anxious to assure him of my feelings, to let him know that I felt the same way he did, that I tripped over my own feet and fell forward.  In an instant I was in his arms.

"Are you okay?"

I looked up and found him staring down at me with such concern it made my knees weak, and I almost collapsed again. But his arms stayed strong around me, supporting my weight, keeping me safe, and just like the day we met, I was certain that no matter what happened he would always be there to catch me.

His unyielding confidence made me feel strong, and I felt like I could do anything...but at that moment, with him holding me tight and his strong hands pressing into my lower back, there was only one thing that I wanted to do.

With all the courage I could muster, I raised my self up on my tiptoes so that our faces were only inches from each other, and placed both my arms around his neck. I was sure I was moving way too fast, and was just waiting for him to pull away...but he didn't.

Instead he wrapped his arms even tighter around my waist and pulled me nearer, molding our two bodies together. We were so close I could feel his heart pounding through his shirt, and it was beating as rapidly as my own. Slowly he leaned in, and as our lips met, I closed my eyes.

The first kiss lasted only a few sweet seconds, and when we pulled away I was reluctant for it to end. The look on Aidan's flushed face told me he felt the same. So I leaned in again and pressed my lips hard against his, pulling myself closer to him, and in return he squeezed me tighter. The kissing deepened, both of us breathing heavily, and when his tongue gently grazed my bottom lip, I shivered. When we finally stopped, it was Aidan who pulled away.

I was suddenly self-conscience.

"What's the matter, did I do something wrong?"

"No you didn't do anything wrong," he said lightly touching my cheek. "You're amazing, it's just that...well we don't have much time."

"What do you mean?"

"When I told you that I tried to come see you, I was telling the truth. But there are people in my life that think I shouldn't be with you, and they kept me from coming."

"Are you talking about your friends from the other day?" I asked, moving away from him and sitting on the bench.

"How did you know I was talking about them?"

"I saw the way they looked at me, and it was like they thought I wasn't good enough for you."

"Selkie, that's not it at all."

"Then why don't they want you to be with me?"

"I told you, my life is complicated...and I'm sorry, but I don't have time to explain it right now."

"Why not?"

"Because they'll be here any second."

"You mean your friends are coming here, now?"

"Yeah, and there's something else you should know. They're not just my friends...they're my brothers."

That was even worse.

"Your brothers hate me? But they don't even know me!"

"They don't hate you."

"But they don't want me to be with you, and they're going

to be here any minute. So what now?"

"Let's just try and figure out when to meet next, and I promise I'll do whatever I can to get there."

Since I didn't have a car we needed to find a place I could easily walk to, and we quickly agreed to meet at the pharmacy by my apartment in three days. I didn't have a cell phone either, so I gave him my work number just in case he couldn't make it. That way he could at least leave me a message and arrange a new time to meet.

Once our plans were set, I stood up and walked over to where Aidan was still standing, placing my hands on his chest. He pulled me close, lightly running his fingers through my hair as I rested my head against his chest.

"Can I ask you something?" I said, looking up.

"Anything."

"Sometime in the future, could you please explain to me why everything in your life is so complicated?"

He stopped stroking my hair and was silent for a moment, and then he gently kissed the top of my head, and said, "I'll do my best."

It wasn't exactly the answer I was hoping for, but it would have to do for now.

I started to step out of his arms, thinking the moment had ended, when he grasped my shoulders, and said, "Where do you think your going?" before pulling me close once again and kissing me.

I could have kissed Aidan like that for hours, but when we heard someone clear their throat, and we realized we were no longer alone, we both regrettably released each other and turned to face our audience.

Standing in front of us were the three guys I had seen Aidan with last week, who I now knew to be his brothers, and I couldn't believe I hadn't noticed it before. All of the brothers looked very similar, with the same lean build, olive skin, and short hair as Aidan. At first glance, the only thing that kept them from looking exactly alike was their difference in height, but examining them closer, I also noticed that everyone but Aidan had green eyes, and none of them had lips that could compare to his.

Suddenly, the tallest brother stepped forward, and in a low voice said, "Aidan, it's time to go."

Aidan grabbed my hand, and then smiling at his brother, he replied, "Brendan don't be rude! Introduce yourself."

When Brendan didn't say anything, Aidan took it upon himself to make things more awkward.

"Fine. Selkie, these are my two younger brothers Ewan

and Liam, and the angry looking one in the middle is my older brother Brendan."

"It's nice to meet you," I said in a quiet voice.

Both Liam and Ewan nodded in my direction. They looked nice enough.

Brendan, however, did not look very nice. In fact, he looked kind of scary. He just stood there with his arms crossed against his chest, glaring at me with that same look of disgust I had seen last week.

I lowered my eyes to the ground.

"What are you doing, Aidan?" Brendan asked curtly. "You know you're not suppose to be here."

Aidan stepped closer to his brother, lowering his voice. "Brendan please, don't be like this, can't you just…"

"No Aidan I can't," Brendan interrupted. "And stop turning me into the bad guy here. We already talked about this and we all agreed."

"I didn't agree on anything, Brendan, and you know that."

"It doesn't even matter, little brother. Either you come willingly, or I will drag you out of the park myself!"

I stood there, completely dumbfounded, as the two brothers faced off with each other; Aidan with his fists clenched tight by his sides, and Brendan with a face full of fury.

What had I gotten myself into?

Finally realizing he wasn't going to be able to sway his brother, Aidan turned back to me, and said, "Selkie, I have to go." He started to take a step toward me, but Brendan placed one hand on his shoulder, restraining him.

He wasn't even going to let him say goodbye.

Well he might be able to hold back Aidan, but he couldn't lay a finger on me. Defiantly I glared at Brendan as I moved forward to stand directly in front of Aidan, and then with a smile I leaned in and kissed him one more time.

When the kiss finished, Aidan beamed at me with that brilliant smile, and loud enough so everyone could here, he said, "See you soon."

Brendan stepped forward and stood next to Aidan, but when he looked at me this time, I was surprised to see that his eyes were no longer filled with anger. Instead they were filled with compassion as he said, "No offense Selkie... I'm sure you're really nice and all, but you won't be seeing Aidan again."

He turned his back on me then, taking Aidan with him, and as they quickly walked away from me my heart sank.

Was Brendan right? Would I ever get to see Aidan again?

As if he could read my mind, and before I could allow the thought to contaminate my heart, Aidan whipped his head around and winked.

I had my answer.

**Chapter 7**

**Feeling happier than I had all week I skipped all the way home, unable to conceal the joy that permeated my entire body.** As I pranced down Main Street, I passed several people who looked at me like I was crazy, but I just smiled at them and kept skipping, too consumed with thoughts of Aidan to care what people thought about me.

I couldn't stop my mind from replaying every glorious minute of our unexpected reunion. The feel of his hands as they caressed my skin, and the taste of his lips on my tongue drove my heart into high speed. I had never kissed a boy before Aidan, and I never wanted to kiss another as long as I lived.

I was in love. It was undeniable. Every part of my soul knew it was true. It was insane and incredible and scary and wonderful, all at the same time. What was weird though was the fact that for the first time in my life, I didn't want to keep my feelings to myself. I wanted to share them. I needed to share them. The only problem was that the person I wanted to talk to about it didn't exist, at least not to me.

Countless times in my life I had dreamt of her. I envisioned her as the most beautiful woman on earth, with skin as pale as a porcelain doll and fiery red hair that was wild and lovely. In my dreams she would find me and we would do the most ordinary things, like shopping at the mall, or painting our nails. And when I was sad, I imagined her holding me as I cried, and rubbing my back as I rested my head in her lap.

But they were only dreams, and I always woke up to find myself alone with no mother to guide me through the pain. I wanted so badly to know her. Yet as I grew older, I realized my dream of having a mother would never become a reality. She didn't want me then. She wouldn't want me now, and no matter how hard I wished I could never change that.

Falling in love for the first time is a tremendous moment in any girl's life, and I should have been able to share it with my mom, just like every other girl in the world got to do. Instead she had chosen to abandon me, leaving me helpless and unprepared.

So then how was I supposed to know what to do? When I needed help picking out my clothes or styling my hair, who could I turn to? When I was confused and unsure, who was going to give me advice and teach me what to say? I needed someone to tell me what to do. If not her, then who?

Sadly, I didn't have that many friends. My mistrust in people had always kept me distant, confining me to a life of solitude. The few friends I did have were mostly people I worked with. They were nice to chat with during lunch, but I didn't feel comfortable going to them with my love problems. Which narrowed my options down considerably. Honestly, I knew there was only one person that I could turn to, and it was a good thing she was talking to me again.

*　　*　　*

Before our fight I had been too proud, or too scared, or a combination of both to let Tabitha in, and it wasn't just the last few days that I had kept her at a distance. My entire life had consisted of hiding out or running away from my problems. I was good at keeping my head down, staying out of the way. Most people never even noticed me. Others, however, thought that with the right attention, and the right clothes, and the right home, I would become the kid that they wanted, and I would make them happy.

But what about me? What about my happiness? In the end, it never really mattered; I never stayed around long enough to ask them.

The last time I ran was right before my seventeenth birthday, from this elderly couple that I had lived with for a few months. Their children were all grown up, and they thought that adopting me would make them feel young again. They were nice enough I guess, but they were always trying to fix me. Make me normal. They kept trying to make me who they wanted me to be, instead of just loving me for who I was. I didn't want to settle. I didn't want to change. So one day I packed up my things, and when they were out getting groceries I left without so much as leaving a note. It sounds cruel, but they would have realized sooner or later that I wasn't what they wanted. So I just left them before they could leave me.

When the cops picked me up, I had such a record of running that I was forced to see a therapist. I had to see this lady once a week for two months. She sat in her comfy chair, with her three-piece suit and coffee, analyzing my behaviors and probing me for answers that I was unwilling to give. She read my file and made her weekly observations. At our last meeting she finally decided that I had serious abandonment issues, due to the fact that I never knew my parents, which was why I acted out in the ways that I did.

She thought she was so smart, but I could have told her that, and I wouldn't have needed to read my file. She recommended that I continue to see her, but since it wasn't mandatory I walked out of her office that day and never looked back.

Now thinking back on it, maybe if we had gotten past all the bullshit she might have been able to help me. The problem was, I didn't know I needed help. Not until my fight with Tabitha. Until recently, no matter how hard I pushed Tabitha away she was always there for me when I needed her, and I had taken it for granted. It wasn't until she finally gave up on me and walked out my door, that I discovered how much I needed her.

But what's more, I saw how much pain our silent struggle was causing her, and I realized it was time to stop being selfish and be there for Tabitha, just like she had always been there for me, so many times before.  I had been letting her do all the work in our friendship, assuming she would always be there, but giving her nothing in return.

I had been so wrong.  I knew if I didn't do something quickly I would lose the only real friend I ever had.  So it was up to me to mend the bond between us that I alone had so cruelly damaged.  After three horrible days of silence, I managed to patch up my relationship with Tabitha, but getting her to forgive me hadn't been easy.

*   *   *

The days leading up to our reunion were tense.  Tabitha was always hiding out in her room, or worse, actually going to work just to stay away from me.  Whenever she was in the same room with me, which was not very often, I would try to start a conversation, but she would immediately cover her ears and hum as loud as she could.  For as long as I tried to talk, she would hum, and eventually I would get pissed off and just walk away.

I understood that she was upset, but she was still being childish and stubborn.  I knew if I wanted to talk I would have to soften Tabitha's stubbornness, and in order to do so I would need something to attract her attention.  So when I came home from the mall with a stack of her favorite magazines, the scene played out just as I had expected.

As I approached her door, I took a deep breath to ready

myself and then lightly knocked three times. When only silenced followed, I wasn't sure if she was sleeping or just ignoring me, so I knocked a little harder.

"No," she growled.

"Tabitha, can I...?"

"I said no, Selkie."

There was no way she was going to invite me in, so it was time to pull out the big guns. I took one of the magazines I held, her favorite of course, and slid it halfway under her door. I knocked again.

Silence.

"I got you something." I held my breath while I waited for her reply. There was more silence, but after a minute or two I heard a rustling of sheets and then footsteps approaching the door. She was coming to retrieve her gift. Sucker.

When she pulled the magazine from beneath the door, I said, "I got you some other ones too. They look pretty juicy. I could give them to you, if you would just open your door and let me in." I knew I was pressing my luck, but when the doorknob turned I released a big sigh, pleased that my plan had worked— so far.

Tabitha stood there in her doorway staring at me, waiting for me to make my next move. As I stared back at her, I noticed her hair was a mess and her eyes were all bleary, maybe she had been sleeping. But when I looked at her shirt and saw that it was wet at the collar, I realized she must have been crying. It was time for me to fix this. I handed her the rest of the magazines, and said, "Can I come in?"

She just shrugged and walked back to her bed, plopping herself down atop the covers. It wasn't really an answer, but at least she didn't slam the door in my face. I slowly walked over and sat on the edge of the bed facing her.

Trying to lighten the mood I smiled, and said, "You're not going to start humming again are you?"

She didn't think that was funny. She crossed her arms over her chest and with a sour expression replied, "I already told you I don't want any of this bullshit, Selkie. I'm done playing games with you, if you want to talk...talk. But if you just came in here to make yourself feel better, than you better leave, because I'm through taking care of you."

"That's not why I'm here."

Her face betrayed her angry exterior and she looked hopeful as she said, "It's not?"

"No, it's not. Look Tabs, I know that I haven't been easy to live with, or even easy to be friends with sometimes."

"True dat."

I smiled a little and continued, "But I want to make it up to you, and not just by buying you things or even apologizing. Which, by the way…I'm sorry."

She looked down, not meeting my eyes. "It's okay."

"No it's not," I protested. "You deserve more than that. So from now on, no matter what, I'm going to be honest with you, and I'm going to stop pushing you away. You're my best friend Tabs, and it's time I started being a best friend to you, and maybe even take care of you for a change."

She looked at me then, and her face was once again stained with tears. "I don't need you to take care of me, Selkie," she said, wiping them away. "I can take care of myself. I just want you to tell me what's going on with you, without me having to beat it out of you, or ignore you for a week. You're my best friend too, and I love you, but sometimes I just feel like you don't want me to be a part of your life. And even though I love you, sometimes you make it difficult for me to like you."

"I know. I have a lot of things I need to work on, but I promise I am going to make it up to you. And just so you know, I will always want you in my life. I've just been a stupid jerk about everything, and I can't believe you've put up with me for so long."

"Well girl, it hasn't been easy."

All the tension that we had built up inside us the last few days suddenly exploded and we started to laugh. It was strange to be laughing, but it felt great. When the laughter died down, Tabitha said, "How 'bout some tea?"

"Tea sounds awesome."

As we left her room and walked to the kitchen, I asked, "So are we okay?"

"Well, that depends. Are you ready to tell me what's been going on with you lately?"

I placed my arm around her shoulder, and said, "Where should I start?"

Even though it was hard and uncomfortable, we spent the rest of the evening talking about me, about us, a lot about Aidan, and the worst of it all, about my reoccurring nightmares. We laughed and cried together, and when we were both thoroughly exhausted we fell asleep, both curled up underneath her comforter.

\*     \*     \*

As I skipped across the street that led to our apartment, the anticipation was killing me. I couldn't wait to see Tabitha and tell her what had just happened. She wasn't my mom, but she was my best friend, and I was just happy to have someone to talk to. Unfortunately, she was just as naïve about love as I was, and after years of liars and cheats, she was way more cautious.

"Selkie are you insane?" Tabitha stood in my doorway

with her hands on her hips, glaring at me like I was a child. "Why the hell would you kiss a guy you don't even know? He could have a disease or something. What were you thinking?"

I glared back at her, fighting back tears as I said, "I was thinking that my best friend would be excited for me."

"Selkie, are you kidding me? You act like kissing a total stranger is normal. You act like you're living in a dream world, but you are certainly no fairy tale princess. You're just an eighteen-year-old girl who's gonna end up pregnant or diseased if you're not careful."

"It was just a kiss, and it's not like you haven't done way worse." That was a low blow, but she was being ridiculous.

"Whoa, do not bring me into this. I may have made some mistakes, but that's why I am trying to help you now, before it's too late."

"I don't want your help, Tabs. I just wanted to tell you about Aidan. I promised I would tell you what was going on with me. Remember? But if you're going to act like this, then maybe we shouldn't talk about him."

I turned my back to her, pouting, and waited for her to leave me alone.

She didn't.

"Look Selkie...I'm sorry." She came and sat down on the

bed next to me. "I didn't mean to jump on you like that. I just don't want you to do something you might regret later on. Besides, he stood you up and any guy who does that once can do it again."

I turned to face her. "I know you're just looking out for me, and I know you won't understand this, but Aidan is different."

"How do you know that?"

"It's hard to explain, but I just know. When I'm with him..."

"Which has been like, ten minutes all together..."

"It doesn't matter. When I'm with him, I feel complete. I think...no...I know I love him."

I swallowed hard, afraid of what her reaction might be. She didn't say anything. She just sat there with her mouth slightly open and her eyes bugged out. Finally she managed to squeak out, "You...love...him? You don't even know what that means, Selkie."

"I don't need to know what it means, I just need to know how it feels, and just those few minutes together was enough to make me certain that what I feel is real."

"And what about him?" She folded her arms over her chest and stared at me with dubious eyes.

"Well he hasn't said it...but I think he feels the same."

"This is what I'm talking about, Selkie. You don't know what he feels, because you don't know him, and I think you're on the verge of getting seriously hurt."

"You're wrong!"

"Well for your sake, I hope you're right," she said, standing up and walking to the door.

"You just have to trust me, Tabs."

"If that's what you want, I will. Honestly, I think you're crazy, but I want you to be happy." Then she threw her hands in the air, and said, "So what the hell, be in love, just don't be mad when I tell you I told you so."

"Should we make things interesting?"

"You mean a bet?"

I nodded, a smile spreading wide across my face.

She thought about it for a moment, and then grinning back at me, she said, "Bring it on."

## Chapter 8

**The following morning Tabitha and I headed to work, both chatting excitedly at the prospects of winning the bet.** She was aching for a new guitar, and I was dying to prove her wrong. The fact that she was betting I would get my heart broken should have upset me, but I was so confident about Aidan that it didn't even faze me.

When we walked into the supermarket, our good moods instantly vanished as we both grimaced at the sight before us. Our annoyingly friendly boss Stephen, with a smile plastered permanently to his face, stood near the two registers Tabitha and I claimed daily. They were the closest to the bathrooms and the staff break-room, which were great places to disappear to on slow days. Those registers were highly coveted, and we made sure to arrive early every day to get them. Unfortunately for us, if we wanted to snag our favorite workspaces, it appeared we would have to have a chat with our rather irritating supervisor.

As we grudgingly made our way over to Stephen, I noticed he wasn't alone. Standing next to him was a young guy with black wavy hair, and skin almost as pale as mine. He had his hands in the pockets of his tight black jeans, and he was tracing invisible lines on the floor with his boots, looking bored already. He was also leaning against the register. My register.

"Good morning girls," Stephen's high-pitched voice rang out.

"Morning," we said together, sounding completely indifferent as we approached the two men.

Reaching the register, I slid past both of them and laid my bag and sketchbook under the counter, securing my space. Tabitha continued walking to the register directly beside mine to stake her claim as well. When I straightened up, I found Stephen still standing there with a goofy smile on his face. The new guy was there too, but he wasn't looking at the floor anymore. His dark coal-like eyes were looking right at me.

After one uncomfortable moment, I said, "So...what's up?"

"Selkie, this is Gabriel," Stephen said, gesturing to the slouching boy, who immediately stood up straight to reveal his true height, which was at least six feet or more.

"He's our newest bag boy, and I would like for you to help him get acquainted with how we do things around here. If you have any questions," he said, turning to Gabriel, "just come and find me. But don't you worry," he said, walking away with a slight bounce in his step, "you are in excellent hands."

"That guy is weird."

The voice that spoke, Gabriel's voice, was a lot deeper than I had expected, and as I looked over at him I saw that he was once again leaning on my register.

"Yeah, I guess. Look would you mind?" I said, motioning to the register.

"Oh yeah! Sorry," he said, moving quickly away to go stand at the end of the counter next to the plastic bags.

Tabitha came over then and cheerfully introduced herself.

"Hey, I'm Tabitha. Gabriel right?"

He didn't look at her as he answered, "Just Gabe."

She looked at me confused and a little wounded, but I just shrugged and remained silent.

She tried again. "Okay Gabe. So what brings you to this horrible establishment?"

He grunted and turned his head in her direction. "I needed a job, and this is the only place in town that would hire me."

She smiled, glad that he was paying her some attention, and then jokingly said, "What, are you some kind of a bad ass or something?"

"Something like that."

She beamed at him, and I could already see her undressing him with her eyes.

"Okay," I said trying to distract her. "Not that this isn't

super interesting, but we should probably start to at least look like we're doing something."

"Sorry Gabe," Tabitha said with a frown. "You managed to get paired with the only person in this store that actually does some work around here," and then she sauntered back to her register, moving her hips a little too much, and pulling a magazine off my shelf as she went.

I shook my head at her, and then turned to hit the power switch on the register. When I looked down to find the switch, I discovered a folded piece of paper propped up against the machine. It had my name on it. As I reached down to retrieve it Gabriel spoke. "So Selkie...that's an unusual name. Your parents must have had an imagination?"

"I wouldn't know," I said indifferently as I unfolded the tiny note.

I guess he didn't know what to say after that because he was silent for a few moments, which gave me time to concentrate on the paper in my hands.

*Selkie,*

*I couldn't wait. Come to the stock room.*

*Aidan*

My heart started to race as I glanced around for any more signs of him, and I didn't even realize Gabriel was still talking to me until I was halfway down Aisle 13.

"Selkie?"

"I'll be right back," I called as I practically sprinted down the aisle.

Pushing the swinging doors of the stock room open, I saw that the lights were still off. No one had been in there yet. I had no idea where to look, so I just whispered, "Aidan?"

A voice whispered back to me, "Over here, next to the Pringles."

I had no idea where the Pringles were, but I followed his voice, and within a few steps I was standing directly in front of him. I reached out to touch him, but thinking of Tabitha's words I pulled my arm back at the last second.

"What are you doing here?" I asked with excitement in my voice.

"I couldn't wait to see you."

"How long have you been here?"

"Not long."

"Should I even ask how you got in?"

"Does it really matter?"

He smiled at me, and I was a goner.

"Uh uh," was all I managed to say.

"Good, because I have something for you."

"For me?"

He reached into his pocket and pulled out a little black object. It was dark in the room, so it was difficult to make it out.

"What is it?" I asked.

"Well I know you don't have a car, and I didn't like the idea of you always walking around at night, so I thought you might need this."

He pressed a button on the object, and a bright light came pouring out from one end.

"You bought me a flashlight?" I said a little disappointed.

His smile faded. "You don't like it."

"No of course I do," I said, instantly regretting my words. "I just wasn't expecting it. It's a great gift. Very thoughtful."

He tried to smile, but I could see he didn't believe me.

"Hey!" I reached out and grabbed the flashlight, putting it in my left hand and keeping my right hand in his. "Seriously, this is perfect. It was so sweet of you to think about that, and now I can have something that reminds me of you."

"So you don't think it's lame?"

"I think it's awesome."

Leaning in, I gave him a quick peck on the cheek, but as I started to pull away he held my hand firmly and gently pulled me close again. His lips brushed my cheek, then traveled across my face and locked with mine. It was a gentle kiss, but it made my body churn with passion for him.

I quickly broke free of him. "Aidan...I...I don't want you to take this the wrong way but..."

"But you think we're moving too fast."

"How did you...?"

"It makes sense. We've barely known each other for a few days. It's just that I feel so connected to you and..."

"And it makes it hard to keep your distance..." I interrupted. "Trust me...I know. I just don't want you to think that I'm the kind of girl who goes around kissing guys she doesn't know...or worse."

I lowered my eyes and concentrated on the white circle of light at me feet.

"Selkie, I know you're not like that, and I hope you don't think that I would make you do something..."

"No of course not," I interrupted again. "I just wanted to make sure we were on the same page. So...maybe we could just…take it one step at a time, and try not to get carried away?"

"Absolutely," he grinned, and then raising his left hand, he said, "I promise to be on my best behavior."

We both laughed then, and I was glad we understood each other. We stood there for a few more seconds, until I remembered where I was. "Well I should probably get back to work, but we're still on for Thursday, right?"

"I wouldn't miss it!"

Suddenly a thought came to me and I was nervous when I asked, "What about your brothers?"

"Just let me take care of them," he said, walking me to the door, and then gently caressing my face he whispered, "See you in a few days."

"Okay…oh and thanks for the flashlight!"

"No problem," he said, sneaking in one more peck, and then he quickly disappeared into the darkness of the stockroom, and I headed back to work.

When I got back to my register, Tabitha was busy flirting with Gabriel. There were no customers in the store yet, so she had no reason to even think about working. She was leaning against the counter, her hands in the back pockets of her jeans, giving Gabriel and anyone else who was watching a great view of her chest. She was out of control.

"Sorry about that," I said. "Did I miss anything?"

"Tabitha was just giving me the low down on all the good hideouts here," Gabriel answered.

Tabitha radiated happiness at his words.

"How productive," I said while feigning a smile.

Tabitha quickly picked up on my sarcasm and spat back, "Where were you, anyway?"

"I had to check out something in the stockroom. Is that alright with you, nosey?"

Tabitha narrowed her eyes at me, but before she could go any farther I focused my attention on Gabriel, and said, "Hey, would you mine going into the break room and grabbing a few aprons for us?"

He glanced between us clearly sensing the tension, and then mumbled, "Uh...sure. Be right back."

As soon as he was gone, Tabitha erupted. "Selkie, what the hell?"

"Just read this," I said as I handed her Aidan's note.

As she read it, I could see the anger in her face begin to recede.

"Well, that explains your disappearance," she said,

returning the note. "I can't believe he was here, how did he get in?"

"I don't know."

"Well, what did he want?"

"He wanted to give me this." I pulled the flashlight out of my pocket and handed it to her.

"A flashlight," she giggled. "Really?"

"Oh, shut up!"

Embarrassed, I took it back from her and shoved it into my pocket, and then crossing my arms over my chest, I said, "He didn't want me walking home in the dark. I thought it was cute."

Thankfully, Gabriel came back then with the aprons, distracting Tabitha and protecting me from her unwanted ridicule, as Stephen's cheery voice sounded over the loudspeaker, "Attention all employees, this morning we have a new addition to our team. Please make sure to take some time today to welcome Gabriel Smith to our family. It is now eight o'clock and the store is open, have a happy day." At the end of the announcement, Tabitha and I groaned in unison, and then grabbed an apron from Gabriel and headed to our registers.

The rest of the morning ticked by slowly. Gabriel was a fast learner, so it only took me a few minutes to explain his duties and make sure he understood the incredibly difficult technique of shoving groceries into bags. Once he had a few customers under his belt, I stopped worrying about him, and disappeared into my head for a while.

I couldn't stop thinking about Aidan's gift. I kept the flashlight in my apron, and every once in a while, I would pull it out under the counter to examine it. It was small, but it looked really heavy duty. It was made out of some kind of metal, and on the top of the flashlight, where the light bulb was, the metal protruded out, encasing the fragile bulb within a jagged sharp wall. Though tiny, it looked like it could easily be used to shatter someone's skull, or at least leave a pretty bad bruise.

As I continued to study it, I found on the bottom of the flashlight two letters that had been etched into the metal. The letters were an S and an R, which I quickly deduced to be my initials. SR. Selkie Reid.

It was funny though, I didn't remember ever telling Aidan my last name. So how had he figured that one out? I thought about it for a while, but then I realized that if he could manage to sneak into a locked grocery store unnoticed, I was pretty sure he could figure out my last name without me telling him. In fact, I was pretty sure that he could figure out anything he put his mind to.

Aidan continued to occupy my mind all morning, and as I walked to the break room for lunch, the flashlight safely hidden in my apron, he was still secure in my thoughts. When I entered the room, I was surprised to find Gabriel sitting at a table in the corner reading.

"Hey, are you on break too?" I asked.

"No," he said shortly, lifting his eyes from the page for only a moment before returning his gaze to the magazine.

"No? So then your just sitting in here?"

This time he didn't look at me, but just flipped to the next page as he said, "Yes."

I didn't know what to say to that.

"So...uh?"

"Care to join me?" He closed his magazine and pulled the chair next to him out for me to sit in.

I hesitantly went to sit in the chair, pulling my lunch and sketchbook out of my bag and placing them both on the table. For some reason Gabriel, with his dark eyes and rebellious behavior, made me nervous. I quickly grabbed my peanut butter and jelly sandwich and started ripping off small pieces and shoving them into my mouth.

For a few seconds we just sat there in silence, then finally he spoke, "So, have you worked here long?"

"Yep." I continued to scarf down my sandwich.

"How do you stand it?"

"I don't have much choice. I need the money and don't have that many options."

"A pretty girl like you? I'm sure you have plenty of options."

My sandwich was gone, so I grabbed my apple and took a big bite, trying to ignore his compliment and the weird feeling it gave me.

He waited for a response, but when I didn't give him one, he said, "You don't talk much, do you?"

"I talk enough."

Just then Tabitha came in, and I breathed a grateful sigh.

"Here you are. I see you've found one of the hiding places…but if you want to keep your job you probably shouldn't sit here all day. Stephen's been looking for you."

"Really? That's too bad, 'cuz I was just getting to know Selkie here." He stood and walked towards the door. When he reached Tabitha, he said with a smirk, "Your friend is…interesting."

"You have no idea."

As I watched them disappear back onto the floor, I was grateful for their departure, happy to be alone. I finished eating my lunch and with still fifteen minutes left of my break, I opened my sketchbook, needing to find some peace of mind. I was feeling a little strange from my conversation with Gabriel. He was charming, that's for sure, but his bad boy attitude, if I was being completely honest, scared me a little.

I stared down at the blank page, waiting for my next inspiration. When nothing came, I impatiently tapped my pencil against the paper and lifted my head in silent frustration. There, directly in front of me, sat a dying ivy plant, and my next endeavor.

The poor plant that had once been vibrant and green was now brown and withered. Stephen had brought it in a few months back, thinking it would cheer up the room a little. But I guess he had forgotten about it, because it was clear from its haggard appearance that it hadn't been watered in quite some time.

I quickly went to work sketching the ivy, but instead of drawing the pathetic plant in front of me, I tried to recreate what it had once been. I made the vines long and abundant, with flourishing green leaves and strong vines that cascaded over the pot, giving the appearance of a leafy waterfall.

Just as I was putting the finishing touches on the picture, Claire, another girl who worked at the store, came in for her lunch break, signaling the end of my own. Not wanting to have Stephen come looking for me, I quickly packed up my things and headed to the door.

"Hey Selkie," Claire called from behind me.

I turned around to find her sitting at the table I had just left with a confused look on her face.

"What's up?" I asked.

"Who watered the plant?"

Now I was the one with the puzzled face. "What do you mean?"

"Look," she said as she pointed her finger toward the place where the dying ivy sat.

Except, it wasn't dying. On the contrary, the lengthy vines were blooming with green leaves. It looked just like my...

"Hmm...that's weird," I said, staring at the plant, unsure of what I was seeing.

"Yeah," Claire agreed. "But it looks nice though."

"Yeah...it does."

What was going on? That plant was practically dead just a few minutes ago, and now I was sure I was seeing a beautiful, living plant.

But how was that possible? There was no way that it could have...miraculously come back to life. So then what could explain this unbelievable transformation?

I so badly wanted to stay and figure out the mystery, but I had prolonged my break too much already. So with a bewildered expression on my face, and a thousand questions whirling around in my head, I left the break room and went back to work.

## Chapter 9

**"Excuse me, are you open?"**

I slowly lifted my head from my sketchbook to find an old woman standing in my aisle with a cart full of cat food, pudding, and several bags of bread. I didn't know how long she had been standing there, because I had been looking at the same picture for the last few hours, unable to concentrate on anything else.

"Uh...yeah...of course," I stumbled as I quickly closed my sketchbook and pushed my hair behind my ears, trying to collect myself. The old woman smiled kindly at me, and I could see the traces of pink lipstick on her teeth. As she reached into her cart, I watched patiently as she grasped each item with shaking hands, and carefully placed them on the conveyor belt.

Once I had scanned everything, I asked, "Do you have a discount card with us?"

She pulled her wallet out of her purse. "Oh yes, it's in here somewhere."

"It's *quitting time*," Stephen sang out as he approached my register. "Selkie and Gabe, make this your last customer and then turn out your light."

It had been a long confusing day, and I couldn't wait to get home. I turned back to the old lady now instantly impatient. She was still searching through her wallet, and in the process she had pulled out several receipts, a few expired coupons, and a wrinkled picture of a small bucktoothed child, but no discount card. I could see this could go on for a while, so I quickly scanned my own card and completed the transaction.

As the old lady hobbled away with her groceries, I gladly switched off my light, took off my apron, and gathered my things. Gabriel was nowhere to be seen. He had walked away without a word as soon as the last can of cat food had been bagged. To be honest, I had spent most of the afternoon ignoring him, so it wasn't as if I was expecting him to say goodbye.

I was walking to the break room to drop off my apron when Tabitha caught up with me and expressed her need to use the bathroom before our walk home. I had spent all day cooped up indoors and was in desperate need for some fresh air. So Tabitha took both of our aprons and dropped them off on the way to the bathroom, as I headed outside to wait for her.

It was a chilly night, and the evening air blew hard around me. I should have been freezing without a coat, but I relished the way the brisk breeze invigorated my fatigued body. I lifted my head to look up at the sky and saw that it was completely dark, without a single star visible through the heavy cloud cover. Not even the moon emanated any light, leaving the parking lot's only streetlamp to insufficiently illuminate the night around me.

From what I could see, except for Stephen's ratty old bug,

the parking lot was eerily vacant, and I felt strangely anxious standing alone in the dark. I had never been a scaredy-cat. In fact, I was probably the only child alive who had never been afraid of the dark. So it was weird that at that moment, for the first time in my life, I should be terrified of it.

I timidly moved forward several feet into the parking lot, when out of nowhere came the sound of crunching gravel and quickly approaching footsteps. My body tensed with unexpected fear, and I immediately grabbed my flashlight from my purse and started to back up closer to the store's entrance.

It was so dark outside I couldn't precisely pinpoint where the sound was coming from. I turned on the flashlight and nervously scanned back and forth, and when my light landed on the face of a dark figure I screamed in surprise.

"Would you mind lowering that light a little?" Gabriel asked as he cringed away from the bright light, shielding his face with his hand.

"Oh...sorry," I said, quickly lowering the light. "What were you doing? You scared the hell out of me."

"Sorry about that," he frowned. "I was just getting my bike."

He gestured to his right, and sure enough leaning against his hip was a large and dangerous looking motorcycle. As he moved closer with the deadly machine, the light from the store reflected off a silver streak that ran down the entire bike. It made it look sleek and sharp. If I didn't think motorcycles were stupid and unsafe, I would of thought it looked cool. He was only a few feet away when I noticed, etched on the side of the bike closer to the engine, a red skull and crossbones.

"Nice touch," I said, pointing to the emblem. I tried my best to suppress the sarcasm in my voice.

"Thanks. I thought it would give it an edge."

He seemed to believe my comment was a compliment. I had to stifle a laugh. He was being serious.

"And I'm guessing you thought by riding this bike it would give you an edge, too?"

His dark eyes smoldered with intensity. "Well, doesn't it?"

For an instant I held his gaze unable to look away. There was something about the way he stared at me. It was so powerful. I felt like his eyes could burn a hole right through me. It was almost hypnotic.

It was also kind of scary.

What was I doing?

I quickly averted my eyes from his face and stared at the ground, once again aware of the uncomfortable feelings his attention generated. My face felt hot, but my body was strangely cold.  I no longer wanted to stand so close to him.  I casually took a few steps away from him as I wrapped my arms protectively around myself, still keeping my eyes on the ground.

"Are you alright?" he asked.

I looked up hesitantly, trying my best to look at him but avoid his eyes. "Oh…yeah…just a little cold I guess."

"Well how 'bout you hop on and I'll give you a ride home?"

"Oh that's nice of you…but…I'm waiting for Tabitha so…"

"Well how about another time then?"

He was persistent.

"Um…actually I'm kind of seeing someone…so I don't think that would be a good idea."

"Really?"

He sounded surprised.

I was immediately defensive. "Yes, really!"

"Well, if you ever change your mind…"

"Change your mind about what?" Tabitha asked cheerily as she walked towards us.

"Nothing," I said quickly.  "Where have you been?"

"Freakin' Stephen!  I was almost out the door when he

caught me. Wrangled me into working tomorrow. It freakin'
sucks! Hey, is that your bike?"

Gabriel swung one leg over the motorcycle positioning
himself on the leather seat. "Yeah, it is. Want to take a ride?"

"Are you kidding me?" Tabitha shrieked. "I would love to!"

I grabbed her arm. "Hey, we were supposed to walk home
together."

She pulled her arm out of my grip, and then trying to talk
quiet enough so Gabriel wouldn't hear, she said, "Uh, earth to
Selkie. You walk home by yourself all the time, and he is freakin'
hot. There is no way I am going to pass this up!"

"Tabs you don't even know him!"

"It's just a ride. Chill out! I'll be back before you even get
halfway home."

With her hands on her hips she walked away from me and
hopped on the bike behind Gabriel. Once she had secured her
helmet, Gabriel started the engine, and as she wrapped her arms
securely around his waist the bike took off, leaving me once
again alone in the dark.

I just stood there and watched unbelieving as Tabitha and
the bike disappeared into the night. Just yesterday Tabitha had
scolded me for taking my relationship with Aidan too far, too
fast. But look at her. She had just left her best friend in the

middle of a dark parking lot to ride home with a strange guy she knew nothing about. What a hypocrite!

My face felt hot with frustration, and my breath was coming in short, heavy bursts. I began to walk quickly across the parking lot, feeling the need to work off my irritation. As I walked, my feet collided hard with the pavement while my trusty new flashlight shone bright ahead of me, guiding me forward away from the store and onto the sidewalk.

The cement on the path was old and broken with weeds growing out of every crack. In front of me I saw that some parts of the pavement had deteriorated into small, rocklike pieces. Still feeling upset about Tabitha, I violently kicked them out of my way and listened intently as they scattered, unable to see in the dark where they would land.

A few minutes into my walk, the wind began to blow in strong gusts sending shivers down my spine. Realizing I was no longer numb to the cold, I quickened my pace, and the light ahead of me bounced up and down in sync with my body's rapid movements.

Unexpectedly, my foot caught on a spot of raised up pavement and I tripped. While trying to avoid smacking my face on the hard cement, I accidentally dropped the flashlight, and as it hit the ground the light vanished.

"Crap," I said as I knelt down to retrieve the flashlight.

There were no streetlamps where I was standing, so I blindly searched the pavement, moving my hands back and forth across the cold hard ground. When my hand lightly brushed across the handle of the flashlight, I released a grateful sigh, but when I pressed the button to turn the light back on nothing happened.

"Oh, come on!"

I stood up and began to vigorously shake the light. When it didn't turn on, I slammed my palm against the bottom, confident that a little jostling would make it work. It didn't.

Then out of the darkness came a sound like the hissing of a snake and I froze. I had never encountered a snake before, so I wasn't quite sure what I was supposed to do. I decided to just remain still, in hopes that it would just ignore me and slither on by.

My hopes were quickly dashed, however, when the sound not only remained but also began to move closer and grow in volume. I was positive that one snake could not make all the noise I was hearing. Which meant that more than one snake was moving through the dark night toward me. Just my luck!

The hissing continued to grow louder, but it was hard to tell where the sound was coming from. When I had first heard it, I was sure it was behind me. So I slowly and quietly turned to face it, not wanting to be caught by surprise, but as I did so the hissing noise echoed loud to my right. They were moving fast, and they sounded angry.

Feeling extremely vulnerable, I began to rattle the flashlight around, praying that it would finally turn on, or even better, scare away whatever kind of serpent was making that hideous sound. The rattling seemed to do the trick and the flashlight turned on, temporarily blinding me thanks to the light bulb pointing directly at my face. Once the white dots faded away, I used the light to inspect the ground around me. The hissing was louder than ever, but I saw nothing slithering toward me.

I began to move forward, seeing that no scaly bodies were approaching and not wanting to just stand there waiting for them, when something moved in the grass to my right. I quickly shined my light on the spot, but found nothing. Whatever had been there was now gone.

I was about to give up on the search and keep walking, when a bright light flooded my vision, making everything around me glow and blinding me for the second time in just a few minutes. It wasn't until I heard the rumbling of an engine and the familiar, raspy laugh of my roommate that I realized Tabitha and Gabriel were driving up to meet me.

Once the bike was no longer in motion, Tabitha unwound herself from Gabriel and got off the bike; thanking him for the ride by giving him a quick peck on the cheek. Gabriel gave her a smile in return, and then turned his head to me and gave me a quick wink, before putting the bike into gear and driving out of sight.

"What happened, I thought you were supposed to be at home by now?" I said with obvious irritation.

Tabitha pushed her lower lip out and gazed at me with that pitiful puppy-dog face she knew I couldn't resist. "Selkie, don't be mad. I felt bad the moment we drove away. I shouldn't have left you by yourself...'Cuz God knows I would have been pissed if you had done that to me," she said, back to her normal self. "But I was stupid...and he was too hot to resist." Then she gave me the puppy-dog face one more time, and asked, "Can you forgive me?"

It was a stupid question, and she knew it. How could I be mad when she looked so pathetic?

"Fine," I sighed.

"Yippee," she squeaked as she hopped up and down, pleased she was off the hook.

"But don't ever do that again!"

Taking in my stern expression she stopped jumping, and with total seriousness, she said, "I promise. Cross my heart and hope to die."

## Chapter 10

**My feet were aching when we finally reached the apartment complex, and thanks to the bizarre events of the day, my mind was feeling just as exhausted.** After listening to Tabitha blab about Gabriel for a while, I brushed my teeth, put on my favorite oversized pajama shirt, and collapsed into bed; hoping that a good night's sleep would bring me some peace of mind. I ought to have known it wouldn't be that easy.

I shouldn't have been surprised that I dreamt that night, or even that I woke up gasping for air and covered in sticky sweat. No. I should have expected it since it happened every night, but I still wasn't used to the menacing shadows. I still couldn't control my fear of the mysterious face that haunted my thoughts, and to make matters worse, my dreams no longer tortured me in depressing silence but plagued me with an ominous chorus of hissing snakes. I didn't know why, but the nightmares were getting worse, and the thought that more bad nights were still ahead terrified me.

When my alarm went off the next morning, against my better judgment I rolled over and smashed the off button. Unwilling to except the fact that I needed to get out of bed and go to work, I remained on my back and stared up at the ceiling.

My apartment complex was old and in much need of

repair; one reason Tabitha and I were able to afford it. Unfortunately, every day I noticed some different piece of the apartment that was failing, and I didn't even have to leave my bed to detect one.

On the ceiling above my head I noticed the many layers of off-white paint were beginning to crack and chip. I immediately scanned the rest of the ceiling for deterioration and found the first signs of mildew beginning to creep up in the form of little gray dots around the air vent.

Gross!

The thought of sleeping under a fungus filled ceiling no longer seemed appealing. So I quickly made a mental note to pick up some bleach from the store and to also check Tabitha's room for any similar decay, before rolling over onto my side and pushing myself up into a sitting position.

I slowly pealed back my covers, exposing my bare legs to the early morning chill, and then hastily hopped out of bed and headed to the bathroom; hoping a nice hot shower would relieve me of the million goose bumps that were now covering my skin.

The warm shower did wonders for my aching body, but I still felt drowsy. I could have easily just crawled right back into bed, but the rent was due soon, and although I really wanted to, I couldn't afford to skip work.

With my towel wrapped securely around my body, I

headed to Tabitha's room to make sure she was awake. When I reached her room I was pleasantly surprised to hear her shower going. She hardly ever got up on her own accord, especially when she had to go to work. I thought about what might have encouraged this behavior, and that's when I realized she wasn't getting up to go to work. She was getting up to go see Gabriel. Tabitha always made the wrong choices when it came to boys, and I had a feeling that getting involved with Gabriel was not such a good idea, but I didn't have time to confront her about it now.

I walked back to my room to finish getting ready. Once I had put on my boring white shirt and khaki pants uniform, I went into the kitchen to pack my lunch and pour myself a bowl of cornflakes, but when I glanced at the clock on the stove I saw that I was running late and wouldn't have time to eat anything. I decided to throw a couple pieces of bread into the toaster and eat them on the way to work.

I would have loved a sandwich for lunch, but we had run out of lunchmeat the previous day and neither of us had any money to buy more. So instead I packed a measly lunch consisting of an apple, some string cheese, and a bag of potato chips, and then went back to the bathroom to blow-dry my hair and put on some makeup.

Usually I had very clear skin and hardly ever had to wear foundation, but with all the sweaty, restless nights I'd been having, I had to apply a lot of foundation and concealer to hide the darkness around my eyes and the red dots that were popping up everywhere. My pores felt like they were suffocating under the layer of cosmetics, but it was all I could do to not look like a hideous pimpled zombie.

Completely out of time I blow-dried my hair just enough so that it wasn't soaking wet, and then quickly ran a brush through my hair so it wouldn't tangle; putting it in a low pony tail at the base of my neck. As soon as I had brushed my teeth and put on some deodorant, I ran back to my room to grab my sketchpad and purse, and then ran to the living room where I found Tabitha impatiently pacing back and forth in front of the door.

"Selkie, come on! What's taking you so long? We're gonna be late."

"Since when do you care if we're late?"

"Since now. Now get your stuff together and let's go!"

"I'll be ready to go in like five seconds. So chill out!" I threw my purse over my shoulder and leaned down to grab my green hoodie that was conveniently lying on the floor next to the door. I couldn't remember how long it had been sitting there. So to be safe, I lowered my nose to the fabric to check for any unwanted smells. Happily, I found no unpleasant odors, just the lingering scent of my sweet pea body spray. It passed the test.

"Alright, I'm ready."

Tabitha rolled her eyes at me and then opened the door and made her way down the steps, leaving me behind to lock the door. When I reached the street she was already a good distance down the road.

"Tabitha, wait up!"

"Walk faster," she called back to me.

I quickened my pace, but my short legs were no match for her long stride.

"What was the point of waiting for me, if you're not going to walk with me?"

She slowed down a little bit, but didn't stop walking. When I finally reached her I was completely out of breath, and sweat was beginning to drip down my lower back.

Feeling a little annoyed, I asked, "What is going on with you today? Why are you acting so crazy motivated?"

She didn't look at me, but kept her eyes forward as she said, "What are you talking about?"

"You know what I'm talking about. Usually I have to drag you out of bed and beg you to go to work, but this morning you were up before I was."

"So what? I didn't want to be late."

"Why?"

I already knew the answer, but I wanted her to say it out loud.

"Because I've been late a lot and I don't want Stephen to get mad."

"Bullshit! You could care less what Stephen thinks. I know what this is all about, Tabs. You just want to see Gabriel. Admit it!"

Tabitha stopped walking, and I could see by the way she stood there, looking defiant with her arms wrapped tight across her chest, that the conversation we were having was about to get ugly.

"Okay. Fine," she replied. "So what if I am? What's the big deal? You should be happy. I'm finally going to be on time for work. Who cares if I'm excited to go just because Gabriel's going to be there?"

"I care, Tabs. I mean just because Gabriel is cute, that doesn't mean he's the right guy for you. I think he's dangerous."

"Uh...this coming from a girl whose boyfriend breaks into grocery stores and keeps all of the important stuff in his life a secret from you."

"That's different."

"Oh really? I don't think so. So Gabriel wears a lot of black and drives a motorcycle...ewww scary!"

"That's not what I mean. He's more than just a bad ass. He just doesn't seem like...a guy who's going to treat you right. Honestly, he reminds me a lot of Jason."

The second his name came out of my mouth I regretted it, but there was no taking it back. Jason had been Tabitha's first real love, but we never talked about him. Ever. They had met two years ago while shopping at the mall. Well, Tabitha was shopping. Jason was shoplifting.

The moment they met Tabitha was smitten with Jason's cute face and found his rebellious lifestyle exciting. They started to date, and at first Jason was surprisingly committed. They did everything together, and Tabitha would have done anything for Jason. After only a few weeks of dating Tabitha was sure she was in love with him and she thought the only way to show him how she felt was with her body. So she slept with him.

A few weeks later when she found out she was pregnant, Tabitha ran straight to Jason looking for support, but found only rejection. He told her he never loved her and that he wanted nothing to do with her or the baby. She was heartbroken and completely alone. When the time came to make a decision, she realized she could never put a child into the horrible system she had grown up in, and so she decided she would keep the baby. But a day later she had a miscarriage and lost it.

We never talked about Jason or the baby because it was too hard for Tabitha to deal with. I had brought him up trying to prove my point, but I could tell by the expression on her face that this time I had gone too far.

"What did you just say?" she said, stumbling back a step.

"Tabs, I'm so sorry." I reached for her but she pulled away. "I should never have said that."

"Damn right you should have never said it! God Selkie! Why do you have to ruin everything?"

That hurt.

"I wasn't trying to ruin anything. I was just trying to help. I love you, and I don't want you to get hurt."

"Well you should have thought about that before you mentioned him."

I could feel tears welling up in the corners of my eyes, as I said, "I don't know why I said it. God, I'm so sorry. Just please...please don't be mad at me."

I thought I could resist the impulse to cry, but I was wrong. A long stream of tears poured down across my cheek, but I quickly brushed them away. I wasn't the one who should be crying.

"Jesus, Selkie! Stop crying. I'm not that mad. I'm just

pissed you ruined my buzz."

I wiped my eyes one more time and took a deep breath. "So you don't hate me?"

"No, I don't hate you. I just want you to calm down and let me have some fun. I'm not stupid, I won't let anyone do what...Jason did."

"Alright. I'll try to relax. But I want you to be careful. I don't trust Gabriel."

"Well that's not surprising, you don't trust anyone."

"That's not true," I argued. "I trust Aidan...and I trust you." Then I smiled, and added, "Sometimes."

"Well then trust me now and let me do my thing."

"Fine. But just promise me you'll be careful."

"I promise. Okay? Now stop worrying!"

She pulled her phone out of her pocket and checked the time. "Damn Selkie, now we're gonna be late, and I wanted to get on Stephen's good side today." She started walking again, and I had to practically run to keep up.

"I don't get it. What's the big deal? Why do you want to impress Stephen so much?"

She slowed her pace, noticing that I was struggling to

keep up with her, and then linking her arm through mine, she said, "Because dummy, I want Gabriel to be my bag boy."

## Chapter 11

**Once we arrived at work, Tabitha didn't waste time snagging a register next to mine or dropping her lunch off in the breakroom.** Instead she eagerly carried all her belongings with her as she ran up and down the aisles in search for Stephen. It didn't take those lengthy legs of hers very long to locate him in aisle 12, discussing the layout of the cereal shelves with Bobby; one of the stores underpaid stock boys.

I watched from my register as she patiently waited for Stephen to finish his conversation and then turn his attention to her. I couldn't make out what she was saying, but I could tell by her rapid speaking that she was very nervous. Stephen just stood there smiling as she rambled on and on, and when her mouth finally stopped moving she took a deep breath in, obviously expecting the worst. Stephen stood there for a moment, clearly unsure of what to do, and then finally made his decision. He barely had time to finish speaking before Tabitha was hugging him.

When she managed to calm down enough to release herself from Stephen's awkwardly gangly body, they spoke for a few more moments and then ended their conversation with the shaking of hands. Since I was too far away to hear what they were saying, I could only guess that he was permitting Tabitha to work with Gabriel as long as she agreed to certain conditions.

My speculations were confirmed when Tabitha came bouncing back over to me. "He said yes. Can you believe it? And all I had to do was promise him that I would like...work and not just talk...and stuff. It was so easy."

In her excitement, she grabbed a candy bar from the shelf by the register and attempted to tear the wrapper, but before she could succeed in opening it I grabbed it from her, and said, "But can you actually do what you promised?"

I waved the candy bar in front of her face. "I mean it's not like you're the employee of the month here." Then placing the candy bar back on the shelf, I asked, "Can you honestly work with Gabriel without actually talking or... I don't know...flirting with him?"

"Of course I can," she said, folding her arms in outrage. "And it's not like Stephen's going to be watching us the entire day."

"So you do plan on talking to him."

"Oh don't be stupid, Selkie! Just because you can go all day without talking to anybody doesn't mean the rest of us can. I'm smart. I can work and socialize at the same time...and Stephen will never know the difference."

"Whatever you say."

Turning away from her I reached down to power up my

register, and just like the day before, propped up against the on switch was a little note with my name written on it. I quickly grasped the tiny piece of paper, turning my back completely on Tabitha to get a little privacy, and then slowly, with my heart thudding hard inside my chest, I opened it.

There was only a single word neatly printed on the slip of paper, but that one word was enough to make my heart pound ever faster.

*Tomorrow.*

A huge smile appeared, spreading across my entire face as I re-read the word over and over in my head.

Tomorrow. Tomorrow. Tomorrow.

Nothing existed in that moment but that small piece of paper cupped gently between my two hands, and the sound of my living, thriving heart pounding so loud I could feel it echoing inside my ears. The thought that Aidan and I would be together, alone, in just a few short hours made my whole body burst with excitement.

I could hardly contain my happiness. I whirled around, eager to share Aidan's note with Tabitha, but she was no longer standing beside me. She stood a few registers down, not at her normal register next to me, but at the only register that was left unoccupied after her chat with Stephen...and she wasn't alone. She stood there already flirting with Gabriel.

Tabitha was attempting to work and focus on Gabriel at the same time, but she was failing miserably. Her station was untidy and needed to be stocked with bags and merchandise. Gabriel wasn't even bothering to look like he was doing anything. He was just lounging against the counter, unaware that any work needed to be done, watching transfixed as Tabitha seductively tossed her hair from in front of her face and smiled at him.

He leaned closer to her and gently tucked a piece of her hair behind one ear, lingering for one moment on her cheek. She blushed, and then quickly turned away to focus on her neglected register.

And that's when it happened.

With Tabitha's back to him, Gabriel slowly turned his head and looked directly at me. He stared at me with his deep dark eyes, and it was obvious, by the way he was staring, that he was conscious that I had been watching them. As he continued to look at me and my bewildered expression, the corners of his lips began to turn upwards, forming a sly smile. I cringed away from the smile, but could not release the hold his eyes had over me. From the corner of my eye I saw Tabitha turn to face Gabriel again, but before she could see where he was looking, he gave me a wink, released his gaze, and then turned back to her with a smile. He was up to something, and I didn't like it.

For the rest of the morning I didn't so much as glance in their direction. Tabitha tried to get my attention a few times, no doubt wanting to impress me with how well she and Gabriel were getting along, but I just acted as if I hadn't heard her. I was afraid that ignoring her might ignite a new feud between us, but I would have rather dealt with that then dare to link eyes with Gabriel one more time.

Besides, I didn't have to look at them to know that they were enjoying themselves. Every few seconds one of them would burst out in ridiculous laughter, and everyone around them couldn't help but glance their way, hoping to figure out what was so hilarious. Everyone but me.

I just couldn't understand it. The way he looked at me. The way he flirted with her. Staring at me as if we shared some incredible secret, but talking and laughing with her as if nobody else even existed. How could he act so smitten with her, but then look at me the way he did?

I had no idea what he was trying to do, but one thing I was certain of; if he really liked Tabitha he wouldn't be sneaking looks at me when her back was turned. He was obviously just having some fun stringing her along, but I would never dare to tell her that. She would just get angry and say that I was being jealous, which of course I wasn't.

I mean how could I ever be jealous when I had someone as amazing as Aidan in my life? He was the perfect guy, who had not only lifted my spirit with his smile, but also claimed my heart with a single touch. He was everything I could have ever dreamed of having, and Gabriel was nothing like him. Gabriel was just a rebellious jerk who liked to play games with girl's hearts. Girls like Tabitha. And I wasn't going to let him use me to hurt her. I could care less about him and his affecting eyes. The only person that mattered was Tabitha. I had no idea how I was going to convince her that Gabriel was up to no good, but I had to think of something quick, before she was as smitten with him as he was pretending to be with her.

It turned out that the universe was on my side, for once, and I wasn't going to have to try hard to keep them apart at work. Stephen did that for me. After several flustered attempts to motivate Tabitha and Gabriel to do some work, Stephen saw that it was a hopeless cause and decided the store was too busy to allow their misbehavior any longer. He quickly separated them, thankfully placing Gabriel with another cashier that wasn't me, leaving Tabitha without anyone to bag for her. Once everything had settled down, Stephen disappeared into the breakroom for a while, only to reappear with a bright yellow sign that was to be hung on the wall behind each register. The sign read:

**Things that should be done when you do not have a customer:**

**(Not talking to other associates)**

Clean your belt and bagging area

Overstock put in correct place

Magazine racks neat and organized

Meet and greet your customers

Bag for the person next to you

Make sure you have enough change

Fill your bagging areas with plastic

Then at the very bottom, as if it wasn't already extremely obvious, written in bold letters and then highlighted in orange was the phrase:

**DO NOT TALK TO OTHER ASSOCIATES!**

I felt horrible that Tabitha had to be so publicly humiliated, but if it meant that she would be safe from Gabriel and his undoubtedly questionable behavior, then I was honestly glad for it.

Besides Tabitha's disgruntled looks toward Stephen, and Gabriel's evident disdain for any type of work, the rest of the day passed quickly, with little to no disruptions. I had a quiet lunch by myself where I was able to peacefully sketch the view of the street outside the break-room window, and of course daydream about Aidan, whose note, which I kept in the front pocket of my pants, was now wrinkled and worn due to my obsessive reading of it.

It was a little after six o'clock, and the sun was still shining brightly through the windows at the front of the store when I signed off my register. It was the only day of the week I didn't have to stay until closing, and I was thrilled to be able to walk home when there was still light in the sky. I had gathered all my things and was just about to leave the breakroom and escape the store for an entire day when Gabriel came in, blocking the door and my only exit.

"Hey, I'm glad I caught you!"

Careful to keep my eyes on my shoes and not on his face, I said, "Well that makes one of us."

"What's that supposed to mean?" he asked, leaning up against the doorframe.

"You know what it means," I spat back at him, and then finding strength in my anger I lifted my eyes, and said, "You might think that just because you're cute, every girl is just going to fall all over you, but you're wrong. Tabitha is my best friend and if you think I'm going to let you hurt her, well you're damn wrong."

"Excuse me?"

"You heard me. Tabitha likes you, which means no matter what I say about you won't matter. But I know the kind of guy you are, and if you think I would let you mess with my friend, well, you better think again."

Gabriel crossed his arms over his chest, unwilling to budge from his spot in front of the door, and then smiling, he said, "Selkie, you've got it all wrong."

"Oh? Do I?"

"Yeah, you do."

"Well I don't think so. So stop acting so innocent. I've seen you looking at me."

We stood there for one tense moment staring at each other, and then out of nowhere he relaxed his stance and began to laugh.

"What's so funny?" I asked.

"Seriously, Selkie? I was just messing with you."

"What?" I said, feeling the energy instantly drain from my body and embarrassment flood my face.

"No offense," he shrugged, "but I wasn't trying to pick you up or anything. I was just having some fun. I mean, yeah when I met you I thought you were cute, but you made it clear the other night that you were seeing someone. So that's why I started talking to Tabitha."

"Then why do you keep looking at me?" I retorted.

He dropped his smile, not looking as confident when he said, "Okay. I admit it. I was flirting...a little. But I didn't think it would bother you like this."

"Why wouldn't it bother me? You're hanging out with my best friend."

"I guess I didn't think about it."

I shook my head, amazed at how casual he was being about all of this, "Okay...well...it did bother me, and I'd like it if you wouldn't do it again. Like I said, Tabitha is my best friend and she doesn't deserve to be treated like that. If you like her, then fine, but if you're just messing with her then you better back off."

"Alright," he said, stepping out of the doorway and letting me pass. "I got it. But just to let you know, I do like Tabitha and I hope we can still be friends."

I stopped walking and slowly turned to face him. I tilted my head to one side, considering him carefully. He looked earnest enough, but looks could be deceiving. Tabitha really liked him, but I still didn't quite trust him. I thought about it for another second and then decided I would just have to take my chances, for Tabitha's sake.

"Okay," I said, raising my hand. "Friends."

Gabriel repeated the gesture, and as we shook hands I smiled, glad to be right about one thing. There was no tingle. No spark. He was nothing like Aidan.

## Chapter 12

**The sun was slowly fading, giving way to the night, as I climbed the last few steps leading up to my apartment.** I had taken my time walking home, in no hurry to be anywhere or do anything. I walked past the harbor, letting myself get lost in thoughts about Aidan, while enjoying the sound of the waves crashing against the rocky shore. The longer I walked the chillier the evening became, but the breeze coming off the bay was warm and welcoming. I unzipped my jacket, allowing the misty air to lightly brush against my cooled skin. It was so peaceful. So invigorating. I could almost forget that I hadn't slept in days. Almost.

Once I was back in my apartment, I rummaged through our desolate pantry for dinner, hoping I would find something delicious hiding behind one of our many boxes of mac and cheese; which we couldn't make since we had no milk or butter. The best I could find was a can of peaches and a half-eaten bag of cheese curls. I quickly devoured the bag of cheesy goodness, licking every bit of cheese off my fingers, and then moved to the peaches. I decided since this was the last of our food I would savor every last bite. Take my time. Make it last.

I grabbed a fork from the sink and hastily ran it back and forth under the hot water for a second, too lazy to take the time to properly wash it, and then snapped the lid off the can of peaches and headed to the living room. I hit the power button on the TV remote and began scanning for something decent to watch. After a few minutes I lucked out, discovering an all-day marathon of *The Office*, and then remembered I still had the uneaten can of peaches in my hand. I happily settled into the couch, turned up the volume and began the feast. At the end of the first episode all of the fruit was gone, but I still felt hungry. So I lifted the can to my mouth and drained it of all its sweet syrup.

A few more episodes had passed when Tabitha arrived home with some leftover pizza in hand. Gabriel had taken her out to dinner after work, but she had refused to let herself eat more than one piece in front of him. Knowing I would be starving, she brought the rest home and together we demolished it in less than two minutes. Feeling stuffed for the first time in forever I said goodnight to Tabitha, and then went to my room to get ready for bed.

The temperature had dropped outside, making my room colder than usual. So instead of my normal oversized shirt and bare legs, I changed into some flannel pants and a long-sleeved t-shirt. I flung my work clothes onto the chair by me desk, and then went to the bathroom to wash my face and brush my teeth. Worried that Aidan might think I was hideous with my skin all covered in pimples, I applied an extra amount of acne medicine to my face, before going back to my room and crawling under the covers.

As soon as I lay down, I remembered Aidan's note in the pocket of my pants.  Not wanting it to end up being destroyed in the washer, I turned my little lamp on and got back out of bed to get it.  I placed the little sheet of paper in the side table next to my bed, where I also kept Aidan's first note and the flashlight he had given me.  It made me feel safe knowing he, or at least some things he had touched, were close by me as I slept.  With Aidan in safekeeping, feeling immensely secure and content, I turned off my light, closed my eyes, and fell asleep.

The next morning, I awoke with the sun streaming through my window onto my face.  What time was it?  I glanced over at my clock.  It was almost noon.  Had I slept through the entire night?  I stretched my arms above my head and yawned, amazed to find my body so rested.  As I sat up and threw off the covers, I tried to remember any nightmares or dreams from the previous night, but I couldn't recall anything.

I stood up and went to the bathroom, unable to quiet my bladder that was screaming at me, and was astonished when I looked in the mirror.  The darkness under my eyes was gone, and the blemishes that were so apparent yesterday were hardly even noticeable.  I looked like myself again.  I was so happy with the turn of events that right there in the middle of the bathroom I started to dance.  I was shimmying my shoulders and shaking my hips when Tabitha walked in.

"What the hell are you doing?" she asked with the tiniest bit of amusement in her voice.

I stopped immediately.

"I wasn't doing anything," I said, feeling foolish.

"Yeah, sure," she said, raising her eyebrows. "Um, I'm gonna forget I saw that...but only if you promise me that you will never dance like that again." A loud chuckle escaped her lips. "I mean, damn girl! You are so white."

"Thank you," I said, completely humiliated. "I hadn't noticed."

Once Tabitha was done embarrassing me, she left me alone to get ready. I had only an hour until I was supposed to leave to meet Aidan. I was running late...again. I took the fastest shower of my life and got out to dry off, just to realize that I hadn't washed the conditioner out of my hair. So unfortunately, I had to get back into the shower, get all wet again, wash all the conditioner out of my hair, and then get out and dry off for the second time.

Back in my room with my towel still wrapped around me, I rushed to my window and pushed it open to feel the outside temperature, and was suddenly assailed with a bitter, biting wind. It was freezing. Great! I went to my dresser and found a bra and some underwear, then went to my closet and pulled on a red sweater and a pair of jeans. I put on my favorite knee length black boots that zipped up the side, and then grabbed my purse and sketchbook and sprinted to the bathroom. Thanks to my two showers, I had just enough time left to throw on some makeup and dry my hair, before screaming goodbye to Tabitha and running out the door.

I reached the pharmacy with two minutes to spare. Aidan wasn't standing outside, but it was so abnormally cold I just assumed he was inside waiting in the warmth. I entered the store and walked past the racks of greeting cards and the medical merchandise, past the old fashioned soda shop counter where Mr. Wilkes makes the most delicious limeades, past all the old ladies conversing about their present ailments, and had made it all the way back to the front of the store without catching a single glimpse of Aidan. I was hoping he would be at the store waiting for me, but he still had time, there was no reason for me to worry.

I felt silly just standing in the store not buying anything, so I went back outside to wait on the street. I kept my hands in my pockets to try to keep them warm, and watched as my breath became visible in the air in front of my face. I could tell my nose and cheeks were starting to turn red from the cold, and I was just about to go back inside when I heard Aidan call my name.

"Selkie."

I turned around at the sound of his voice, but I couldn't see him anywhere.

"Aidan?"

"Over here, in the alley."

Looking around I discovered a little door, almost like a fence, in between the pharmacy and the adjacent building that hid the tiny alley from the public. I walked over and gently pushed the door open and found Aidan there waiting for me with a smile on his face. Without question, Aidan was the most handsome person on the planet, and he was mine.

In two steps I was standing in front of him, and in less than a second after that, I was kissing him. Our faces were both frozen from the cold outside air, but his warm lips on mine filled my whole body with an incredible heat. He started to pull away, but I couldn't let him go, not yet. Instead I lifted my arms and wrapped them around his neck, meshing our two bodies tighter together. He tasted so sweet. When I finally pulled away we were both out of breath and Aidan's hands were still holding firm to my lower back.

Realizing I had just pretty much attacked him, I blushed, and said, "Sorry. I guess...I really missed you."

"Why are you apologizing? That was amazing!"

"Because we said we were going to take things slow, and I just screwed it up. I just can't resist you when you smile like that."

"Smile like what?" he asked.

"As if you don't know," I said with a smile of my own.

"No really," he said sincerely. "I don't know what you mean. Tell me."

"Oh…" I said, a little flustered. "I don't know…it's just that…you have the most amazing smile, and when you smile at me, I just feel…"

"What?" he asked as he looked at me even more serious this time.

"You'll just think I'm being stupid."

He placed one hand on my cheek and my whole body began to melt as he said, "Selkie, I could never think that you were stupid." He smiled again, and the feeling that came over me was so intense, so mind-blowing, there was no way I could deny what I felt.

I took a deep breath. "Well, when you look at me that way, I can't help but…love you." There was silence for a split second, and then Aidan's face lit up with a smile so radiant that my heart began to race.

He wrapped his arms tighter around me and lifted me up off the ground. He was so strong. His lips met mine again, and this time the kissing was gentle, but just as amazing. He continued to hold me tight, my feet dangling, as his lips moved from my lips, to my cheek, and finally to the space below my ear. My body was shaking with delight, and when he began to nibble on my ear I became putty in his hands.

I thought nothing could be better than that moment...but I was wrong...because what happened next changed me forever. With Aidan's arms holding me tight, and his sweet lips just an inch away from my ear, he whispered the words I never thought I would ever hear. "Selkie Reid, I love you."

## Chapter 13

**I stayed where I was, frozen in his strong embrace as I tried to make sense of what he had just said.** I knew exactly how I felt about Aidan. How much he meant to me. From the first time we touched I knew how much I needed him. I should have been overjoyed when he spoke those three amazing words to me; words that no one had ever said to me in my entire life. But instead I was surprised. It just didn't make sense.

Aidan must have sensed my unease, because he slowly lowered me down, my feet once again resting on the hard pavement, and then taking my two small shaking hands in his own, he asked, "Selkie, what's the matter?"

I repeated out loud this time the only thought that kept appearing in my head. "It just doesn't make sense."

"What doesn't make sense?" he pressed.

Separating our two warm bodies, I took a step back from him. He didn't bother moving forward to bridge the gap, but stood there strong as a statue, waiting for me to speak.

I was timid when I finally spoke, "You say you love me, but why?"

"How could I not?"

"That's not really an answer."

"I'm sorry," he apologized. "It's kind of hard for me to explain…"

I took a step toward him. "Please, could you try?"

With a smile he casually reached up and began to twirl a few locks of my hair around his finger. The sensation of him touching me was out of this world, but I remained calm. He kept playing with my hair, driving me wild, as he took a few seconds to collect his thoughts, and then with a sigh, he said, "I don't know why I love you."

That was definitely not what I was hoping for.

He quickly continued. "Oh crap, please, don't take that the wrong way. I told you this was hard to explain."

I didn't say anything, but just let him continue.

"Okay. Remember that day in the park, the first day we met?"

I smiled. "How could I forget, you hit me with a Frisbee."

"You're not making this easier," he said with a grin.

"Sorry, I'll shut up." I mimed locking my lips with a key and threw them farther down the alley.

"I don't know what happened, but when I was face to face

with you, and you touched my hand, it was like an explosion went off inside of me."

I could remember every moment of that touch, the one that set my heart on fire.

"Well after that," he continued, "It was impossible for me to do anything but think about you. It was like you were burned into my memory and there was nothing I could do about it. You were instantly a part of me."

"And that doesn't scare you?" I asked.

"Are you kidding me? Of course it does. It terrifies me." Then with both of his hands cupping my face, he said, "But what terrifies me more, is living a life without you in it. And if that's not love, I don't know what is."

I couldn't breathe. I couldn't think. My brain was mush.

"Selkie?"

Silently I stood there, feeling my legs might collapse at any moment, unable to comprehend anything but that this amazing, incredible guy was truly and irreversibly in love...with me. It was insane. It was impossible. I had no idea what to say.

So I just blurted out the first thing that came to my mind. "Green!"

He stared at me, perplexed. "Excuse me?"

"My favorite color…is green."

He began to laugh under his breath, a big smile spreading across his face as he said, "Selkie Reid, you are the strangest girl I have ever met, and I love you even more because of it," and then he leaned in and lightly grazed his lips against my nose.

His hands were still cupped softly around my face, warming my skin and sending tingles through my entire body. I placed my hands on top of his, and his whole body visibly shook.

"What's yours?" I asked.

"My favorite color?"

I nodded.

He moved his hands from my face to the top of my head, running his fingers through my hair as he answered, "I thought it was obvious."

"Okay," I said, trying my best not to blush. "How old are you?"

"Nineteen."

"And where did you go to school?"

"Actually, I didn't go to school, not exactly. I was homeschooled. Alright, now it's my turn," but before he could ask me a question, we were unfortunately interrupted…again.

When the door to the alley swung open, there was no doubt in my mind who would soon come walking through it. I was hoping, praying, that it was anyone else but him.

As Brendan walked toward us, my heart sank with the realization that Aidan would very soon by leaving me. My hands clung to his chest, my fingernails cutting into his shirt, unwilling to let him go. If I was hurting him he didn't show it. Instead he just wrapped his arm protectively around my shoulder and waited for what was sure to happen next.

"Selkie," Brendan growled. "I'm afraid I can't say it's nice to see you again. Aidan, let's go!"

I didn't wait for Aidan to move or speak; I was too angry at Brendan and this ridiculous situation, which I still knew nothing about, to keep quiet. "Why are you doing this? Can't you see that you're hurting your own brother? What's the matter with you?"

I was no longer next to Aidan, but had taken several steps forward, and was standing with my fists clenched only a few inches from Brendan. He didn't move, he barely even breathed. He just glared at me and in a voice so hurtful, he said, "You have no idea what you have done. I'm not the one messing everything up here, you are!"

"Brendan, that's enough," Aidan yelled. "If you want me to go, then I'll go, but just leave Selkie out of this."

"How am I supposed to do that, Aidan? Can't you see what she's doing to you, to all of us?"

What was Brendan talking about? What had I done? Why was he so against me? I'd never done anything to him. The tears started to fall before I could even try to stop them.

"Aidan, what is he talking about?" I cried.

Aidan grabbed my hand and pulled me to him, trying to comfort me with his loving touch, but I didn't want any more tingles, I wanted answers.

I tried to push him away, but it was he this time that was unwilling to let go. Unable to release myself from his grasp I simply lifted my head, hoping to find the answers I desired in his compassionate eyes, but they weren't looking at me. No, they were glaring with hatred at his brother.

When Aidan spoke I was alarmed at the way his voice sounded, so deep, so intimidating. "How dare you blame this on Selkie, Brendan. She has nothing to do with this. You're the one who can't seem to realize how much she means to me. You're the one who keeps ruining everything!"

Aidan was so angry his whole body was shaking. I tried to get his attention, but he was so caught up in his fury he hardly noticed me shaking him. He just continued to stare at Brendan, and then his voice became only a whisper as he said, "You're my brother and I love you, but if you ever hurt Selkie again, I swear you'll regret it."

Aidan's words echoed eerily off the alley walls, and then it was silent. No one moved. No one spoke. No one dared to even breathe.

After what seemed like a lifetime of waiting, Aidan slowly turned to me, and his face was once again filled with love. "Selkie, I have to go."

"I know," I said sadly.

"But you'll be okay?" he asked, truly concerned.

"No, but I'll manage," I shrugged.

"Just remember what I said, okay? I meant every word of it."

Feeling a little shaky, and unsure if I could trust my voice not to break, I just nodded.

Aidan placed his hands on my shoulders and pulled me in for one last hug, but not even a thousand sweet kisses from him could make me feel better. He was leaving me again. He was walking away and I could do nothing to stop him. He was already through the door and back on the street. He was gone, and I had no idea when I would see him again.

My feet began to move before my brain understood what I was doing. When I busted out of the alley, I saw they were already halfway down the street, almost out of view. I ran faster, my boots thudding hard against the sidewalk. They were about to turn the corner. I couldn't let him go, not yet. I ran as fast as I could, and when I finally reached them I was out of breath.

"Aidan, wait," I gasped.

He immediately turned around to face me, ignoring his brother's commands to keep moving. "Selkie?"

"I need to tell you something," I said, and then looking at Brendan, I added, "I need to tell you both something." Brendan stared at me with hard eyes, but he didn't protest. I looked back to Aidan, and with a smile on my face I repeated his words. "I don't know why I love you. I just do. I have since the moment we met. You make me feel safe. Something I have never felt in my entire life, and I can't imagine living without you...and I won't live without him," I said firmly, turning to Brendan. "So go ahead and take him, but I just want you to know that I will be fighting for him, and nothing you do is going to change that."

Feeling stronger than I had in my entire life, I leaned in and planted a kiss on Aidan's cheek. He didn't say anything, but as I pulled away I could see that his gorgeous gray eyes were filled with pride. I quickly glanced over at Brendan to find him looking a little shell shocked, and then turned back to Aidan, gave him a wink, and said, "See you soon."

**Chapter 14**

**My whole being was brimming with elation as I strutted away from Aidan and his horrible brother.** Part of me, a big part, wanted to turn around when I reached the corner, just to see if Brendan was still standing there with that stupid look on his face, but I was afraid that one glance from Aidan might soften my resolve and just send me running right back into his arms. I couldn't, wouldn't give Brendan the satisfaction.

I needed to be strong, and for once in my life I was going to take control of my destiny. I wasn't going to let Aidan's bully of a brother decide how my life was going to turn out. Determined, I kept my eyes forward and continued down the street, never once glancing behind me.

I didn't know when I was going to see Aidan again, but for once I wasn't worried. How could I be? Aidan, literally the man of my dreams, was in love with me. He wanted to be with me. I knew without a shadow of a doubt that he would find a way to see me again. I just had to be patient and wait.

I was halfway home when I realized that it was Thursday afternoon, and I shouldn't be walking home, but walking to the grocery store to pick up my paycheck. Payday was officially scheduled for every other Friday, but one Thursday, while grabbing some pens from Stephen's office, I stumbled upon a big pile of checks. When I asked Stephen about them, he told me that the checks had to be made out in advance, and as long as I didn't tell anyone I was welcome to pick mine up early. I wasn't able to keep it from Tabitha, so of course she begged Stephen to get hers early too. Ever since then, as long as I found Stephen in a good mood, which was pretty much all the time, I was guaranteed to obtain my check early.

I arrived to find the store bustling with activity, much more than usual for a weekday, and of course we were understaffed. Typical. I located Stephen at register four bagging for Susie, our sixty-eight-year-old cashier who only worked when no one else could. Susie had terrible arthritis, which made it impossible for her to lift anything over two pounds, and she was constantly leaving her station to use the bathroom. Stephen would have loved to have fired her a long time ago, except for the fact that she was just a volunteer, and you can't fire someone who doesn't even get paid.

He looked a little frazzled, his hands all full of groceries needing to be bagged, when I asked him for my check, but he didn't refuse me. He placed the groceries back on the conveyor belt and told Susie he would return shortly. Once we got into his office, he seemed more like his cheery self, and I figured he was just grateful to have a solid excuse to ditch Susie for a few minutes.

I had already signed for my check, and he was just about

to hand it over, when Tabitha busted in.  I was sure Stephen didn't mind giving me my check early because I was his hardest working employee and he wanted me to stick around, but he always seemed a little put out when Tabitha asked for hers; probably because she never really did anything to deserve it.

He was reluctant, but he wasn't stupid.  Stephen knew far too well that Tabitha could have a horrible, and somewhat terrifying attitude if she didn't get what she wanted.  Which is why he always ended up handing it over without too much protest.

With our checks in hand, we gladly strolled across the street to the bank, thankful that it was still open, and then returned to the store, our wallets bulging with money, to shop for some much-needed groceries.  We spent the next hour and a half pushing our cart down every aisle, buying all the essentials and anything else that looked appealing.  When we reached the chip aisle, we were both so hungry, we couldn't resist grabbing a bag of our favorite cheese curls and ripping it open.  We both stuffed a handful into our mouths, and then placed them in the cart next to our purses so that we could continue snacking on them while we shopped.

Our cart was practically overflowing when we reached the check out, and even after our employee discount it took almost all of our money to pay for the groceries, but we didn't care, we were just happy to have food again.  We didn't realize until after everything was bagged how much there was to carry, and we struggled to load all of the bags onto our arms, wrists, and hands. Before we even left the store, the plastic was already cutting into my skin, but I didn't complain.

As we walked home we had to stop every few seconds to re-adjust the bags or take a rest from the heavy load. At one point, a bag full of cans broke, spilling our precious food all across the sidewalk, and we had to put everything down and try our best to relocate the fallen items into different bags. By the time we had walked half the way home the sun was beginning to set, making it harder to see our way, and forcing us to move even slower. When our apartment complex was finally in sight, we breathed a sigh and hobbled on, excited to be so close to dinner and rest. We had just one more block to walk before we were safely at home, when the awful hissing sound returned stopping us both in our tracks.

"What the hell is that?" Tabitha shrieked. "Is that a freakin' snake?" She closed her eyes and frantically moved her head side to side. "Because girl, you know how much I hate snakes."

"Tabs, calm down," I said soothingly. "Let's just keep moving."

"Good idea, let's just keep..."

Before she could finish the noise intensified, swarming

around us and sending chills down my spine.

"Jesus, Selkie. What the freak?"

Tabitha, looking completely terrified, quickly ran to my side. Clumsily slamming her body into my hip, she dislodged all my bags from my hand, sending them and all of their contents crashing to the ground.

"Tabs," I whined. "Now look what you did!"

"I'm sorry," she said. "I'm just really freakin' out here."

"Fine, but don't just stand there. Help me pick this stuff up."

The hissing continued to grow, and with shaking hands we threw the groceries back into the bags, not caring if we smashed or broke anything. It took us only a few seconds to gather up the bags again, but before I stood up I retrieved my flashlight from my purse and turned it on.

"Thank you Aidan," Tabitha crooned as she stole the flashlight from me and began to shine it all around her feet.

"Try the grass," I said in a shaky voice.

She shined the light into the grass, but we couldn't see anything.

"Where the hell is it coming from?" she asked.

"I don't know, but I heard it the other day and…"

We both saw it at the same time. There was something dark skittering in the grass towards us, but we couldn't make it out because it was being very careful to stay out of the light.

It only took us a split second to react, and then we were both screaming and running. When we got to our door, I dropped my groceries and scrambled inside my purse to find my keys. Once the door was unlocked we ran inside, pulling the groceries along with us, and then slammed the door behind us. Tabitha quickly locked the door and then we both collapsed to the floor, clutching our sides and gasping for air.

It was silent for a moment, and then Tabitha spoke, "We…are so…out…of shape!"

We couldn't help ourselves, we both started to laugh, and once we started we couldn't stop. We just lay there, looking up at the grungy ceiling, and giggling at how silly we were. Running around screaming like two little girls. How ridiculous.

When the laughing subsided, we stood up and began to put the groceries away. Most of the food had survived the adventure, except for a few crushed eggs and two squished bananas, which was pretty amazing. With all the groceries stashed away, we popped a few hot pockets into the microwave, opened a bottle of soda, and went to the living room to watch a movie.

I never understood how people could fall asleep during movies, especially ones that were supposed to be their favorite, but Tabitha could never keep her eyes open past the first ten minutes.  I could have just turned the movie off and went to bed, but after all the excitement I was too wide-awake to sleep.

Tabitha had chosen *Ten Things I Hate About You*, which I had seen about a thousand times, so I decided to paint my nails while I watched.  I touched up the bright red paint that was already on my toes, and then used the same paint for my nails.  Halfway through the movie my stomach started to growl.  So I went into the kitchen and popped some popcorn.  By the time the movie was over, I had devoured a large hot pocket, two bags of butter popcorn and half a liter of soda.  I threw a blanket over Tabitha, turned off the TV, and then went to the bathroom for my usual evening routine.

Back in my room, I still found myself too wired to fall asleep, and the caffeine from the soda wasn't helping.  There was no way I was going to sleep any time soon, so I went and sat down at my desk.  I hadn't drawn in a few days, and so I opened my book and started to sketch.

I heard Tabitha moving around a little while later.  She must have gotten cold on the couch and turned the heat up, because the air vent under my desk started to blow hot air all over me.  My room became very stuffy, and even after taking off my pants and socks, I was still really warm.  I leaned over my desk, opening my window to let some cool air in, and then went back to sketching.

The hissing started just a few seconds later. I was in the middle of drawing a rose pedal when I heard it, and I pressed so hard on the paper that I broke the tip of the pencil right off. My heart started to beat faster, and the same chills from earlier traveled down my back, making my whole-body quiver.

Without making a sound I went to my purse and found my flashlight. I returned to my desk, and leaning over it I peered out the window. My flashlight was small but powerful. With the light shining on the ground I could clearly see every blade of grass, but there was no sign of the snakes.

I was starting to feel really uncomfortable, and was considering going into Tabitha's room and climbing in bed with her, but she would just want to know what was wrong, and I didn't want to freak her out. There was no reason for us both to be scared.

I quietly shut my window and then curled my legs up against my chest, wrapping my arms tightly around them. I kept staring out the window, waiting to see something jump across my vision, but nothing ever did. I didn't know what was lurking outside my window, but it was definitely scaring me, and I really didn't want to be alone. I wanted to feel safe, protected, and there was only one person who could make me feel that way, but I had no idea where he was, and had no way of contacting him. I settled for the next best thing.

I sketched his lean and lengthy frame, his round muscular shoulders, and every gorgeous detail of his face. I placed him on a ground of soft grass and encircled him in a forest of trees. I darkened the sky with the side of my pencil, and then outlined the portrait with a window frame. There he was standing outside my window, his arms outstretched in front of him like he was calling out to me, begging me to come down and join him. He was my own personal Romeo.

The picture was a perfect likeness of the view outside my window, except for one thing. Aidan. The picture I had drawn was too good to be true, because Aidan wasn't standing there waiting for me. He wasn't calling me down from my balcony. It was only a picture, a fantasy.

Aggravated, I closed my eyes and covered my face with my hands. Usually drawing made me feel happy, energized, fulfilled, but the only thing I felt at that moment was anxiety and frustration. Sitting at my desk drawing silly pictures was not helping me feel better about my problems. I breathed a heavy sigh, and then removed my hands from my face.

At first, I thought that I was still looking at the Aidan in my sketchbook, my fantasy Romeo. But slowly my brain began to identify some unfamiliar qualities around him, like the color in the grass by his feet, and the way the wind blew steadily through the trees that enclosed him.

I hadn't drawn with color, had I?  No, I still held the gray pencil in my hand, and how could I have captured the wind?  I was certainly not talented enough to make a simple picture come to life.

So then what was I looking at?

I decided to just forget about the landscape and focus on what was important.  I looked closely at his face.  His beautiful gray eyes were sparkling, and his lips...his lips were moving.  He was speaking, but I couldn't hear what he was saying.  I leaned closer, and that's when I hit my head against the pane of glass.  My hands quickly moved to the window and I pushed it out of my way.

"Selkie!"

I could hardly breathe.  My Romeo was calling for me.

"Aidan?  What are you doing here?"

"Come down, and I'll tell you."

I didn't even stop to think about what I was doing.  My every thought was of him.  I hastily put on my pants that were lying at my feet and then slipped on my black boots, not even bothering to put on socks.  I ran out of my room and was at the front door in mere seconds.  I had forgotten to pick up my hoodie, so I grabbed the fleece blanket off of the couch and wrapped it around me, before opening the door and bolting down the steps.

When I reached the bottom floor, I sprinted to the side of the building where my window was and found Aidan standing there smiling at me. I ran all the way to him, and then launched myself into his arms. He caught me without difficulty and held me firm against him. The blanket had fallen below my waist as I jumped into his arms, but lowering my feet to the ground he reached down and replaced the blanket around my shoulders.

"What are you doing here?" I asked, unable to hide my excitement.

"Don't you know," he replied with a grin.

"No, should I?"

"Selkie," he said, his hand lightly caressing my face. "You have no idea how special you are."

"Me? Special? What are you talking about?"

"Selkie, there's something I want to tell you. It might be hard for you to understand...but I can't go on like this...with you not knowing."

"Okay," I said, feeling a little worried, but not knowing what else to say.

He took a deep breath. "Remember when I told you that my life was complicated?"

I cautiously nodded my head.

"Well, the thing is…"

He abruptly stopped speaking. Aidan's gentle face became rigid and pale, and his eyes began to frantically scan the area around us. Something was wrong. His whole body suddenly tensed, and then I heard it. The hissing.

"Selkie," he said firmly. "Get behind me!"

Feeling extremely confused, I asked, "Aidan, what's going on?"

"I'll explain everything later, but for right now get behind me and try not to make any noise."

"But…"

"Selkie," he begged. "Please, just trust me."

I nodded my assent and he gently pulled me against his back, and then from underneath his shirt he pulled out a large ornamented silver dagger. He wrapped his fingers firmly around the handle, and as he lifted the weapon into the air the blade burst into light. I was immediately blinded from the light emanating out of the blade, and I had to use Aidan's shoulder to shield my eyes from the glow.

As I cowered behind him, my fingers tensely digging into his shoulders, he remained strong, but I knew he could feel my stress.

"Don't be afraid," he said. "I'm here, and I will always protect you."

My voice was barely a whisper when I replied, "What's…out there?"

"We call them Shadows."

"But what are they?"

"They can take many forms. But the important question is not what are they…but what are they made out of?"

"And what is that, exactly?"

"Pure unyielding evil," he growled.

"So they're dangerous?"

A smile played across his features. "Extremely."

"Okay," I gulped. "But what do they want?"

He turned to look at me then, and this time there was no trace of a smile on his face, as he answered, "You."

## Chapter 15

"Me?"

My lips slowly formed the word, but my voice did not respond, and I quickly discovered my body was failing me too. My arms, which suddenly felt too heavy to hold up, fell limp by my sides while my lungs constricted tight behind my ribs, cutting off my air and making my head swim. I had never thought myself to be the fainting type, but I was about to prove myself wrong. I began to sway back and forth and was about to go under when Aidan's strong voice resuscitated me. "Selkie...Look at me..."

I rapidly blinked my eyes and did as he requested.

"You don't need to be afraid." His voice was a sweet whisper. "I said that they wanted you, but I didn't say that I would let them have you." With his hand still holding the dagger high in the air, he turned and leaned his forehead against my own. "They're coming now..."

I swallowed hard.

"...But I swear on my life that I will never let them hurt you. I will always be here to protect you."

"Why?" I asked barely above a whisper.

"Because Selkie...it's what I was born to do," and then

with a smile, he added, "But more importantly...because I love you!"

"I love you too," I said without missing a beat.

"And do you trust me?"

Never taking my eyes off of Aidan's face, I lifted my hand and placed it on the middle of his chest where his heart would be, and then with complete confidence, I murmured, "With my life."

He placed his unoccupied hand on top of mine, lacing our fingers together, and then gently kissed the palm of my hand, before releasing it and turning back to face the darkness.

In just those few moments with Aidan, the hissing had become my life's soundtrack, lightly playing in the background as my future unfolded. I had almost forgotten about the repulsive music until I realized that it was no longer playing. The world around us was silent. The only sound I could here was the pounding of my heart.

"Is it over?" I asked

"No," he replied. "It's just beginning. Hold tight to me, and whatever you do...don't run."

They came as silent as the dead, slithering on the ground like serpents, growing in height and shape with every wicked swish. When they were but a few feet away, they were as tall as

Aidan, and resembled the silhouette of a human. Their bodies were constantly shifting, never settling on a single shape, and their faces, complete with ferocious red glowing eyes, were void of all expression.

I recoiled from them, hiding myself behind Aidan's sturdy frame as he lowered his weapon, ready to defend. The hissing started up again, but when it reached my ears I was surprised to hear a different tune. The song was no longer just an instrumental piece. The Shadows had added words.

No, not words, one word. One name.

My name.

"Sssseeelkie," they hissed. "Sssseeelkie."

Again and again they taunted me with their malicious voices. I wanted to scream at them to stop. I couldn't bear the sound of my name on their lips. I wanted to run, to be anywhere but where I was. I started to back up, but Aidan reached out and took hold of my hand.

"Don't move," he said. "That's what they want...that's what they're waiting for."

Fearfully, I moved closer to him, but I couldn't stand it. I had to get their voices out of my head. I covered my ears with my hands and began to nervously rock back and forth.

"Please Aidan," I begged. "Make them stop!"

"Shhh…I'll make them stop…just stay right where you are."

I could tell by the way he spoke that he wanted to pull me into his arms and comfort me. He hated the fact that I was hurting, but he had to focus, he had to protect me.

With the dagger still radiating the bright light, Aidan took a step forward. "If you want her…you'll have to get through me…" and then lowering himself into a fighting stance, he yelled, "Now stop wasting time and come get me!"

Everything happened so fast. All at once I felt a rush of freezing wind, and then Aidan's blade burst into flames. He was ferociously cutting through the air, his gleaming blade tracing streaks of light through the darkness, but the Shadows were ready and they were fast. They darted from side to side, gracefully dodging every swipe of his blade. We were being pushed back, and it looked like Aidan was losing, until the tip of his blade sliced through a Shadow, making it screech in pain and then explode into a million pieces and disappear.

The two remaining Shadows howled in protest, and then moved with even more determination toward us. As Aidan struck out with the dagger, the light brightened his face, and I could see a glint of sweat on his brow. He continued to violently slash out against the Shadows, but it was no use. We were being pushed farther back into the dark woods around my apartment, and soon they would overtake us completely. Aidan was strong, but these Shadow things had the upper hand. They had the numbers, and Aidan was tiring. His legs were moving slower with every step, and his arms were carelessly flailing around, no longer decisive. This was it. A few more moves and Aidan would be defeated, and then they would have me.

One of the Shadows rounded on Aidan, attempting to grab me from behind his body, but this only encouraged Aidan to fight harder, and as quick as lightening he whipped his blade around, slicing thick into the Shadow's neck, beheading the creature and destroying it.

There was only one left. It quickly lunged towards us and Aidan had to stumble backwards to stay out of its reach. I was pushed back during the scramble, and my foot caught on a root of a nearby tree. As I fell to the ground, my ankle made a nasty popping sound, and I screamed out in pain. Aidan, concerned for my wellbeing, glanced back at me to see what had happened. It was only a split second, but that was all the time the Shadow needed. The Shadow rushed Aidan, slamming hard against his chest, knocking him off his feet and sending him flying into the trunk of the tree behind us. He hit with incredible force, and then crumpled to the ground.

"Aidan!"

I tried to stand up and run to him, but my ankle was so sore I instantly fell back to the ground, unable to put any weight on it. I quickly got on my hands and knees and started to crawl over the hard roots of the tree towards him.

"Sssseeelkie," the single Shadow hissed.

I froze in place, unable to move a muscle.

"Sssseeelkie."

It sounded so close.

I slowly rotated my head, and when I discovered the Shadow looming just a few steps away, I flipped my body over so that I was sitting on my butt with my hands behind me and my legs outstretched before me. If this thing was going to kill me, I wanted to face my death head on.

I cringed as the Shadow's hand reached out to grab my neck and instinctively I leaned back, cowering away from the touch. An immense cold air rippled off the Shadow's body, chilling me to the core, and as the hand began to imprison my neck I released a terrified gasp.

Aidan's dagger came out of nowhere. It soared past me, just missing my head by a few inches, and struck the Shadow directly in the chest. Fire exploded from the weapon, and then the Shadow went up in flames, writhing in agony for a few seconds, before disintegrating into ash.

"Aidan," I cried.

His voice was rough when he answered, "Selkie, are you

alright?"

With my arms and my one good foot, I began to pull myself along the ground towards him, and when I finally reached the base of the tree where he still lay on his back, I wrapped my arms around his body and began to kiss every part of him.

"Ouch," he yelped. "Careful Selkie, I'm..."

"Oh my God. You're hurt!" I pulled myself up to look at him. "What's the matter? What can I do?"

"I'll be okay, don't worry about me. The important thing is that you're safe. How's your ankle?"

It was pounding with pain, but I lied, and said, "Oh it's fine. Seriously, don't be ridiculous. You're in pain. There must be something I can do."

He stubbornly shook his head and then tried to sit up, but before he even moved a few inches he winced with pain and fell back to the ground.

I couldn't bear to see him hurting. "Aidan, please, let me do something!" I was practically hysterical.

He took a deep breath, grimacing again from the movement, and then said, "In my pocket, you'll find my cell phone."

I carefully placed my hand on his leg, not wanting to cause

him anymore pain, and then reached into his pocket to retrieve the tiny black flip phone.

"Open it up, and dial one," he said.

I opened the phone, pressed the one key and then hit send. The caller I.D. popped up and I saw Brendan's face staring back at me. The phone only rang once before he picked up.

"Aidan?"

I placed the phone to my ear and timidly said, "Brendan, its Selkie."

It was very quiet for a moment, and then the phone began to beep.

"I think he hung up," I said.

Aidan sighed and closed his eyes. "Good."

"Good? Aidan, what's happening?"

"Don't worry, Selkie. Everything is fine. Brendan is coming."

"How is that good? He hates me!"

"I told you, he doesn't hate you. It's just..."

I didn't let him finish. "Yeah, yeah, I know. It's complicated, right?"

Aidan, seeing my frustration, gingerly lifted his arm up and grabbed my hand, holding it tight as he said, "Selkie, I'm sorry. I know this is a little confusing for you?"

"A little confusing?"

He rephrased. "Okay, a lot confusing. But I promise, I will explain everything to you…"

"When?" I interrupted again.

"Soon," he said with a smile. "In a few minutes Brendan will be here…"

I frowned.

He squeezed my hand. "It gets worse."

"Worse than this?"

"He's going to take me away…and you're not going to be able to come with me."

"You're just going to leave me here? But look what just happened. What if those things come back?"

"Don't worry, I'm not going to leave you alone for a second, and as soon as I can, I'll be back for you."

I was so frustrated and scared and confused. I couldn't help but cry.

With the tears frantically rolling down my cheeks, I said,

"But what am I supposed to do now, Aidan? I mean, I have no idea what's going on and I'm really scared, and you keep telling me everything is going to be alright, but what just happened was not alright with me, and to make it worse you're leaving me...again! Do you have any idea how that makes me feel?"

It took all of his energy, but Aidan pushed himself up on his elbows and then raised his hand to my face, wiping away my tears as he said, "Selkie, I am so sorry. I wish that I could tell you everything right this second. I wish that I could stay here and hold you and never leave you again. It kills me every time I have to walk away from you. I can't stand it, and I know it's worse for you, not having a clue about what is happening...but right now I don't have any other choice."

I was about to start arguing again, but he stopped me. "Selkie, when the Shadow attacked me...it did some damaged, and without immediate treatment...well...I just have to go." His hand was still resting on my face, but he moved it down then placing it on my heart. "The whole time I'm gone, I'll be thinking about you. Every second."

I didn't say anything at first, but just leaned over and tenderly kissed him. He responded to my kiss with enthusiasm and when we pulled away, I said, "It's okay. I don't understand what's going on, but I can wait, because you're more important to me than anything, and if you say that you need to go, then I'll let you go."

He looked at me for a moment, and then smiling he leaned in and kissed me again. Our lips moved in perfect harmony together. He moved his hand from my heart to my neck, entwining his fingers in my hair. My whole body was tingling. I cautiously placed my hands on either side of his face and kissed him more deeply. I explored every contour of his face, trying to memorize it for when he was gone, while he playfully tickled my neck with his fingertips...and that's how Brendan found us.

"Selkie, get out of my way," Brendan roared.

I had barely unlocked my lips from Aidan's when Brendan grasped my arm and started to pull me away from him. When he noticed that I couldn't stand on my ankle he just pushed me to the side, allowing me to fall roughly to the ground, and then took my place beside Aidan.

"Brendan could you not..."

"Shut up, Aidan! Where is it?"

Aidan grumbled something under his breath and then said, "My chest."

With his bare hands Brendan ripped Aidan's shirt in half, and I gasped, horrified by what I saw. Aidan's entire body was very pale, except for the skin on his chest where the Shadow had struck him, which was a hideous collaboration of black and blue splotches. It looked like the pictures I had seen in health class of people who had gotten frostbite from staying out in the cold for too long. Only his chest looked worse, way worse.

"We need to leave now," Brendan commanded.

Aidan looked down at his mangled body, and said, "I'm not going to argue with you this time."

Brendan nodded his approval, and then called out, "Liam, Ewan, get over here."

The two younger brothers came running out of the darkness. I noticed they were both carrying daggers; similar to the one Aidan had fought with.

"We've checked the perimeter," Liam said. "If there were anymore, Aidan must have scared them off."

"Okay," said Brendan. "We need to move now, before any more damage is inflicted on this wound. Liam, Aidan won't be able to walk, so grab his feet. Ewan, you stay here with Selkie, and don't forget to pick up the dagger."

They all moved with great speed to perform their tasks. Ewan, the youngest, ran over to pick up Aidan's weapon, and then brought it over to Brendan who slid it in the back pocket of his jeans. Brendan and Liam then attempted to lift Aidan off of the ground, but he screamed so loud that they put him right back down again.

"Let me help," I said.

All four of the brothers looked at me, but Aidan was the only one smiling.

"It's okay guys, she knows she can't come with us, but this really hurts and I need her." When no one budged or said anything, Aidan spoke in a more commanding tone, "I *want* her beside me."

He didn't have to tell me twice. I went hobbling over to him and grabbing his hand, I said, "I'm here. Now I know this hurts, but you need to go and get better, so just look right at me, okay?"

A thick layer of sweat was visible on his face, and he was looking paler every minute, but he firmly nodded his head and taking a deep breath, he winked at me.

"Okay," I said. "He's ready."

"On the count of three."

"Don't take your eyes off of me," I said.

"Never," Aidan replied.

"One...two...three."

They tried to lift Aidan without jostling him too much, but I could tell he was in a lot of pain. He didn't make a single noise, but he squeezed my hand so tight that I had to fight to not cry out. Once he was up, we walked briskly to a gray van in the parking lot. With every step I took, my ankle protested, sending sharp pains shooting up my leg, but I just kept moving. They had removed all of the seats in the back of the van, so they were able to lay Aidan right on the floor. I climbed in with him, hoping maybe they would forget that I was there and drive away with me still inside, but they weren't that stupid.

Of course Brendan was the one to say it. "Alright Selkie, it's time for you to get out. We appreciate you helping us, but let us take it from here."

I looked down at Aidan, but he just nodded, and said, "It's time. Don't worry, I'll be okay, and you'll see me again in no time."

I knelt down, and after kissing his hot forehead, I whispered, "Don't forget about me."

Aidan grinned, and then with the last bit of strength that he had, he lifted his hand, placed it on my heart, and said, "Impossible."

## Chapter 16

**I stood like a statue on the sidewalk, unwilling to budge, and watched with sad eyes as the van and Aidan disappeared into the night.** I should have been worried about my ankle, which was as swollen as a tennis ball and throbbing like hell, but I was only concerned with the deep, lonely burn of my heart. It seemed like every time Aidan left he took a little piece of my heart with him, leaving my body sore and incomplete. My heart felt fragile, weak, like any minute it could cease to function, and if that happened, how was I supposed to go on living without it?

I remained on the sidewalk looking off into the distance for quite some time; wondering where Aidan was and how he was doing, and hoping he was missing me as much as I was missing him.

I had forgotten Ewan had stayed behind to protect me, until he started to speak, "Selkie, if it's okay with you, I think you should go inside now."

I awkwardly hopped around on my good foot to face him. "Sorry, I forgot you were here. I guess I'm just a little...shook up from everything." I attempted to take a step forward, but finding it extremely difficult, I said, "Hey, I don't think I can make it back up to my apartment like this, would you mind giving me a hand?"

Eager to help, Ewan rushed to my side, and said, "Oh yeah, of course, whatever you need."

"Thanks."

I wrapped my arm around his neck, grateful to take some of the strain off of my foot, as he timidly wrapped his arm around my waist, careful not to touch my hip with his fingers. He was about as tall as I was, maybe a few inches taller, but his round cheeks and soft muscles made him look a lot younger.

"Ewan, how old are you?" I asked him as we walked.

"Fifteen," he answered, then looking at me with curious eyes, he said, "Why?"

"Oh...well, it just seems like you're a little young to be out here so late at night, with all those Shadow things around."

"I'm not too young," he whined. "I'm exactly the right age to be a..."

He stopped talking and quickly turned his head away from me.

"Exactly the right age to be a...what?" I pressed.

He shook his head. "Sorry, Selkie. I can't tell you anything," then he looked at me again, his eyes more playful as he said, "But I think you already know that."

"Oh come on, Ewan. No one needs to know. It could be

our little secret!"

"I wish I could, Selkie...for Aidan's sake, but I just can't."

We were finally at my door. "What do you mean, for Aidan's sake?"

He lifted my arm from around his neck, and then placing his hands in the front pocket of his jeans, he said, "Look, all I can tell you is that Aidan really cares about you, and that makes things, for all of us, really difficult. But he's my brother, and I want him to be happy. So I hope things work out, but it's not up to me, and I can't afford getting in trouble, not when I just started. So I'm sorry...but I just have to keep my mouth shut."

Ewan turned and started to walk down the steps.

"Wait," I yelled, stopping him in his tracks. "I know you guys said that those Shadow things were gone and everything, but...I still feel really uneasy for some reason, and to be honest, I'm scared out of my mind. So...I was wondering if maybe you would come in and hang out with me for a while. You know...just until I can get to sleep."

Ewan, with his gentle features and innocent eyes, released a sigh. "On one condition."

"Okay, what?"

"Promise me that you won't tell Brendan, because if he found out that I was inside with you, he would say that I wasn't doing my job, which would only get me in trouble and..."

"Let me stop you right there," I said. "If there is one thing we can agree on, it's that Brendan has no right sticking his nose in other people's business."

Ewan smiled at me. "Yeah, okay then, it's a deal...but I can only stay until you fall asleep."

"That's all I'm asking."

When we got inside I went right to the couch to unzip and remove my boots, and then propped my enormous ankle up on a bunch of pillows. Ewan didn't waste any time getting comfortable either. He went to the other couch and flopped down on his back, grabbing a few pillows to stuff under his head.

"Are you tired?" I asked.

"Umm...no not really," he said as he rolled over on his side to look at me. "You?"

"Well...yeah...but that never really seems to matter. I haven't been sleeping well lately."

"Why?"

Usually if a complete stranger started asking questions about me, I would just shut down, refuse to keep up the conversation, but the way Ewan looked at me, with his soft eyes and sweet sincere face, he reminded me a lot of Aidan. It was comforting.

"Well," I replied slowly. "I keep having these terrible nightmares, and after what I saw tonight, I don't even want to think about closing my eyes."

"I know how you feel," he said.

"You do?"

"Oh yeah. The first time I ever saw a Shadow, I couldn't sleep for days."

"Really?"

"Yeah, but don't worry, it'll pass."

"When?"

"Probably not soon enough, but eventually you'll wake up and you won't be thinking about them so much, and then you won't be able to remember a dream with them in it. I guess you just get used to them...you know?"

"I don't think I could ever get used to them."

"Well I hope you do," he said, and then he smiled a very familiar smile.

"You know Ewan, you remind me a lot of your brother."

He quickly sat up. "Please tell me it's not Brendan."

"Oh God no!" I shrieked.

"Thank goodness," he said, flopping back onto his side. "Because I don't know if you've noticed...but Brendan can be such an ass sometimes."

"I know, right?"

Suddenly we were both laughing. It was the kind of giddy, carefree laughter that made your stomach hurt and your legs and arms flail uncontrollably. The worst kind of laughter to have when your foot, which was attached to your flailing limbs, was injured. My foot slammed down hard against the pillow and I grimaced.

"You should really ice that and then wrap it up," Ewan commented, still fighting back the giggles.

"Oh right! Okay..."

I started to push myself up, but when my foot accidentally hit the ground I winced, and Ewan quickly intervened.

"Here, why don't you just sit down and I'll get the ice."

When he returned from the kitchen with a dishtowel wrapped around a bag full of ice, I said, "Well you're resourceful."

"Thanks. Now where can I find an ace bandage?"

"There might be one in the first aid kit under the bathroom sink."

"Okay, I'll be right back."

While he scampered down the hallway, I placed the icy bag on my ankle, and then looked around for a blanket to throw over my foot.

"Oh crap!"

"What's the matter?" Ewan asked as he returned with the kit.

"I dropped my blanket outside somewhere."

"Oh, well I'll go and get it."

He dropped the first aid kit on the couch and headed for the door, but as he passed me I grabbed his arm. "Don't...don't worry about it," I said, quickly. "I can get it tomorrow. You don't have to go right now."

Ewan silently moved back to the couch, sitting beside my foot, and as he wrapped my ankle with the bandage, he said, "You know Selkie, you don't need to be afraid. We would never let anything happen to you. You're in safe hands."

"No offense...but I don't know what you're talking about, remember? I just wish I could see Aidan."

Ewan lowered his eyes, concentrating very hard on his wrapping job.

I decided to give it a try. "Ewan, do you know where Aidan is?"

"Of course I do," he said, never taking his eyes off my foot.

"Could you take me there?" I asked apprehensively.

He raised his eyes to look at me, and his face was firm and strong, as he said, "Absolutely not!"

"But why? You just said that you hoped things worked out between me and Aidan, and I need to see him."

"Selkie, you can't. It's impossible. Even if I wanted to take you, I couldn't."

"Do you want to take me?"

"That's not important!"

"Of course it's important."

"No Selkie, it's not. No matter how I feel, I can't take you to him. It is absolutely forbidden."

"Why?"

"I can't tell you."

"Bullshit! I want to know what's going on. I mean this is my life we're talking about, and I am sick of people telling me what I can and cannot do, and I'm tired of all this sneaking around crap...

If you don't take me to Aidan, then I'll just follow you."

Ewan was silent for a second, and then he smiled, and said, "I see why Aidan loves you so much."

His comment shocked me, leaving me speechless.

Ewan didn't seem to know what to say after that either, so we just sat there staring at each other; Ewan nervously tapping his fingers against his leg, and me desperately holding my breath, until finally he spoke, "You have no idea how much trouble I would be in if anyone found out."

I started to breathe again. "Then we will just have to be really careful."

He scratched his head. "If I do this, you will have to listen to me and do exactly what I tell you."

"Of course."

"No one can know."

"Who am I going to tell?"

Ewan stood up and I watched anxiously as he began to pace back and forth.

"It's going to be tricky, and your foot is going to slow us down."

I quickly stood, ignoring the pain in my foot. "Don't worry

about that, I won't slow us down."

Ewan ran his hands through his hair, and then releasing a sigh, he said, "Aidan is really going to owe me big time."

I squealed with delight and flung my arms around Ewan, hugging him tight.

He gently pushed me away. "Don't celebrate right now. We haven't done anything yet."

"But we will," I said with a smile.

"Yeah, okay. Now go get a coat, it's cold outside."

I hopped as fast as I could to my room, not caring if I woke Tabitha up, to get a pair of socks and a jacket. When I got back into the living room, Ewan wasn't there. Instead I found him in the kitchen, sticking his head into the fridge.

"What are you doing?" I asked.

Keeping the fridge door open, Ewan stood up and turned his head toward me.

"Well, I'm about to break all the rules for you and Aidan, and I will most likely be grounded for the rest of my life because of it. So if it's okay with you, before we go I'm going to have a soda." Then grabbing the half drunken soda bottle off the top shelf and unscrewing the cap, he lifted it into the air, and said, "Cheers!"

## Chapter 17

**I didn't want Ewan to change his mind about taking me to Aidan, so I just stood patiently in the kitchen while he gulped down the rest of the soda and then waited, without argument, as he went to use the bathroom.** When we finally left the apartment, I bounded down the steps as fast as my foot would allow, and even made it to the parking lot before Ewan.

"See slow poke, I told you I wouldn't slow us down," I teased.

Ewan chuckled and then pointed to the back of the parking lot where a small blue Honda was parked. "Over there. That's Aidan's car. He usually leaves an emergency key. I hope it's still there, 'cuz otherwise we're going to have to walk."

We hurried across the parking lot, and thankfully the key was hidden right where Ewan said it would be, under the car by the driver's side tire, in a little black magnetic case. He unlocked the doors and we hopped in. As soon as my seat belt was buckled, we took off into the night.

It was a little after two a.m. and all of the streets, with their red blinking traffic lights, were eerily quiet. Ewan was very silent as we drove. Focused. I glanced over at him a time or two, but he never noticed. He was too busy checking his mirrors every five seconds and keeping his eyes on the road ahead of him. At first I thought he might be checking to see if anyone was following us, but as we continued to weave through town, I realized how cautious he was being; taking every turn very slowly and insisting on using his blinker, even though nobody else was around.

"Ewan, do you have your license yet?" I asked.

"Uh…not exactly…but I have my learners permit and I drive all the time with my parents."

"And what would your parents say now if they knew you were driving without them?"

He swallowed uncomfortably. "Well…they would probably kill me. Which is why they are never going to find out, right?"

"Mums the word!"

He scrunched his face up, looking confused. "What does that even mean?"

"I have no idea," I shrugged. "But they always say it in the movies."

"Okay, well let's just say that if we get caught, which we most likely will, you drove us here."

Ewan had his eyes plastered to the road, but I could still see all the tension and anxiety in his face. I really wanted to see

Aidan, but I felt terrible having to drag Ewan into it.

"Hey," I said, placing my hand on his arm. "I want you to know that I really appreciate you doing this. I know you don't have to and..."

"Selkie, don't worry about me," he interrupted, shaking my hand away. "I can take care of myself."

"I know, but I just don't want to see you get in any trouble."

"It's not like you kidnapped me or anything. I was the one who made the decision," and then with a smile, he added, "Although, if we do get caught, maybe I could use that as my excuse."

"You wouldn't," I laughed.

"No...I wouldn't," he said quickly. "But you have to admit, it's not a bad idea."

We drove in silence after that. Ewan turned his attention back to his driving, while I busied myself inspecting Aidan's car. I was surprised to find the vehicle extremely tidy. I checked out the backseat and all of the random compartments, I even rummaged around the glove compartment, but I didn't find a single piece of trash. It was strange. Who kept their car so clean? I continued to poke around, and was almost convinced that Aidan was obsessive compulsive when I found the envelope. It was on the floor by my feet, half hidden beneath the car mat. I picked it up, curious to see what was inside, and then quietly lifted the flap.

Inside the envelope were a bunch of photos. I eagerly pulled them out, skimming through the pile, and immediately discovered a trend; something that all the pictures had in common.

Me.

In one photo I was sitting on the bench in the park, and in another I was walking down the street with my umbrella. There were several photos of me at work, and even a few of me sitting at my desk in my room.

A normal person might have been creeped out by the photos, maybe even been scared for their life, but I knew long ago that I wasn't normal, and the photos didn't scare me, they thrilled me. He had been there all along. Watching me. Protecting me. Loving me. Each photo represented all the times he had wanted to see me, but couldn't.

I looked through each photo again; trying to remember what I was thinking about the moment they were each taken, but it really wasn't too hard to figure out. No matter where I was, or what I was doing, Aidan was always in my thoughts.

I was still flipping through the photos when Ewan slowed down and pulled off the main road into a small parking lot. I swiftly put the photos back into the envelope, and then shoved the entire envelope into the front of my jeans.

Ewan turned the headlights off, but kept the car running. "Okay. We're here, but before we go inside, there are a few things we need to get straight. First, just because it's late at night, does not mean that everyone is sleeping. In fact, this is the busiest part of the day for us. I think you can guess why. So put your jacket on and cover your head with your hood.

"Also, I told you I would help you get to Aidan, but I didn't say how long you could stay. So if I tell you it's time to go, no matter what, you have to leave."

I didn't argue, but just sat there quiet and attentive.

"Finally, your relationship with Aidan is no secret. Everybody knows about it and for as much as I can tell, everybody disapproves. So nobody can find out that you snuck in, because if they do, you'll go straight to the Council, and you're not going to like what they have to say."

He paused for what seemed like a lifetime, and then asked, "So, are you sure you still want to do this?"

I didn't hesitate. "I have to see him, Ewan."

"Okay," he sighed. "Then let's go."

When we got out I put on my jacket and then walked around to the front of the car where Ewan stood waiting for me.

He reached out his hand and I took it willingly.

"That's where we're going," Ewan said, pointing through a cluster of trees to a white steepled building, and then clambering up a muddy slope we arrived on the well-groomed front lawn of the First Church in Belfast; one of the oldest church buildings in Maine, and one I had even attended a few times over the years.

"You guys live in a church?" I asked, wrenching my neck to check out the large clock adorning the tall tower.

"Uh, not exactly," Ewan replied. "We sort of live under it. You'll see."

We reached the church stairs in a few more steps, but instead of just walking through the two large wooden doors at the front, we went around the building to a poorly lit side entrance. Ewan pulled a small white card out of his pocket, and then proceeded to walk over to a nearby bush. He pushed a few leaves back, revealing on the side of the building a small black card reader. He scanned his card back and forth in front of the machine, and when a little green light appeared, I knew we were in.

The door unlatched, and we both took a deep breath. Ewan cautiously opened the door, and holding his hand up for me to wait, poked his head inside. He returned with a smile on his face.

"I don't see anybody."

"That's good, right?" I asked, feeling extremely nervous.

"That's really good. Come on."

He grasped my hand again, and together we entered the building, making sure the door closed silently behind us.

As we tip toed down the hall, I glanced around for anything that might look suspicious, but with its white cement walls covered in crucifixes and pictures of Jesus, it looked like any other church. How could anyone, especially some secret order of Shadow killers, live here?

We turned the corner and sprinted down the adjacent hallway, where Ewan then directed me to a flight of stairs. Without making any noise, we descended the steps to the basement.

"Okay, this is where it gets tricky. Wait here," he said, pointing to the small alcove beneath the stairs. "I'm going to go in and check things out, and when the coast is clear, I'll come back for you."

"You're just going to leave me here?"

"Don't worry, you're completely safe within these walls. People might not like the fact that you're with Aidan, but they will always protect you." He moved closer and placed his hand on my shoulder. "Nobody here is your enemy, okay?"

I nodded my head. "Okay, but still don't take too long."

"I'll be back before you know it," he said, and then he disappeared into the basement, leaving me cowering beneath the stairs.

To keep my mind from going crazy while I waited alone in the creepy cold basement, I decided to count to myself. It was a trick I had learned as a child, and one that I practiced often. Whenever I was worried about something, instead of dwelling on it and freaking out about it, I would start to count down from one hundred, and usually by the time I got to zero, I would have forgotten about whatever was bothering me.

I started to count. 100, 99, 98, 97, 96, 95, 94...

It seemed like forever, but I had only just reached ten when Ewan reappeared.

"Selkie, we're in luck," he said with a smile. "The Council has assembled a meeting, probably to talk about what happened with you and Aidan earlier, so we've got a clear path to him, but we need to move quickly, just in case somebody decides to leave the meeting and check on him."

I instantly abandoned my counting, no longer needing its assistance, and then stepping forward I grabbed Ewan's hand, and said, "Well then, what are we waiting for?"

## Chapter 18

**With Ewan in the lead, we moved away from the stairwell and continued further into the basement, into a large rectangular shaped hall.** We quickly cut through the center of the hall, having to clumsily zigzag our way through the many rows of long white tables, before coming to a dark hallway of doors.

"What's behind all the doors?" I asked, my voice a low whisper.

"Classrooms mostly," Ewan replied. "The church uses them for Sunday school and stuff."

As we crept down the hall, I peeked through the windows of the classroom doors and found them all very similar. In the center of each room was a round wooden table, and on one of the four walls hung an ancient green chalkboard. Nothing seemed unusual about these rooms either. I was starting to think that Ewan had taken me on a wild goose chase.

"Ewan, are you really taking me to Aidan, or are you just messing with me, because this whole place looks very..."

"Shhh," Ewan prompted. "This is it."

We had walked all the way down the hallway and were now standing in front of the last door. It had no window for me to peek into, but there was a black sign mounted on the door, and etched onto it with gold lettering were the words, MEDITATION ROOM.

"Aidan's in there?" I asked, pointing to the closed door.

"No. We still have to go a little further, but this is where the church ends…and we begin."

He reached forward to open the door, but when his hand was only an inch away from the knob, he hesitated.

"Is something wrong?" I asked.

Ewan still frozen in place kept his eyes on the knob as he said, "It's just that, no one like you has ever gone where I'm taking you, and it just feels a little…strange to me."

"So, does this mean you're changing your mind?"

Ewan pulled his gaze away from the door and looked directly into my eyes. "Just tell me one thing. Do you love my brother?"

I returned his penetrating gaze and without blinking, answered, "More than anything else in this world."

Ewan didn't say anything else, but simply nodded once and then placed his hand on the knob and opened the door. The room was dark when we entered, but Ewan slid his hand along the wall to our right and found the light switch. We had been walking in the dark for quite some time, so as the bright fluorescent light above our head came on, I had to shut my eyes for a moment and then open them slowly so they could adjust to the change.

Once I could see properly, I watched with curiosity as Ewan walked over to a three-tiered metal stand covered in multicolored votive candles. He reached down, and lifting his pants leg up retrieved a dagger from a sheath attached to his calf. He then proceeded to slowly insert the silver blade of his dagger into the keyhole of a drawer directly beneath the stand. In a single motion he twisted the dagger counterclockwise, and then removed the blade from the drawer. He moved to my side and taking my hand he said, "Okay, as soon as the door opens, we're going to have to move fast."

I looked behind us, but the door we had just entered was still open.

"Not that door," he said as he closed it behind us. "That door."

I looked at the spot where his finger was pointing, but all I could see was a small hand carved wooden table sitting on a granite stone platform. On the table, placed on top of a gold and silver table runner, was a plain wooden cross. There was no door.

"Ewan what are you..."

I stopped speaking mid-sentence, and watched with amazement as the platform began to shift towards us, revealing a staircase that had been hidden beneath it. Ewan moved to the secret passage, pulling me behind him, and without any more conversation we began to descend the concrete steps. As soon as my feet left the bottom step and landed on the floor, the platform slid back to its original position, trapping us below the building.

The room we were standing in was cramped with our two bodies, and the rocky ceiling was only a few inches above my head. The only light we had was coming from a torch that was hanging on the wall, but the flame was small, and we could barely see anything past our noses. I had always been a little claustrophobic, and standing in such a small space was really freaking me out. My heart was pounding fast and my breath was coming in short heavy bursts, and as I tightened my grip around Ewan's hand, I noticed my palm was clammy with sweat.

"Ewan, can we please get out of here? I think I'm starting to lose it."

"I can get us out of here in no time, but I'm going to have to have both of my hands to do it."

I released him and then wiped my slimy hand against my leg, before crossing my arms tightly across my chest. Ewan took two small steps forward, and then placed his hands against the wall in front of us. Suddenly, a bright yellow light appeared on the surface behind his hands and I jumped in surprise. Ewan didn't budge however, but kept his hands pressed firmly against the wall. After a few seconds, the light turned green and Ewan removed his hands, and as the wall swung forward, he said, "Here we go," before grabbing my wrist and pulling me into the light.

The torches lining the stony gray walls were blazing with fire, and as we made our way down the narrow hallway, the flames licked at my face making my cheeks flush. The air underground was so warm that my shirt was starting to stick to my back with sweat, but after my earlier experience with the Shadows and their unsettling cold touch, I didn't mind the heat. In fact, I welcomed it.

As we continued through what seemed like a maze of hallways, Ewan began to pick up speed, and I awkwardly followed behind him, my boots clunking loudly against the uneven stone floor. For a while, I tried to keep track of the path we were taking, but all the corridors, with no significant markings or signs, looked exactly alike, and it seemed to me like we were just running around in circles. It was so confusing. How could anyone find their way around?

We ran for what felt like an eternity; stopping only a few times so that Ewan could check around corners for any unwanted visitors, and I was just about to tell Ewan that I could go no further, when he slowed his pace down to a walk.

"Around the next corner is where we'll find Aidan," he

whispered.

My lungs were aching, and my legs felt like mush, but knowing Aidan was so near gave me a burst of energy. I started to run again, but Ewan still had hold of my hand, and he quickly restrained me.

"Hold on a minute. Someone could be in there, and if so, you can't just go barging in to see him."

"So what are we going to do?" I asked as I wiped away the salty sweat from my forehead.

"You are going to wait here, while I go and check the room."

"But what if somebody sees me?"

"Then we're screwed," Ewan replied with a smile.

I watched uneasily from around the corner as he made his way to the large wooden door. He opened it a few inches, just enough to steal a look inside, and then after only a moment he smiled at me and waved me over. When I reached him, my heart was beating fast with excitement, and as Ewan opened the door for me to slip inside, I gave him a quick kiss on the cheek and then entered.

Unlike the rest of the underground lair, with its ancient gray rock and hot stale air, this room had smooth walls that were painted a pleasant pastel blue, and the air, which smelled faintly of alcohol, was clean and refreshing. In the center of the floor lay a large navy rug, and lying with his eyes closed on a small cot in the corner, with a thick woolen blanket pulled up to his chin, was Aidan.

He looked so weak, and his face was still unusually pale. If I hadn't been able to detect the gentle rise and fall of his chest as he steadily breathed in and out, I would have thought that he was dead, but thankfully he was only sleeping.

There was so much I wanted to ask him about, so much I needed to know, but it would just have to wait for a while. He was resting so peacefully, and he had been through so much for me. I just couldn't bear the thought of waking him.

I quietly crept across the room to the chair beside his cot and sat down. I would have been perfectly content to just sit beside him all night while he slept, but when his eyes fluttered open, I couldn't resist the urge to speak. "Aidan?"

He sleepily rolled his head to the side, not quite making eye contact. "Selkie?"

I leaned closer. "Yeah, it's me."

"Selkie," he repeated, his eyes struggling to stay open.

"Shhh, don't try and talk," I said. "Just go back to sleep."

"You're here," he said with a grin.

"Yep," I said as I lightly caressed his arm. "Ewan snuck me in."

Aidan's smile quickly disappeared and he was instantly awake, his eyes wide with fear and focused right on my face. "Selkie, what are you doing here?"

His voice was surprisingly strong.

"I told you, Ewan snuck me in."

"Snuck you in?" he asked frantically.

"Yeah, through the passage beneath the table. Why? What's the matter?"

"You shouldn't be here," he said as he pulled the heavy blanket off of his chest and pushed himself up into a sitting position.

"Are you okay?" I asked as I took in the many layers of bandages that had been wrapped tightly around his torso.

"I'm fine, but you're not listening to me, you can't be here."

"But I wanted to see you," I cried, feeling a little hurt by his tone.

He placed his hands on my face to soothe me. "I know, and I am so glad to see you, but you can't stay any longer." He removed his hands. "You have to leave, now!"

"But..."

I could have continued to argue, but there was a sudden commotion on the other side of the door that distracted me. We both turned our heads toward the noise.

It started out as just talking, but the conversation quickly turned into a shouting match. Someone was yelling at Ewan to step aside. They wanted to come in, but Ewan was blocking the door with his body and screaming at the person to leave. There was a scrambling of footsteps, and then Ewan shrieked in pain. There was silence for a moment, and then the knob of the door turned and Brendan came busting in.

"So it's true," Brendan yelled as he took us both in.

Aidan put a protective arm in front of me. "Brendan, I can explain."

"Save your breath for the Council, Aidan. Right now I have more important things to do." In less than two strides Brendan was standing above me. He grabbed my arm and pulled me out of the chair.

"Let go of me," I yelled as I tried to wiggle my arm out of his grip.

"Not likely," Brendan smirked.

He started to drag me towards the door, but Aidan made it there first.

"Get your hands off of her," he said forcefully.

"Not a chance. She has an appointment with the Council. I can't wait to hear what they have to say about this."

He tried to push Aidan out of the way, but Aidan refused to budge.

"I said...let her go!"

"Or what Aidan?"

"Or I'll make you."

"Oh yeah," Brendan said with a sneer. "I'd like to see that."

Brendan moved forward and placed his hand on Aidan's shoulder to push him out of the way, but Aidan easily shrugged it off and then punched Brendan right in the face. Brendan staggered back a few steps, and as his nose began to pour blood, he released my arm to cup his injured nose with his hands, giving me the chance to escape.

Completely shocked, Brendan said, "Aidan, what the freak man?"

Aidan ignored Brendan and looked at me. "Are you alright?"

"I'm fine," I said.

He touched my cheek. "Good. Now could you do me a favor? Could you go get my shirt and dagger from the table?"

"Why, what are you going to do?" I asked as I retrieved the items for him.

"*We* are going to leave," he said with a smile.

Brendan spoke up again. "Aidan, I can't let you do that."

"You think you could stop me?" Aidan challenged.

Brendan took a step forward, still cupping his nose, his shirt covered in blood. "Why are you doing this Aidan? Why are you fighting me? I'm your brother, your family, your blood, and she...she's nothing!"

Furious, Aidan shoved Brendan backwards and pinned him against the wall. His face was filled with conviction as he said, "Selkie is everything to me. I tried to tell you that a million times, but you wouldn't listen. You don't care about me. You only care about impressing the Council. You spend all of your time hiding behind this place and their ridiculous rules, instead of supporting your own family."

Aidan, fuming with anger, released Brendan and came to stand beside me, gently placing his arm around my waist. "We're leaving now..." he said to his brother, "...but I want to make sure I make myself perfectly clear. I love Selkie, and that is never going to change. She is the most important thing in my life, and until you can realize that, you're no brother of mine." Then he opened the door and we walked out into the hallway, leaving Brendan alone and bleeding.

## Chapter 19

**As soon as the door closed behind us, Aidan staggered forward and slumped against the wall, clutching at his chest.** I reached out to him, but he just waved my hands away, and said, "Don't worry about me, I'll be fine."

"Are you sure?"

The corners of his lips lifted slightly. "I'm just a little tired, that's all. Just let me rest for a second."

"And then what?"

"And then we need to get you home and off of that ankle."

"Oh, it doesn't even really hurt anymore," I lied, but in reality, it hurt like hell, and after all the running around Ewan and I had done, I couldn't wait to sit down and take a load off.

Where was Ewan anyway? I looked around and was startled to find him just a few feet from us. He was sitting crossed legged on the floor, silently sobbing as he rocked back and forth, his right hand cupping his left wrist. I went and knelt down beside him.

"Ewan, are you okay?"

He lifted his tear-drenched face to look at me and in a small voice said, "I think Brendan broke my wrist."

"Oh, well if it makes you feel any better, I think Aidan broke Brendan's nose."

Ewan's face instantly lit up and he looked at his brother with admiration. "Really Aidan? You broke his nose?"

Aidan pushed himself off the wall and came to stand beside me. "Yeah, he had it coming...and man did it feel good," he added, making a fist. "But I don't want to hear what mom is gonna say about it."

"Don't worry about mom," Ewan said. "She'll be so concerned about my hand and Brendan's stupid nose, she won't even bother with you."

"I hope you're right," Aidan said as he offered his hand to me.

I took it gladly, and then once I was standing I reached my hand out to Ewan. He laced his good hand around my wrist and then I pulled him to his feet.

"So now what?" Ewan asked excitedly.

"Now I take Selkie home," Aidan answered.

"Okay, I'll come with you," Ewan said with a smile.

"No Ewan, you need to stay here."

"But we're a team! I mean, I am the one who got Selkie here after all."

"So?"

"So…that proves that you need me!

Tired and frustrated, Aidan pinched the bridge of his nose. "Ewan, I don't have time for this. I need to get Selkie out of here before anyone else shows up, so just stay here." We turned to walk away.

"But I have to go with you," Ewan whined behind us.

Aidan spun around and his voice was firm when he said, "Ewan…you are going to stay here…and that's final."

Ewan's determined face crumbled, and it looked like he was about to cry again. I couldn't stand it.

Pulling on Aidan's arm, I asked, "Aidan, why can't he come with us?"

"Yeah, give me a good reason," Ewan insisted.

"Okay, fine." Aidan sighed. "You can't come with us because you have more important things to do."

Ewan's eyes became wide with surprise. "I do?"

"Yes," Aidan said seriously. "I need you to keep Brendan off my back, at least until I can convince the Council that I'm right about all of this…but more importantly, I need you to pass on a message."

"I can do that," Ewan said enthusiastically. "What's the message?"

"I want you to tell everyone that I've made up my mind, and I've chosen to leave, and I'm not coming back until they decide to start seeing things my way."

"Aidan, are you sure?" Ewan asked, his face filled with concern.

Aidan wrapped his arm tightly around my waist and gently pulled me to his side, "There's not a doubt in my mind. If they won't listen, then this is just how it's going to have to be."

Ewan nodded and then reached into his pocket and pulled out the car keys. "Here, you'll need these."

Aidan still held his shirt and dagger in his hand. Letting go of me, he swiftly tucked his weapon into a leather sheath on his waist, and then put on his shirt, careful not to rub the fabric against his chest. Once his hands were free, Ewan tossed him the keys and Aidan caught them easily with one hand.

"We'd better get going," Aidan said as he took my arm and steered me away from Ewan.

"Wait," I protested.

Aidan stopped immediately, anxiety flooding his face. "Selkie, what's the matter?"

"I didn't get to say goodbye," I said with a frown.

The tension in Aidan's body released and a gentle smile spread across his face.

"I'm sorry," he said. "Go ahead, but we only have a few moments."

"I'll be quick," I said as I limped my way back to where Ewan stood, my ankle suddenly very stiff and sore.

Ewan observed my labored stride and said with a frown, "You really should put some more ice on your ankle when you get home."

"Look who's talking," I said, pointing to his swollen wrist.

"Yeah, I guess we've seen better days."

Aidan cleared his throat impatiently.

I hurried on, "Yeah...well...we have to go, but I didn't want to leave without thanking you for what you did...so...thanks...for everything," and then I leaned in and hugged him. It took Ewan a few seconds to respond, but he managed to place one arm lightly around my back, before I released my arms from around his neck and pulled away.

I felt Aidan's hand lightly grasp my shoulder. "It's time to go. We can't waste any more time."

I smiled once more at Ewan, and then we turned and

started walking briskly down the corridor. My navigation skills were not always the best, but I was sure that we were walking in the opposite direction of the way Ewan and I had come, but then I realized that there were probably many ways to get in and out of this place, and Aidan was just taking us a different way. We had reached the end of the corridor and were about to make a left into another identical hallway, when Ewan yelled, "Hey, Selkie!"

Aidan, nervous about being detected, refused to stop walking, but not wanting to hurt Ewan's feelings I glanced over my shoulder, and called back, "Yeah?"

"Sweet dreams," he said with a grin.

I smiled back, and said, "You too," before turning the corner to find a tall gray-haired man marching towards us.

My smile immediately disappeared.

Aidan stopped in his tracks and pulled me behind him.

With a scowl on his face, the burly man approaching, asked, "Aidan, what have you done?"

His voice was deep like a growl and it rang through the corridor, shaking me at my core.

Aidan pushed me back around the corner. "Dad, I can explain."

Dad?

"There's nothing to explain," his father roared. "You've made a terrible mistake, and now there must be consequences."

Aidan stepped back into view and reached out his hand to me. As I took it, he raised his chin in confidence, and said, "I'm sorry dad, but that's not going to happen," and then we spun around and raced back down the corridor we had just left. I looked behind us and saw that Aidan's father was right on our heels, his long legs conquering the distance between us quickly. He was only a few feet away from us when Ewan's foot "accidentally" got in his father's way, slowing him down, and giving us the time we needed to make our escape. We reached the end of the corridor in a few seconds, but before we rounded the corner, Aidan slowed slightly and yelled back to his father, "Tell mom I love her," and then we sped up once again and took off down the hall.

## Chapter 20

**The torches were only smoldering blurs as we sprinted through the intricate maze of hallways.** My body was once again drenched with sweat, and as it trickled down my face I had to fight the urge to wipe it away. We were still being pursued; the loud thud of boots behind us an ever-present reality, and any attempt to remove the perspiration, which was stinging the corners of my eyes and dripping down my nose, would only slow us down.

To make matters worse, the pain in my left ankle was no longer tolerable, and every step I took became excruciating. Several times the toe of my boot caught against the irregular stone beneath it and I stumbled. Luckily, my hand was securely inside Aidan's strong grasp and he always kept me on my feet, encouraging me to continue forward.

"We're almost there," Aidan said breathlessly as he slammed his hand against a small red button on the wall to our left.

A doorway opened in front of us, and we ran through it, cramming ourselves into the small entryway below the meditation room. Aidan quickly placed his free hand against the wall, and as the platform slid open above our heads, we took to the stairs two at a time.

Once inside the room, Aidan didn't waste any time. He pulled me across the room, my shoulder protesting all the way, and led me out into the hallway. The seemingly unoccupied building was still very dark. I followed Aidan blindly as he weaved me through the many chairs and tables, up the stairs to the hallway, where we then reached the door to the outside, and our freedom. We were only a few steps out of the door when Aidan stopped running and slumped to the ground.

"Aidan? What's the matter?" I asked worried.

Aidan tried to placate me with a smile. "It's nothing, Selkie. I just need to rest for a second."

Not trying to rush him, but scared to be standing out in the open, I asked, "Do you think that's a good idea? I mean your dad is probably right behind us."

Aidan shook his head. "You don't need to worry about him."

"If I don't need to worry, why were we just running from him?" I asked confused.

"Help me up, and I'll explain."

I grabbed Aidan's arm and gently pulled him to his feet. Even though he said he was okay, it looked like he was struggling to stay standing. I carefully wrapped my arm around his waist.

"Here, lean on me," I told him.

"But your foot..." he started to protest.

"Oh, it's not that bad, really. Let's just get you to the car."

As we walked away from the church, I tried to rely as little as possible on my hurt foot, while Aidan attempted in vain to resist leaning against me, and together we slowly hobbled forward, the crescent moon our only light to guide us. I was still curious why we were no longer being pursued, and was just about to open my mouth when Aidan spoke.

"Well I guess it's time I explain myself," Aidan said with a sigh.

I looked up at Aidan's pale face. "I'm not going to lie and say that I'm not curious, but I understand if you don't feel up to it. You've had a hard night."

Aidan smirked. "You've had a hard night too, and besides...it's time."

Having reached the trees, we passed through them, ducking our heads to avoid the numerous protruding branches, and as the car came into view we both relaxed and breathed a grateful sigh. Aidan, the gentleman he was, opened my door first, and then walked to the driver side, relying on the hood of the car for support.

Once we were both safely inside the car, Aidan placed the keys in the ignition and turned them once, allowing the engine to heat up, and the control panel to turn on. The clock read 3:45. He placed his head in his hands, rubbing at his tired eyes, and then removing his hands and placing them in his lap, he turned to look at me.

"There is so much I need to tell you." He exhaled heavily. "But I hope you will forgive me if I just tell you a few things tonight. I'm just so tired and I want to get you home safely."

"I understand."

"Good. Now the first thing that I want to assure you of, is that you are very safe. I'm afraid you might have misunderstood what was happening back at the Sanctuary."

"The Sanctuary?" I interrupted, obvious confusion filling my face.

"Oh, sorry. That's what our order calls it. It's really just our home, a safe place where we can live and be undetected."

"Ewan told me that no one like me has ever been there before. Is that why your father was so angry at me?"

Aidan leaned over and grabbed my hand. "Selkie, that's another thing, my father wasn't angry with you. It's true, no one like you has been within the walls of our Sanctuary for many years, but it was not your fault you were there. Ewan and I are the ones to blame."

"No," I said a little too forcibly. "I made Ewan take me. He shouldn't get in trouble for me."

Aidan flipped my hand over and gently rubbed his thumb across my palm. "You don't need to worry about Ewan. He's perfectly fine. He might get a scolding, but I can't imagine my father doing anything more," and then with a smile, he added, "My mother wouldn't allow it."

"But I'm still confused," I said, furrowing my brow. "If your father wasn't mad, why was he chasing us?"

"Oh, he was mad alright."

"But I thought you said…"

"He was mad at me, Selkie."

"But why?"

Aidan took a deep breath. "Selkie…I'm a protector. I'm your protector…and on the day that we met I made a very bad mistake. You see, a protector is never supposed to come in contact with their Scaper. We're chosen to protect you against the Shadows, but in secret, and you're never supposed to know that we exist. That's why my father won't follow us. We're in your world now, a world he can't exist in, so he won't expose himself to you within your world."

"I see," I said, not fully comprehending what he was saying, but glad that I was finally getting some answers. I decided to keep going. "What's a Scaper?"

"You're what we call a Lightscaper. Like me you were chosen for a special destiny. A destiny that can be wonderfully fulfilling and completely safe, but I'm afraid that you might be in danger because of my mistake."

As Aidan spoke, a fear began to arise within my heart. I tried to ignore it, but it continued to grow until I was unable to contain it.

"Are you saying that you regret falling in love with me?"

I could feel the tears approaching.

Aidan, seeing my distress, squeezed my hand. "No of course not. I only mean that because of what I've done I have made your life more complicated, but I don't regret a single moment I've spent with you."

"Complicated?"

"Yes, complicated, and a long explanation, which I'm hoping to continue after a good night's sleep, if you can wait that long?"

"I just need to know one more thing, and then you can rest."

"And what's that?" he sighed.

"You said that you made a mistake, but that you don't regret being with me."

"Right."

"But what I want to know is if you plan to stay with me, even though it's supposedly wrong, or if you plan to make up for your mistake and...leave me." The last two words were difficult to speak, but I couldn't let myself hope that everything was going to be okay if it wasn't, and I wasn't going to let another person walk out of my life just because it wasn't exactly how they had pictured it.

Aidan laced his fingers with mine and leaned close so that our faces were only a few inches from each other. He took my face in his other hand, gently cupping my cheek, his hand surprisingly warm, and then in a sweet voice, he said, "Selkie Reid, when I said I loved you, I meant it. And even though this is difficult, I wouldn't change a single thing, because if I hadn't hit you with that Frisbee that day in the park...and again I'm sorry about that...I never would have known how incomplete my life was without you."

My heart skipped a beat in reaction to his words, and I could feel the warmth of his touch spreading through my entire body. I leaned in, powerless to control the longing that was churning within me, and placed my lips on his. He reacted immediately, securing my face with both hands, and pressing his lips harder against mine. My hands eagerly explored his face as well, before travelling to his strong, muscular chest. Aidan suddenly whimpered in pain and I pulled away.

"Oh God, I'm so sorry. I didn't mean to…"

"It's okay," he said, grabbing my hand and kissing the inside of my palm. "It's not your fault, but we should probably get going."

"Yeah, okay."

During the ride home, Aidan held my hand tightly, and I never took my eyes away from his face. The ride took no time at all, and when we got to my apartment we walked arm in arm through the parking lot, both depending on each other to make it to the front door without collapsing. It was a struggle for us to walk up the stairs, me with my foot and Aidan in his weakened condition, but the thought that sleep was only a few steps away was enough motivation to keep us climbing.

When we got inside, I threw off my hoodie and guided Aidan down the hall to my room. Turning on the light I walked to my bed, expecting Aidan to follow, but he just stood leaning against my doorframe, looking concerned.

"What's the matter?" I asked.

"I was just thinking that maybe I should be sleeping on the couch," he replied nervously.

I smiled at him. "I appreciate the gesture, but frankly you're in worse shape, and if anyone should be sleeping on the couch it's me."

"I'm not going to let you sleep on the couch in your own house," he said, squaring his shoulders.

"Then we will just have to compromise. We can share the bed, as long as you promise to be on good behavior."

"Not that you're not tempting," he said with that gorgeous smile. "But honestly all I can think about is sleep, and I'm afraid if I don't lay down right now I might just end up sleeping in the hallway."

"Well, we can't have that, can we?"

I pulled back my covers and gestured for him to come and lay down. He moved cautiously to the other side of the bed and bent down to remove his shoes. Seeing that it caused him pain, I climbed over the bed and knelt beside him on the floor.

"Here, let me do that."

"I can take off my own shoes, Selkie," he protested.

"Just shut up and let me do this," I grinned.

He put his hands up in surrender and then smiled playfully at me.

"There," I said once his shoes were off. "Can I help you with anything else?"

"If you wouldn't mind," he said timidly, "I could use some help getting my shirt off."

I eyed him wearily.

"No, it's not like that," he laughed. "It's just that my shirt rubs against my chest too much and it feels better without it on."

I nodded my head in agreement and then helped him out of his shirt. I also detached his sheath and dagger from around his waist and laid them on the floor next to the bed. Once he was comfortable, I covered him with the sheet and comforter, and then went to the bathroom to clean up and put on my pajamas.

I was only gone a few minutes, but when I got back Aidan was already fast asleep, and snoring lightly. I turned off the light and quietly made my way to the bed, my path clear thanks to the moon shining dimly outside my window. Being careful not to wake him, I eased my way under the covers and lay down. Rolling over on my side, Aidan's body warm against mine, I gently placed my hand on his shoulder and closed my eyes.

After a few moments, I felt his head turn toward me and in a soft voice, he said, "Selkie?"

I opened my eyes to find him looking at me, that same familiar smile spread across his face.

"Yes," I whispered back.

"I can't wait to see you tomorrow."

I moved closer, resting my head on his shoulder, and said, "Me either," before closing my eyes and falling fast asleep.

## Chapter 21

**The Shadow was very close. Its dark tendrils swirled rapidly toward me, and its red eyes glowed with a wild anticipation.** As it approached, I felt the cold, dead air rippling off its dark frame. Rigid with fear, I watched with horrified eyes as the Shadow easily overcame me, draping my body in its evil material. I felt its bitter touch against my skin, and I gasped as its slender fingers constricted tightly around my throat. I called out for him, my loving protector, but with my throat in the hands of the Shadow, it was only a silent plea.

The Shadow leaned ever closer, tracing circles on my cheek with its icy finger, making me shudder with dread, and then a slow hiss escaped his lips. "Sssseeelkie."

"No...please...don't," I managed to choke out as my body began to convulse uncontrollably. The Shadow lifted me off the ground, and I tried to call out for Aidan again, but it was no use. No one could hear me. I was alone, and I was going to die. A single tear rolled down my cheek, and as the Shadow threw me to the ground, I screamed.

"Selkie, wake up," a voice said anxiously.

My eyes immediately flew open to find Aidan leaning over me, his hands cupping my face.

"What happened?" I asked.

"I think you were having a nightmare. You were shaking so badly, I didn't know what to do. Are you okay?"

Before I could answer him, my door swung open and Tabitha came stomping in.

"Seriously Selkie, what the...?" Tabitha froze at the sight of Aidan in my bed, her eyes wide with surprise. "Oh, umm...sorry," she stuttered. "I...I didn't know you had company. I heard you scream and I thought you were having another...umm...never mind. I'll just leave you alone."

I sat up.

"Tabs, it's not what you think."

"Okay," she said as she averted her eyes and quickly left the room.

"I'll be right back," I told Aidan with a sigh, before getting out of bed and following Tabitha out into the hallway.

"Tabs wait!"

She turned around, her face full of displeasure. "Selkie, how could you?"

"I told you, it's not what you think!"

"Well, if it's not what I think," she said, her hands on her hips, "why is there a guy half naked in bed with you?"

"Umm, good question," I stalled. "Aidan brought me home last night, and it was really late. So I invited him to stay over. He wasn't feeling well, and I couldn't just let him sleep on the couch."

"No, of course you couldn't," she jested. "Did you help him take his shirt off too?"

"Well...funny you should ask..."

"Save it, Selkie," she said rather calmly. "Whatever you do in private is your own business." Then forcibly she emphasized, "Just Don't. Get. Pregnant."

"Honestly Tabs, we didn't do anything but sleep. Don't you know me better than that?"

She cocked her head to the side and looked at me. "I guess you're right...I believe you."

"Good," I said, running my hands through my tangled hair.

She looked at me more intently. "Selkie, what the hell happened to you, you're a freakin' mess!"

I looked down at my disheveled appearance and grimaced. "It was a long night, and to top it all off I think I twisted my ankle pretty bad."

"How did you do that?"

"It's a long story. Oh, but that reminds me. I'm supposed to work today…"

"Oh no, Selkie. I told you, never again."

"Please Tabs," I begged. "There's no way I can work on this foot."

"Bullshit Selkie! You just want to spend the day with Aidan!"

I made the puppy-dog face that she always used on me. "Come on…please, please, please do this for me."

Tabitha stewed over my request for a second, and I could tell my pitiful face was working. She shook her head in irritation, and then said, "Fine, I'll work for you, but I'm only doing this because I know Gabe is working and I want to see him."

"Oh thank you, thank you," I said gleefully.

"Yeah, sure. Whatever."

Tabitha turned to leave.

"Oh wait. There's one more thing."

She eyed me suspiciously.

I took a deep breath, and then spoke quickly, "Aidan's had a little disagreement with his family, and I was wondering if maybe you would be okay with him staying here for a while?"

"How long, Selkie?"

"I'm not sure, just a few days?"

She wrinkled her forehead in thought. "It's okay with me, I guess, but I want to know what happened to you last night."

"Deal! I'll tell you when you get home for work."

"Work, ugh," she groaned, and then walked down the hall to her room to get ready, slamming the door behind her.

When I got back to my room, Aidan was sitting on the edge of the bed struggling to get his shirt back on.

"Having some trouble?"

"I think I almost have it," he grumbled.

I helped get his arms through the sleeves and then sat down beside him, pulling my legs up to my chest.

"Selkie, I need to ask you something," he said in a serious voice. "But I don't want you to get mad."

"Go ahead, but I can't imagine you saying anything that would make me mad."

"I was just wondering if you're really going to tell Tabitha about last night, because I don't really think that's a good idea. I mean, I know she's your best friend but..."

"Don't even worry about that," I interrupted. "This

probably makes me a terrible friend, but I never actually thought about telling her the truth. I mean for one thing she wouldn't even believe me, and I just don't want her to be caught up in all of this."

"I'm glad to hear you say that," Aidan sighed. "It makes things a lot easier."

I smiled at him, but when a piece of my greasy hair fell in front of my face my smile faltered, and I said, "Umm...if you don't mind, I'm going to go take a shower, because I feel really gross. Will you be okay here for a little while?"

"Don't worry about me. I'll be fine. But I do have one more question before you go."

The look on his face worried me. He seemed anxious about something. I took his hand in mine, afraid of what was coming next.

"When Tabitha came in, she thought you were having another nightmare. Has this happened before?"

I squeezed his hand to reassure him. "A few times, yes. These last couple of weeks I haven't really been sleeping very well, but they're just nightmares, they're really no big deal."

Aidan didn't look appeased. "Selkie, do these nightmares have to do with the Shadows?"

"Mostly," I said, not wanting to ignore his questions, but

not willing to say anything else.

"Mostly?"

"Well...sometimes I have good dreams," I said, trying to divert him from the subject. "They're all about you of course..."

"And other times?" he prodded.

I sighed, knowing there was no way of getting around it. "Well it's kind of hard to explain, but there's this guy. I don't know who he is, because I can never see his face, but I can sense him hovering on the edges of my nightmares. It's weird, but I can feel his eyes on me...watching me, and it's like he's...waiting for something."

"Waiting for what?" Aidan asked, his eyes full of worry.

"I don't know," I said with a shaky voice. "But if I had to guess, I would say that it was the same thing the Shadows want."

Aidan leaned close and wrapped his arms protectively around me. "I will never let them hurt you," he said confidently.

"I know," I smiled as I cuddled close to him. "But I'm afraid that if I don't get into the shower, you might eventually change your mind."

"Are you kidding me?" he said, grabbing my shoulders and pushing me away to get a better look. "I think you're gorgeous at any time of the day."

"Well that may be true," I said, blushing a little.  "But I'd rather not take the risk."

I gave him a quick kiss on the cheek, avoiding his mouth because I was devastatingly aware of my awful morning breath, and then grabbed some clothes and headed to the bathroom. After carefully brushing every plaque-covered tooth, I stripped off my grimy clothes, throwing them in the dirty clothes hamper, and then turned the shower on.  As the steam from the hot water seeped out from behind the curtain, I propped my foot on the counter to examine it.  My swollen anklebone was bruised black and blue, and was still very tender.  I put icing my ankle on my to do list for the day and then hopped into the shower, careful not to hit my sore foot on the rim of the tub as I lifted it over.

Scrubbing the many layers of dried sweat off my skin took longer than I had expected, but it felt great to feel clean again. Once out of the shower, I put on my clothes and hastily threw my wet hair into a sloppy bun on top of my head, and then happily headed back to my room.  When I opened my door, I was surprised to find Aidan not on the bed but leaning over my desk.

"What are you doing?"

Aidan jumped a little, startled by my presence. "Selkie, you scared me.  I didn't hear you come in."

"I scared you?" I asked as I walked over to him and wrapped my arms around him.  "I didn't think that was possible."

He pulled me closer. "Oh, it's possible. Especially if you sneak up on me like that."

"I wasn't sneaking. I was just walking, and besides you're the one in my room sneaking around," I teased. "What were you doing, anyway?"

"I was just looking at your sketches. Is that okay?"

"Only if you tell me they're amazing," I said playfully.

"Selkie," Aidan said, his eyes intense, "You are the most amazing person I have ever known."

Feeling a little uncomfortable by the sudden change of conversation, I jokingly said, "Well then you mustn't have known that many people."

His eyes warmed at my words. "I have known a great many people actually, but none have ever moved me like you do, and no one I have ever met has been able to do what you can do."

I swallowed nervously.

"And what is that, exactly?"

Aidan reluctantly removed his arms from around me, and said, "Maybe you should sit down."

"Okay," I said timidly as I moved to my bed and sat down, curling my legs up beneath me. Aidan grabbed my sketchbook off of my desk and then came to sit next to me on the bed. He carefully flipped through the pages until he came to the picture I'd drawn of him last night outside my window, and then placing the sketchbook on my lap he grabbed my hand, and said, "Selkie, it's time I tell you the rest of what you need to know...and the truth about who you really are."

## Chapter 22

**"Aidan, no offense,"** I said with a frown. **"But I already know who I am...I'm a nobody."**

"You are not a nobody," Aidan said emphatically. "You have an amazing gift, a power that can change the world!"

"Me, change the world? I don't think so!"

"You don't believe me?" Aidan asked, obviously frustrated.

"No, I don't, and I'm sorry if that upsets you, but there is just no way that what you're saying about me is true." I released his hands, stood up and walked to my desk, embarrassed to declare to his face what I was thinking, and then crossing my arms in front of my chest, I said, "I'm not special, Aidan. I never have been."

Aidan quickly stood and made his way over to me. "But that's where you're wrong, Selkie." He grasped both my hands and gazed lovingly at me. "You have always been special, unique, and I'm going to prove it to you."

Not wanting to give in, but still finding his argument interesting, if not ridiculous, I said, "And how are you going to do that?"

Aidan beamed at me, pleased that I had taken the bait, and

then grabbing my sketchbook off the bed and handing it to me, he said, "Follow me."

After throwing on a sweatshirt and a pair of sneakers we left the apartment, but instead of walking to his car in the parking lot, Aidan led me around the building to the spot where the Shadows had appeared the previous evening. The thought of the Shadow's icy grip around my neck made my body shiver and my feet hesitate.

"You don't need to worry," Aidan said, aware of my trepidation. "The Shadows can't come out during the day. The only thing they fear is light, and so the sun is our greatest weapon against them."

"So there is no way they could show up right now?" I asked, still cautious.

"Absolutely not," he said with an encouraging smile. "You're completely safe," and then he tightened his hold on my hand and pulled me forward.

The sun shone brightly above our heads as we walked farther away from the building, and its warmth relieved my uneasiness. When we reached the edge of the woods Aidan stopped walking.

"Let's sit here."

"What are we going to do out here?" I asked as he sat

down on the damp grass.

"You'll see. Just sit down and face me."

I did as he requested.

"Now what?"

"Now, I'd like you to draw me a picture."

Confused, and a little upset that the butt of my jeans was now moist from the morning dew, I said, "Couldn't we have done this inside?"

Aidan chuckled, amused at my annoyance. "Just humor me, Selkie."

"Fine, fine. What should I draw?"

"How about a flower?"

"What kind of a flower?"

"Anything you like...what's your favorite?"

"It's kind of hard for me to choose. There are just so many beautiful flowers."

"But if you could draw just one..."

"I'd draw a lily," I said confidently.

He gave me a smile and handed me a pencil. Opening my sketchbook and taking a deep breath, I leaned over the page and began to sketch. With the tip of the pencil I traced a long Y-shaped stem with four short branches. All along the stem I drew several curly leaves of different shapes and sizes, and on the end of every branch I placed a bell-shaped pod. Around each pod I sketched five delicate triangular petals, and then added four small ovals attached to short stems in the center of each flower. Once the outline was finished, following the natural curves of the plant I shaded the inside of each flower to give it a fuzzy texture, and then completed the picture by darkening the tip of each petal.

I examined my creation and pleased with the final product I smiled to myself, content, but then remembering I wasn't alone, I looked up at Aidan. "Okay, what next?"

"Now, I want you to close your eyes and imagine the flower you just drew."

"That's it?" I asked skeptically.

"That's all it takes."

"Just close my eyes and think about the flower?"

"Yep."

"And then what?"

"You'll see," he said, the anticipation clear in his voice.

"Well okay," I shrugged. "Here goes nothing."

As soon as I closed my eyes, the beautiful flower appeared behind my eyelids. It was safely nestled within the grass before me; its dew-dropped orange petals, with accents of yellow and pink, glistening in the early morning sun. The wind swept the small flower back and forth in a gentle rhythm, and it happily danced alongside the blades of grass that swayed to the same beat.

"Selkie," Aidan whispered. "Open your eyes."

I slowly lifted my eyelids, sad to leave the happy scene in my head, but found Aidan's face a pleasant substitute.

He smiled warmly at me and then lowered his gaze. I followed where his eyes led, and then gasped at the sight in front of me.

"That's my flower," I said loudly as I pointed to the orange lily that was rooted to the ground between us.

"Yes it is," Aidan said happily.

"But how did you do that?"

"I didn't do anything, Selkie. It was you!"

"But how...I mean...that's impossible."

"Not for a Lightscaper it isn't. I've seen you do it a thousand times."

"But how did I do it?" I asked, extremely curious.

"Isn't it obvious? You have the amazing ability to create a new world just by opening your sketchbook. Every time you draw something and then picture it in your head, it immediately exists, and not just within your sketchbook, or within your imagination, but in the real world."

"So you're saying that this flower is real, and I created it?"

Aidan plucked the flower from the ground and tucked it behind my ear. "It's as real as you and me."

"Wait a minute, you called me a...Lightscaper again, but what does that mean? What's a Lightscaper?"

"Well, this is where it gets a little more complicated."

"A little more?" I said, wrinkling my forehead.

"You're right, it's already complicated, but this might be even harder to understand, so...just bear with me."

Aidan took a deep breath and began, "Okay, depending on who you ask, they might tell things a little differently, but this is the story my clan has passed down through generations.

"Before time began, the only thing that existed besides the Shadows of the deep was God and his angels. He created them all with different gifts, but one in particular had an extraordinary gift. He was called the "bearer of light," and it was said that he could manipulate the space around him and create beautiful things. Most people today consider him to be the first true

Lightscaper, and the story says that God was very pleased with this angel, and many believe that this angel, above all the rest, was God's favorite. How are you doing so far?" Aidan asked, stopping his tale.

"So far, so good. Keep going!"

"Okay. Now sometime later, although God was happy in Heaven with his angelic creations, he felt as if something was missing, so he decided to create the Earth and with it the first human beings. God spent many days perfecting his new creation, and when it was done, he left Heaven and his "bearer of light" to spend time on Earth.

"The angel quickly became jealous of the humans on Earth and was angry at God for ignoring him. He decided that the only way to restore God's attention to himself was to destroy the Earth and all that inhabited it. His wrath overcame him, and the Shadows overtook his pure soul. The angel fell from Heaven, unable to reside there with an evil heart, and entered the place where God's humans lived.

"In the form of a snake he came to them, and with the help of the Shadows the humans were easily defeated, and ever since then this world has been corrupted by the dark. And "the bearer of light," whose name today translates to Lucifer, is no longer God's favorite angel, but a disgrace, and he no longer bears the light of God, but is the ruler of the Shadows...a Prince of Darkness."

"So what does all of that have to do with me?" I asked, thoroughly confused.

"Be patient," Aidan said, reaching over and caressing my cheek. "I'm getting there...once the Shadows claimed the Earth, God couldn't just stand by and allow his treasured creation to be destroyed, and that's where you come in. You were chosen, like so many before you, to be God's "bearer of light" here on Earth."

"Are you saying I'm an angel, or something?"

"No, you're still a human," Aidan grinned. "But you have powers that are not of this world."

"I guess that makes sense...but if I have this awesome power, why didn't anyone tell me? I mean you made it clear that I wasn't supposed to know, but why?"

"It hasn't always been this way, Selkie. Lightscapers used to know about their powers, and they even knew who their protectors were. But just like with God's angels, we were created with free will. He gives us all a choice to do good things, or do bad things, and many decades ago, a Lightscaper decided he wanted to do more with his gift than just make the world a prettier place. He abused his powers, and when the Shadows overtook him...well...many bad things happened.

"So, all the clans around the world decided it was too dangerous for Lightscapers to know their true abilities, and we've kept it a secret ever since. Well, that is, until *you* of course."

"Oops," I said, embarrassment flooding my face.

"Yeah, well there's nothing we can do about that now. We're just going to have to be really careful."

"Why, so I don't go over to the dark side like Darth Vader or something?"

Aidan's concern melted away as a smile lit up his face. "Yeah, something like that. Now let's get you inside and put some ice on that ankle."

"Hold on," I said before he could stand. "I want to try something first."

I flipped to a new page in my sketchbook, and covering the page with my hand I started a new picture.

Aidan was silent for the first few minutes, but unable to control his curiosity any longer, he asked, "What are you doing?" as he tried to sneak a glance at the page.

"Hey, stop peeking, it's a surprise! I just need one...more...second. There! All done. Now close your eyes and I'll tell you when to look."

Once Aidan's eyes were closed, and I was sure he wasn't going to cheat, I closed mine too and envisioned the picture I had just drawn coming to life. Once the picture was clear in my head,

I opened my eyes and was amazed at what I saw.

"Okay," I told Aidan with a smile. "You can open them now."

Aidan's eyes quickly shot open and then his jaw dropped in surprise. "Selkie...this is incredible."

Hundreds of orange lilies, identical to the one that was still tucked behind my ear, along with several dozen tulips and roses encircled our two bodies, their sweet fragrances filling the air around us. Aidan swept his hand through the impromptu garden and pulled up a few flowers of each type, forming them into a lovely bouquet.

"For you my lady," he said as he handed me the bouquet and took my hand.

"Why thank you," I said, standing up, and then wrapping my arms around his neck, I pulled his body close against mine and kissed him.

## Chapter 23

**What started out as a tender kiss quickly intensified into something much deeper as we both realized the extent of our longing for each other.** Aidan's caressing hands slid to my hips and up the side of my body, as his soft lips traveled from my mouth down to my neck, and I, encouraging his advances, leaned my head back and closed my eyes.

"I love you," he said between kisses, and then squeezing me tighter against his body he returned to kissing my mouth, and I responded eagerly, my body delighting in his loving touch.

Suddenly, from inside Aidan's pants pocket came a loud buzzing noise. Flustered, I started to pull away from him, but he grabbed my hand, unwilling to part from me completely, and then reached into his pocket and retrieved his phone. He flipped it open and said with frustration, "What do you want?"

The person on the other end answered, but I couldn't make out their muddled reply.

Aidan turned his back on me, and then staring into the woods, he said, "Yeah that's what I figured, but I'm a little busy right now so..."

He stopped speaking, and I could hear more jumbled noise coming from the phone.

"Well that's really none of your business, Liam," Aidan spat.

I placed my hand on Aidan's shoulder and he turned to look at me.

"Is that your brother Liam?"

Aidan nodded his head and then spoke into the phone, "It doesn't matter, I've made my decision, so why don't you just run home and..."

Aidan stopped again, and although Liam's voice was still unclear, I could tell that he was yelling.

"Fine," Aidan said once his brother had finished. "You've got three minutes," and then he hung up and shoved the phone back into his pocket.

"What was that all about?"

Aidan sighed. "Liam needs to talk to me for a minute. So why don't you go inside and..."

"I'm coming with you," I said forcefully.

Aidan smiled. "That's what I thought you'd say. But we have to go in there."

My eyes lingered on the dark, secluded area in the woods he was pointing to, and I swallowed nervously, before asking, "You're not going to leave me in there by myself are you?"

"No, of course not," he replied.

"And the sun is still up, so there is no chance the Shadows could appear. Right?"

"Exactly."

"Well, then, I guess I have nothing to worry about," and then tucking the bouquet of flowers into my sketchbook, I said, "So let's go."

Hand in hand we walked away from the beautiful flowers that were scattered at our feet into the small forest of trees beside my apartment. A light breeze drifted through the newly budding branches above our heads, and the sound of birds and skittering animals could be heard all around us as we walked. Once in the thicket of trees, I could no longer feel the sun's heat on my skin, and the farther into the shade we went, the more uneasy I felt about my decision to accompany Aidan.

"How far in do we have to go?" I asked as I carefully traversed the uneven, muddy ground.

"We're almost there," Aidan said, squeezing my hand, and then encountering a large fallen tree, he said, "Here, let me help you," before swooping me up in his arms and carrying me safely over the log.

When I was back on my feet, we winded our way through a large cluster of blackberry bushes, careful to keep our bare skin away from their prickly spines, and as the trees before us began to thin, we soon found ourselves within a small clearing, where the sun shone brightly through the blossoming branches of the trees that encircled us. I lifted my head toward the light and smiled, happy to once again feel the sun's affectionate rays on my face.

"What took you so long?" asked a low voice hidden among the trees.

I looked around but couldn't see Liam anywhere.

"Selkie's foot is injured," Aidan called out. "Now skip the dramatics and show yourself. I don't have all day."

"You are always so impatient," Liam said, appearing from behind a tree to our right.

"You're right Liam," Aidan growled. "I am very impatient. Especially when I've got better things to do. So let's get on with it."

Liam, with his bright green eyes and firm set jaw, looked more like Brendan than I had remembered, and as he strolled towards us with a small black bag flung over his shoulder, I noticed another family resemblance. He proudly wore the same ugly scowl his father had worn the night before.

Coming to stand in front of us, Liam threw the bag on the ground by Aidan's feet, and then said matter-of-factly, "This is from mom. I think it's some clothes and a toothbrush, or something. She said she couldn't stand the thought of you running around in the same clothes day after day."

Aidan picked up the bag and tucked it under his arm. "Tell her I said thanks, will you," and then squaring his shoulders he asked in a serious tone, "Now, why are you really here?"

Liam rolled his eyes in annoyance. "I'm here because you are in some serious trouble, Aidan. Brendan should be the one to handle this, seeing as he is the oldest and your first ward, but he can't stand to look at you right now...and Ewan, who practically begged to come and talk to you, is grounded for like...the rest of eternity. So, since you don't have any other brothers, that leaves only me to come and clean up your mess."

"And what did you think you were going to do?" Aidan asked, his voice loud. "You already saw how Brendan tried to clean things up, and unless you want a broken nose to match his, you better not try anything stupid!"

"I'm not here to fight you, Aidan," Liam said, raising his hands in surrender. "Believe it or not, I don't feel the same way as Brendan does."

"That's not what it seemed to me when you helped him keep me away from Selkie," Aidan said, his temper rising.

"What was I supposed to do, Aidan? Brendan is the one in charge, not me."

"You could have helped me," Aidan yelled.

"You mean like Ewan did?" Liam countered.

"Well, he might have made some stupid decisions. But at least he tried. At least he cared enough about me to do something!"

"You don't think that Brendan and I care about you?" Liam roared. "After all we've been through. How could you say that?"

Aidan, lost for words, just stood there glaring at Liam who was now filled with so much rage that he refused to look Aidan in the face, and instead kept his eyes focused on the ground in front of him. The tension in the air was unbearable.

"Excuse me," I said meekly. "I don't mean to interrupt, but maybe we should all just calm down for a second, because I don't think that yelling at each other is doing either of you any good."

Aidan took a deep breath, and wrapping his arm around my waist he kissed the top of my head, and said, "Selkie's right. I'm sorry I yelled at you Liam. I really am...but I can't change what's happened, and if you're not going to help...then maybe you should just leave."

"What do you think I'm doing here, Aidan?" Liam asked outraged.

"I obviously have no idea, do I?" Aidan said irritably. "So why don't you just tell me."

I nudged Aidan in the ribs, unhappy with his disagreeable tone, and then politely asked, "Please Liam, could you just tell us what's going on?"

Liam looked at me for the first time and his hard-set mouth softened into a shy smile. "I'm sorry, Selkie. This must be very confusing for you."

"Well, there is a lot to take in," I said, returning his smile.

"Yeah, I remember how confusing it was when I was younger, and I had years to prepare for all of this. I can only imagine what it's like for you."

"It's been quite an experience," I told Liam, and then looking up at Aidan, I said, "But I was lucky to have your brother with me."

A huge smile spread across Aidan's face, and I blushed.

Liam cleared his throat uncomfortably. "Well, that's kind of what I'm here to talk to you about."

"What are you getting at, Liam?" Aidan asked, his face instantly wary.

"Don't get mad at me, okay? Because remember I'm just the messenger, but as soon as you and Selkie left last night Dad went and notified Jeremiah and the rest of the Council. They've been in assembly all day, and rumors have been spreading all over the Sanctuary. I don't know if this is true, or if anything has been decided, but there is talk about your status as a protector."

"My status?" Aidan asked confused.

"Like I said, I don't know if this is true, but apparently the Council has the ability to remove protectors from their Scapers, if they deem it necessary, and from what I've heard, the Council feels your relationship with Selkie is cause enough to remove you from her guard."

Aidan's face drained of all color, and his arm tightened around my waist. "Liam, are you telling me that I might not be Selkie's protector anymore?"

"Not exactly," Liam said, his face filled with pain. "If what I've heard is correct, and the Council decides against you...you won't be a protector at all."

"What?" Aidan shouted as his arm dropped to his side and his hands curled into fists. "They can't do that!"

"Apparently the law says they can."

"But that's ridiculous, Liam! I was chosen by God to be a protector. They can't just take that away from me. What about Selkie?"

"I guess Selkie would be reassigned a new protector."

"Reassigned?" Aidan yelled. "You know that's not how it works. I was chosen to be Selkie's protector, just like I was chosen to protect. It's my destiny." Then Aidan grabbed my hand, and added, "It's our destiny."

Liam took a step forward and placed his two hands on Aidan's shoulders to calm him. "Aidan, I know," he soothed. "I can't believe that the Council would do such a thing, but remember, nothing has been decided yet, and honestly getting mad is not going to solve anything."

Aidan's voice was shockingly quiet as he said, "So tell me Liam, what am I supposed to do?"

"I don't know, but whatever you decide, I'll support you entirely."

Aidan, with his face full of hopelessness, nodded and then lowered his head. Feeling terrible for Aidan, and not knowing what else I could do to comfort him, I squeezed his hand and he quickly responded by lifting his head and smiling at me.

He gazed deeply at me for a moment, and then without removing his eyes from my face, he said strongly, "Liam, I told you before that I had made my decision, and no matter what happens, I know I've made the right one." Aidan pulled me close and then looked at his brother. "Selkie is my world now, and I promised her that I would always protect her. You know me, Liam. You know I have never taken a promise lightly. So no matter what the Council decides, no matter what they do to me, I will never break my promise to Selkie."

Aidan's confident words warmed my heart and filled me with joy. He was choosing me. His whole world was crashing down before him, but he was willing to let it all fall. He was willing to give it all up...for me.

For me? Give up his family, his life, his destiny, for me? What was he thinking? That was insane. The heat in my heart, which had begun to spread through the rest of my body and make my mind fuzzy, quickly faded away, and I could think clearly again.

"Aidan, you can't do this," I said, my voice uncommonly loud.

"Selkie, what are you talking about?" Aidan asked, surprised by my sudden outburst.

I sadly pulled myself away from him, taking a few steps back. "I'm not worth it, Aidan. I'm not worth losing your life!"

"Selkie, don't be ridiculous."

"No, you don't be ridiculous," I said, tears threatening to spill over. "Don't you see what's happening? I'm just screwing things up."

Aidan rushed to my side and cupping my face in his hands, he said, "You are not screwing anything up! You haven't done anything wrong. I love you, and I want to be with you."

"But you could lose everything," I said, the tears now

flooding down my cheeks. "You could lose everything you've worked so hard for. You could lose your family!"

"Selkie, you still don't understand how important you are to me."

"I do understand, and I know I'm not important enough to just throw your whole life away, to throw your family away. Aidan, I know what it's like to go through life all alone..."

"But I won't be alone, I'll have you," he said with a smile.

"It isn't the same. I'm not enough," I cried, pushing him away, but Aidan wouldn't allow me to escape. He only pulled me closer, forcing me to look into his lovely gray eyes as he said, "Selkie, you're wrong. You are enough, and no matter what anybody says, I know that I am meant to be with you. Even before I was born, I was chosen to be your protector, which means that my body was designed with the specific purpose to protect you, and only you.

"Before that day in the park, I thought that being your protector was enough to make my life worthwhile, and I was happy, but the moment we met, the moment we touched, something changed within me, and being your protector just wasn't enough anymore.

"I needed to see you, to be near you, and I quickly discovered that my heart, just like my body, was designed with a specific purpose." Aidan wiped away my tears and then lightly brushed his lips against my cheek, before saying, "My heart was designed to love you Selkie; to love you, and only you. So you see," he said, gently stroking my face, "your life and heart are entwined with mine, and if I couldn't be with you, well, there'd be no reason for me to exist."

## Chapter 24

**How could I resist him after that?** After he presented me with his unwavering heart and declared his most adamant affection, how could I refuse? Aidan was offering a life I had only dreamed of, and although I feared the outcome of the risk he was taking, I could not dismiss the love he swore to provide. I needed it. I needed him.

So I gave in, and with my arms wrapped snuggly around his waist I smiled through my tears, and said, "I couldn't exist without you, either."

That perfect smile that I loved so much spread across Aidan's face as he said, "I was hoping you would say that."

"You were? Well I'm glad I didn't disappoint you," I beamed at him.

"Never," he said more seriously, and then he leaned in and kissed me passionately.

"Um...I'm still here," Liam said awkwardly.

"Oh, sorry about that," Aidan smirked as he regrettably released my lips and turned to his brother.

"It's fine," Liam said, holding back a smile. "But I have to be getting back soon, and I still haven't told you everything."

"You mean there's more?" Aidan asked indignantly. "What, do they want my dagger too?"

"No…I mean not yet at least."

"Well, then what do they want?" Aidan asked, trying his best to stay calm.

"They want your car," Liam frowned.

"Naturally. Let me guess, dad's idea?"

"Yeah, but don't be mad at him, he's just doing what he thinks is right."

"No Liam, he's doing what he's told to do, there's a difference."

"Well, regardless, I need your keys."

"Fine, take them," Aidan said, handing them over. "But I need to get something out of the car before you go."

Together we walked, a little faster than my foot could handle, back through the woods to the parking lot and Aidan's car. Once Liam had unlocked it, Aidan opened the passenger side door and climbed in. After frantically searching through the glove box, and under every seat, Aidan climbed out and slammed the door.

"I could have sworn I had left it in here," he said frustrated.

"What are you even looking for?" Liam asked.

"Its personal Liam, so it's really none of your business, alright?"

"Alright, geez, I was just trying to help."

"Yeah, I know. Sorry, but if..."

"If I find anything," Liam interrupted, "I'll let you know. Well, I'd better be going. I'll call you if I found out any more information."

"Thanks."

"Hey," Liam said with a shrug, "that's what brothers are for," and then he got into the car and drove away.

*　*　*

"Aidan, what were you looking for back there?" I asked as we climbed the last few steps to my apartment.

"Oh, it's nothing important," he said, obviously trying to avoid the subject.

"Well, you seemed really upset when you didn't find it. So it must be somewhat important."

"Really, Selkie," he said, opening the door, "it's no big deal, don't worry about it."

Feeling uneasy with Aidan's sudden secrecy, I asked,

"Aidan, what's going on? Why won't you tell me what you were looking for?"

"Because I don't think you're going to like it very much, and I don't want you to be upset," he said as he walked into the living room and slumped onto the couch.

"So you think that keeping secrets from me is a better idea?" I asked, my hands sliding to rest on my hips.

"No of course not," Aidan insisted.

"Well, then I think that you should tell me," I said, coming to sit next to him.

"Alright, but just so you know, I wasn't intentionally keeping this from you, but I also wasn't sure how to tell you so…"

"So why don't you just tell me quickly and get it over with."

"Okay. Right. Good idea," he said with a forced smile. "It might sound silly, but I was looking for an envelope that had some pictures in it."

"Hold that thought," I said, standing up. "I'll be right back."

I quickly hobbled to my room and retrieved the small envelope of pictures I'd found in Aidan's car, that were now safely residing in the drawer of my night table and brought them to Aidan with a smile.

"Are these what you were looking for?"

He opened the envelope and scanned the pictures. "How did you get these?"

"I found them when Ewan took me to the Sanctuary."

"And have you looked at them?" he asked cautiously.

"Well, yeah. I'm sorry if that makes you mad, but I was curious and I couldn't help myself."

"Why would I be mad? Shouldn't you be the one that's upset?"

"Me? Upset? Why would you think that?"

"I don't know," he said sheepishly. "I guess I thought that you would think it was creepy, me taking pictures of you when you didn't know I was there...and stuff."

"Actually, I did think about that, but honestly I was kind of flattered."

"You were?"

"Yeah! It made me feel good that you wanted to see me and know what I was doing. It also made me feel safer, knowing you were always there watching over me."

"Selkie," Aidan said, shaking his head, "You are so strange.

Any other girl would have called the cops or something, but you..."

"But me, what?"

"You...surprise me."

"Is that a good thing, or a bad thing?" I asked nervously.

"That's a very good thing. You always keep me on my toes."

"Oh, well in that case," I said, moving to stand on the couch so that I was just a few inches taller than Aidan, "how's this?"

"Perfect," he said with a grin, and then raising himself up on his tiptoes he kissed me.

Once the glorious kiss was over, I asked, "Well, what should we do today?" but before Aidan could open his mouth, his stomach answered for him.

"Oh my gosh," I said with a giggle. "Was that your stomach?"

"Umm...guilty."

"Wow! Okay, then I guess it's settled. Now that you have some clothes, why don't you go take a shower, and I'll go fix us something to eat."

"Sounds good. Oh, but do me a favor...no mushrooms."

"You don't like mushrooms?"

"Nope, I never have. I just can't stand the sliminess."

"Oh...well...good to know. No mushrooms, it is."

"Thanks," he smiled, before giving me a quick peck on the cheek and heading to the bathroom.

Once he was gone, I carefully climbed off the couch, using the armrest for balance, and went straight to work on making a delicious, non-mushroom lunch. I also took the time to ice my ankle, which was still swollen and incredibly sore.

I had already ladled the tomato soup into the bowls, and was just plating the grilled cheese sandwiches, when Aidan appeared in the hallway, his clean red polo covering his bare chest.

"Are you ready to eat?" I asked, picking up his plate and laying it on the counter.

"In a sec, but I'm going to need your help first."

"Sure. What's up?"

He took a step forward and looking around, he asked, "Is Tabitha still here?"

"No, she left for work a few minutes ago. Why?"

"I just don't think she should see this," he said as he lowered his shirt to reveal his wound.

"Oh my God, Aidan," I screeched as I took in the charred looking skin at the center of his chest.

"No, it's okay. It's healing, but it just looks really hideous."

"Are you sure?" I asked, walking over to him. "Because it looks worse than the last time I saw it."

"Yeah, I'm sure. It will heal, eventually, but I do need to get some ointment on it and wrap it up again. Would you mind?"

"No, of course not. Let's go to my room."

While Aidan went to lie on the bed, I rummaged through the black bag Liam had brought and found that Aidan's mom had packed several containers of a strange golden gel, along with some medical gloves and lots of bandages.

"So, what is this stuff?" I asked as I lathered Aidan's mutilated skin with the unfamiliar medicine.

"It's what we call Solas Serum, or light serum."

"Solas? What language is that?"

"It's Irish of course," Aidan said with a grin.

"Irish? Wait. You're Irish too?"

"Yes, Selkie. I would have thought that was obvious."

"Why would that be obvious?"

"Well for one thing, my name is Aidan O'Connor, and you can't have a name more Irish than that…"

"Yeah, I guess so."

"Plus, I'm your protector."

"So?"

"Oh, right," Aidan said, sitting up. "You don't know any of this, do you?"

"Afraid not."

"Okay, well let's see if this helps. Every Lightscaper has a protector, right?"

"Yep, got that."

"Alright, now there are thousands of Lightscapers all over the world. Which means that there has to be protectors all over the world too, right?"

"I suppose."

"Well, you come from an Irish family, which means you are part of the Irish clan…"

"Which is the same clan you're a part of?"

"Exactly."

"Okay, that wasn't too confusing."

"How about this?" Aidan asked with a sly smile. "Protectors have always been chosen by God, and although we still believe that, modern science over the last few decades has helped us discover an extra gene that all protectors carry within their DNA. It's hereditary, but it can only be passed on to one offspring."

"What kind of gene, exactly?"

"I don't know all the science behind it," he said, grabbing the bandages and unraveling them, "but I do know that the protector gene gives me a few important assets to help defeat the Shadows and protect you."

"Like what?" I asked, completely enthralled.

"Well, I can sense when Shadows are near for one..."

"How do you sense them?" I asked, scooting closer and taking the bandages from Aidan.

"It's a feeling I get in the pit of my stomach," he said, raising his arms out to the side, "kind of like the feeling you get when you're riding a rollercoaster and your stomach drops."

"Oh, I hate that feeling," I said as I began to wrap the bandages tightly around his body.

Aidan's face contorted in pain when the bandage made

contact with his wound, but he just took a deep breath, and said, "Yeah, it's annoying, but it gives me an advantage. The feeling even gets more intense when the Shadow's numbers are larger."

"Well, that's cool. What else can you do?"

"My reflexes and strength are more heightened than most humans, and I don't age..."

"You don't age?" I squealed, almost dropping the bandage.

"Hold on, Selkie. Let me finish."

"Oh, okay. Sorry."

"That's alright. But what I was going to say was that I don't age as quickly as most humans."

"Oh," I said as I finished the wrapping and fastened the silver clip. "So you can still die?"

"Most definitely," he said, grabbing his shirt and tugging it over his head.

"Well, that sucks!"

"That's life," he replied, and then lightly touching my cheek, he said, "and I wouldn't want it any other way."

I blushed at his gesture, and then took his hand. "So let's see if I get this right. To be a protector you have to be born with a special gene that's passed down from another protector. This gene gives you special powers, but you can still die."

"Precisely."

"So then what about your brothers? If you got the gene, what do they have to do with everything? They're not protectors, right?"

"That's right. Brendan, Liam and Ewan are what we call wards. They weren't born with the gene, but they were born into a clan family. Which means, they know all that I know, and they fight the Shadows, but they just don't have the same abilities."

"Well, that makes sense, but it sucks that they have to fight those things without the powers you have."

"Yeah, but they don't face them unless I'm overwhelmed. Mostly, they guard you during the day when the Shadows can't come out, which gives me the time I need to sleep and regain my strength."

"So they're kind of like bodyguards."

"In a way, but don't tell Brendan that, he would get seriously pissed."

"Yeah, what's up with that? Why does he have such a bad attitude?"

"Well, that's even more simple to explain," Aidan said, standing up and taking my hand. "Brendan was the first born son, and nine times out of ten, the first born son carries the protector gene…"

"But you have the gene," I interrupted.

"Exactly," Aidan said, leading me out of the room and down the hallway to the kitchen. "When everyone realized that Brendan didn't have the gene, they knew that my mother would have to have another child."

"Have to?"

"Yes. That's another rule I'm not so fond of. All protectors must have at least two children, unless the gene doesn't surface, and then you have to have more children until it does."

"But that's ridiculous, what if you have ten kids and the gene doesn't show up?"

"Well, technically you would have to keep on trying."

"That's terrible."

"I know. It sounds awful, but if you look at it the other way, without enough protectors, Lightscapers would be left to themselves, and the Shadows would overrun them."

"So it sucks both ways then," I said, handing him his food.

"Yeah it does," he said as he took the sandwich from me and eyed it hungrily. "It sucks both ways."

## Chapter 25

**"So what should I draw?" I asked as I placed my uneaten crust on my plate and picked up a pencil.**

Aidan, preoccupied with twisting a piece of my hair around his finger, simply replied, "Whatever makes you happy."

"But there's just too much to choose from," I said, smiling at him.

"Alright, well in that case, how about a rose?"

I shook my head. "No, roses are too easy. I want to really test my abilities. Think of something more difficult."

"Okay," he said, releasing his hold on my hair and standing up. "How about a billion roses?"

"Is that really the best that you can do?" I asked, disappointed with his lack of creativity.

"Hey!"

"Well, sorry, but you're the one who said you've watched me do this a thousand times..."

"I have..."

"Okay, so I just assumed you'd have some good ideas."

"Well, maybe I do, but you caught me off guard. I mean, how am I supposed to think properly when you're sitting next to me, looking like that?"

"Looking like what?"

"Looking so beautiful, that's what! It's incredibly distracting."

"Oh, yeah right," I laughed. "You're just trying to sidetrack me so that you can have more time to think."

"I am not! I honestly have a serious problem thinking about anything else when you're around."

"Okay, sure, but you still haven't given me any ideas."

"Well, give me a sec," Aidan said, turning away to face the window. "Let me get you out of my head first."

Amused by his frenzied behavior, I smiled, and then sat silently as he took several long deep breaths.

"I think I've got it," he said finally, spinning around to look at me. "Why don't you make it snow?"

"What? Are you crazy? It's almost the end of April."

"So? You said you wanted to test your abilities, didn't you?"

"Yes, but that's impossible!"

"Are you sure?" Aidan smirked. "I guess you'll never know until you try."

"But what if someone sees?"

"They'll probably just blame it on global warming or something," he shrugged. "Besides, you can always make the sun come out to melt it all away."

"You make it sound so easy."

"For you, Selkie, it is."

"Alright," I sighed, "I'll try...but don't be surprised if this strange change of weather ends up on the news," and then as Aidan turned to face the window again, I opened to a clean page and began to sketch the wintry scene.

The gray, overcast sky my pencil produced was consumed with an endless layer of flat, dark clouds that hovered close to the ground, overflowing with a flurry of tiny white flakes, which quickly covered every surface they could reach. The newly blossomed treetops within the small, gloomy forest drooped from the weight of the icy precipitation, and the exposed grass below my living room window was blanketed in a thin coat of the glistening snowfall.

With the picture complete, I took one more glance out the window at the glorious sun, and then closed my eyes and imagined my cold, frosty landscape coming to life, before opening my eyes to see the large white flakes silently floating down on the other side of the glass.

"I knew you could do it," Aidan said, coming to sit beside me.

"But how does it work? I mean, I just finished the picture, but outside it looks like it's been snowing for hours. It's like magic."

"Well, your role in the process is pretty simple. All you have to do is draw the picture, close your eyes, and imagine it. God does the rest, and since he is all powerful and everything, I'm guessing that making a little snow appear is pretty easy for him."

"Yeah, when you put it that way, I guess it is."

"So what's next?"

"Well, I'm curious about something," I said, wrinkling my forehead in thought. "If all of this can appear just by me drawing it, what happens when I do this?" I flipped my pencil around and began to vigorously rub the eraser against the page, removing all the snow from the trees and the clouds from the sky. Then I quickly closed my eyes and imagined the layers of snow melting away, and the dark clouds vanishing to make room for the sun.

A beam of light suddenly struck my face and I opened my eyes to find the midday sun resting in a crystal clear sky, and shining brightly through my window. The snow, which had very recently blanketed the landscape, had swiftly vacated the ground and trees, and it was Spring once again.

"Pretty cool, huh?" Aidan said, a proud smile spreading across his face.

"Yeah, very cool," I replied as my eyes traveled down to the picture in my lap.

"And that's not even all that you can do."

"What?" I said loudly as my head shot up in surprise. "You mean there's more that I can do?"

Uncertainty flooded Aidan's face. "Well, yes there is, but..."

"How much more?" I asked excitedly, ignoring his hesitation.

"Quite a bit more, actually, but..."

"Well, what is it?" I interrupted, unable to contain my enthusiasm. "Tell me!"

"I'm sorry," he said quickly, "but I can't."

"What do you mean?"

"I made a mistake, Selkie."

"What do you mean you made a mistake?"

"I mean that I was wrong to say what I said, and I have nothing else to tell you."

"Wait, you just admitted that I could do other things, you put it out there, and now you don't want to tell me?"

"It's not that I don't want to tell you..."

"So there is something else?"

"Yes, but..."

"But what?"

"But I'm not allowed to tell you because it's a lot more complicated than drawing a flower or two," Aidan said, grabbing his dirty dishes and standing up. "If you do it incorrectly, you could cause some serious problems."

"Well, have I done it before?"

"Yes, but you didn't know you were doing it, so your intentions were pure," he said, turning his back to me and heading for the kitchen.

I quickly followed.

"So you think that if I knew what I could do, I would choose to do something bad with it, is that it?"

"Not exactly, but we all have our temptations, and most of the time we fall prey to them."

"But if God gave me a special ability, Aidan, he must have thought that I could handle it, right?"

"I suppose…"

"And if I was going to do something bad you would tell me, wouldn't you?"

"Yes."

"Okay, so then what's the problem?"

"I don't know," Aidan said frustrated as he went to lean against the counter. "I've just made a lot of choices recently that my family and clan weren't happy with, and although I don't regret making them, because they were necessary, I'm afraid that telling you this will just make it harder on both of us."

"Do you really think that it would be harder for me…" I asked, my hands sliding defiantly to my hips, "…or are you just worried about what your friends and family are going to think? Because, honestly, it just seems like you don't want to tell me because you don't won't to get into any more trouble."

"Is that a bad thing?" Aidan asked, his body tensing with disagreement.

"It is if you're not telling me the whole truth. I mean, you're the one who came into my life and brought all this secret crap with you, and it's not fair that you know everything about me, but won't tell me."

"I know this is difficult for you," Aidan soothed, "but everything about our life together isn't going to be simple. As your boyfriend, I want to tell you, believe me I do...but as your protector, I'm bound to keep it a secret, and who knows what will happen if the clan found out that I told you."

"But this isn't just about you," I said, moving closer. "It's my life too, and I have a right to know what's going on."

"I'm sorry, Selkie, but it's just too dangerous."

"So that's it," I said, my anger rising. "You just get to decide what you will and won't tell me, and there is nothing I can do about it?"

"I've told you everything I know, except for this one thing, isn't that enough?"

"No, it's not."

"Well I can't tell you because I made a promise. So I don't know what you want me to do."

"I want you to be honest with me, about everything!"

"I'm sorry, but I can't!"

"You're not sorry," I yelled, my temper now completely out of control. "You've been like this from the beginning. You've always been keeping secrets from me, never telling me what's going on, and you're just going to keep on doing it."

"Selkie, please, it's not like that at all," Aidan said, reaching out for me.

"No, I think that's exactly how it is," I said, backing away from him, my voice threatening to break. "And if that's how this relationship is going to be...I don't think that I can do this anymore."

"Selkie...what are you saying?" Aidan asked as his face contorted with pain.

I didn't know what I was saying...or what I was doing. All I knew was that I was angry and confused, and I just wanted whatever was happening to stop. I wanted to be away from it.

I wanted to be away from him.

So with tears in my eyes, I said, "Aidan, I think that you should leave."

"What? Selkie, please don't do this," Aidan pleaded.

"I have to, Aidan," I said, turning away from him. "You were right, this is too dangerous." Too dangerous for my heart. "We were never supposed to be together, and now I can see why it can never work between us. Now please...just leave me alone."

I had anticipated more argument from Aidan. I had thought that he would try to convince me to let him stay...but he said nothing. We just stood there in silence for a brief moment, the tears now flowing freely down my face, until I heard Aidan walk over to the door and open it.  A strong breeze blew through the doorway into the apartment, sending shivers down my spine, and then the door slammed closed, and it was gone...and so was Aidan.

## Chapter 26

**So it could happen.** I hadn't thought that it was possible. For the second time in my life, my heart, which had once felt the intense smoldering burn of love, was once again an icy chasm of loss, void of all happiness and warmth. In the past, my sketchbook would have served as an incomparable release, a desired distraction from such agonizing pain...but no beauty in the world could divert me from the emptiness inside of me, and to think I might have prevented it...if only I could have resigned myself to live a life of happy ignorance with Aidan.

As I lay on the floor sobbing into my hands, I thought of the initial spark that awakened my heart and ignited the fire that had engulfed my whole being in its passionate flames. Yearning for comfort, I placed my hands against my hollow chest and tried to imagine the heat that my soul had once possessed...but it was no use. Aidan was the one who had set fire to my heart, and he was the only one who could rekindle it. But he was gone...and it was all my fault.

Unwilling to deny my heart the satisfaction of mourning over Aidan, I dragged myself over to the couch and curled up with a pillow, ready to drown my sorrows in endless hours of restless weeping, when I heard a timid knock at the door.

Wiping my eyes against my shirt, I slowly sat up. "Who is

it?" I called out, my voice shaky.

"Selkie?"

Something inside my chest stirred.

"Selkie...are you alright?"

There it was again...that small movement deep within me. His gentle, loving voice was like a jolt to my system. I stood up and silently crept forward. He was so close, just outside the door.

"Selkie, I know you can hear me. I understand why you're upset. I came back to tell you that I was wrong...and that I'm sorry."

My hand slid down the door to the handle.

"I love you, Selkie."

My heart sputtered with anticipation, and I couldn't resist the glimmer of heat. Turning the knob, I cracked the door open and peeked out to see Aidan standing there, his eyes red and swollen.

"I'm so sorry," he said, his gray eyes laden with pain.

I swung the door open and threw myself into his arms. Aidan eagerly wrapped his arms around me, and then nestled his head into my hair. The tears came pouring out again, and I whimpered quietly into his shoulder.

"I don't know what I was thinking," I managed to choke out amidst the sobs. "I was angry, and stupid. I never really wanted you to go."

"I know," he whispered close to my ear. "I only left because I didn't know what else to do."

"It's all my fault."

"No, it's mine," he said, cupping my face in his hands. "I shouldn't have tried to control you like that. You were right. It's not fair."

"But what about your family?"

"I don't know what I'm going to do about them," he said with a frown. "But I do know that I never want to leave you like that again. So I'll tell you all that I know, but it's going to have to be our little secret."

"So many secrets," I said, laying my head against his chest. "Isn't there another way?"

Aidan squeezed me tighter. "Not that I can see."

I sighed, frustrated with the situation before us, but content to be back in Aidan's arms. Back where I belonged. I lifted my head and lightly grazed his chin with my lips. He returned my loving gesture with a tender smile, and then lowering his mouth to mine, he kissed me. His lips tasted salty from the tears he had shed, but I didn't mind. I knew mine were just as tainted.

Once the kiss had ended, we lingered in each other's arms for a few more glorious moments, and then grudgingly made our way back inside to deal with the serious problem still at hand.

"We just had our first fight," I said, my face grim.

Aidan, seeing my distress took hold of my hand. "But hopefully it was our last."

"Very doubtful," I said, shaking my head. "With my stubbornness, I can almost guarantee that there will be a lot more fights to come."

"Well, that might be true, but we shouldn't dismiss my need to control a situation," he said with a smirk, obviously trying to lighten the mood. "That could sure lead to some scuffles down the line."

"I guess, no matter what, this would have happened eventually?"

Aidan nodded.

"So there was no way of avoiding it I suppose, but I wish I had had more control. I feel terrible about making you leave."

"Yeah, that didn't feel so good," he said sadly. "But I guess I kind of deserved it."

Still feeling guilty, and not wanting to drudge up anymore

of those sour feelings, I said, "Let's just say that we both did and said things that we wish we hadn't, and then just leave it at that."

"That would be great," Aidan said solemnly. "But that doesn't really solve our problem, does it? We can both apologize all we want, but that just won't be enough. It's clear to me now that the only way we can fix this mess between us is if I tell you everything."

That news should have made me smile, but instead I found a frown upon my face and feelings of mistrust in my heart. "Aidan, not that I'm disagreeing with you or anything," I said carefully, "but before, you were so adamant about not breaking your promise, and now suddenly you've decided to tell me...and I'm just wondering...what changed your mind?"

"You did...or that is, your face did," he said earnestly. "It was the way you looked at me when we were fighting. You were so angry, so confused...so unhappy. It broke my heart seeing you like that," he said, releasing my hand and looking away, "and knowing that I had been the one to cause you all that pain, well it made me hate myself."

I lightly placed my hand on his shoulder, and his sad eyes slowly returned to my face.

"I hadn't comprehended how serious our fight had become until you kicked me out," he continued, "and I quickly realized that I had no chance of seeing you again, unless I changed my way of thinking.

"So I vowed to myself that if you let me back in I would do my best to always make you happy, promise or not, and I intend to make good on that vow" he said, his eyes now gleaming with a fierce determination.

"You really do love me," I said tearfully, amazed by his unwavering dedication.

"Did you doubt that?" he asked, reaching his hand up to stroke my cheek.

"No, not really," I blushed. "It's just hard for me to accept that someone could love me the way you do. I'm not used to it."

"Well you better start getting used to it," he said, scooting closer so that he could wrap his arm around me, "because I'm not going anywhere."

"Are you sure about that? What if we get into another fight, and I tell you to leave again?"

"You won't," he said with a confident smile. "But just in case I'm wrong, and you do tell me to leave, I just won't listen."

"That's comforting."

"Sorry, but at least it's better than the alternative."

"And what's that?"

"Well, I suppose I would have to restrain you, and then hold you hostage until you were ready to think reasonably."

"Oh, is that all," I giggled.

"No, I'm sure I could think of something else," he said, his eyes flickering with mischief, "but you'd have to give me more time."

"I think I'll just settle for the first option. Thank you."

"No, I don't think so," he said more seriously. "That's still not good enough for me."

"What do you mean?"

"Well, I'd rather we not have to use any of the options. Which means, it's time for me to stop wasting time and tell you what I promised."

"Are you sure?" I asked, my body tensing with an unexpected excitement.

"If it will make you happy..."

"It will, Aidan. More than anything."

"Then I guess we should start at the beginning," he sighed, sitting back into the couch and crossing his arms across his chest.

Grabbing a pillow from behind my back and hugging it to my chest, I settled in close next to Aidan and waited with bated breath for him to begin.

"Selkie, what do you know about your parents?"

"Nothing really," I sulked. "I was only a baby when they gave me up, and I was never given any information about who they were or where they came from."

"Let me see if I can help you with that," he mused. "From what I've been told, your parents were both born in Ireland and met each other during college. They got married and moved to Belfast, which is the capitol of Ireland, ironically enough, and then two years later, October 18, 1990 to be exact, you were born."

"How do you know all of this?" I asked, my voice trembling with astonishment.

"Protectors are not just trained in combat, Selkie. We spend many years learning about our Lightcapers so that we can be better prepared to protect them. I've been studying your life since I was a child."

"Really?" I asked startled. "That must have been a drag. I'm sorry my life hasn't been more exciting."

"Well, actually, that's not quite true," he contested. "Some parts of your history are a lot more interesting than you would think, but they're not pleasant, and I'm afraid that it would hurt you to hear about them."

What could be worse than what I already believe to be true?

"I need to know," I said vehemently.

Aidan's forehead instantly crinkled with worry. "Why doesn't that surprise me," he said, and then taking a deep breath, he continued, "You've always thought that your parents abandoned you because they didn't want you, but that's not the real reason, and you need to know what really happened so that you can stop blaming them and move on."

Aidan took my hand. "They loved you very much, Selkie...and they had every intention of being your parents, forever. But in September of 1991, just before your first birthday, your parents went out to a bar and left you with a babysitter. While at dinner, a bomb planted by an extremist political group exploded on the second floor of the bar, killing 3 civilians and wounding 12 others."

I squeezed Aidan's hand. He stopped talking for a moment and examined me with cautious eyes. Unblinking, I nodded my head for him to finish.

"They died that day in the bar, Selkie."

I released an anguished sigh and closed my eyes.

"It was a horrible thing that happened...and you didn't deserve it...but it wasn't their fault, and it's important you know how much they wanted you."

"What were their names," I whispered, opening my eyes and allowing a single tear to escape and roll down my cheek.

"Your mother's name was Sarah, and your father's was Ronan."

"Sarah and Ronan Reid," I repeated dreamily. "That sounds nice."

"They were nice people."

"How do you know that?" I questioned. "Another one of your studies?"

"No, not mine. My fathers."

"Your father?"

"Yes, Selkie. My father...was your father's protector."

"But that would mean that...that my father was...a Lightscaper," I stammered.

"Yes, he was, and it's very common for Lightscapers to pass their abilities to their children, just like with the protector gene."

"And what about my mother? Was she a Lightscaper too?"

"No, she was just your mother, but although she didn't

give you any magical powers, I do know of one thing you inherited from her," he said as he twisted a lock of my hair around his finger.

"My hair," I blurted out in amazement.

"Yep, or at least that's what my dad says. He told me once that he thought you looked just like her, red hair and all."

"Are you serious? Oh I wish I had a picture of her," I said, running my fingers through my hair, "of both of them, but I guess it's too much to hope that your photographing tendencies are hereditary too."

"That I have no idea about, but judging on what I know about my dad, I would say that finding a picture that he had taken of your parents would be very unlikely."

I released a frustrated sigh.

"Selkie, was I right to tell you about them?"

I looked at Aidan and saw that his forehead was again creased with worry. I smiled meekly. "It's hard for me to imagine that what you say is true, except for the fact that I know you wouldn't lie to me about this...and it's strange to think after all this time that I had parents that loved me and wanted me, but honestly, I've heard stranger things. So in a way," I said, touching his cheek, "it hurts knowing that I've been wrong about them for so long...but I think that it would have hurt me even more if I'd gone on thinking all those terrible things about them."

"So then, your glad that I told you?"

"I'm glad to finally know the truth, yes."

"But are you happy now that I've told you?"

"Well that's tricky," I said, laying my head against his shoulder. "I'm definitely sad for them, and for the fact that I'll never get to meet them or talk to them...but I'm also very happy to know that I have a piece of both of them with me, wherever I go, and you being here, telling me all these things, well I couldn't have asked for a more amazing gift. So I guess, in a weird way, this is the happiest day of my life."

# Chapter 27

**"Maybe I'm stupid," I said, pulling the hot bag of popcorn out of the microwave and dropping it on the counter, "but if I was born in Ireland, how did I ever end up here?"**

Leaning over to open the bag and pour the steaming snack into a bowl, Aidan smiled, "You're not stupid. That's a good question, and I was actually just about to get to that."

"Oh sorry," I said, embarrassed with my lack of patience. "I didn't mean to rush you or anything, but I'm just so excited to finally learn things about my life that, until today, I've only been able to guess at."

"You? Excited?" Aidan asked in mock amazement. "I never would have guessed."

"Oh ha, ha," I said, rolling my eyes at him. "Very funny."

Aidan, unaware of my irritation and completely amused with himself roared with laughter, and then greedily grabbed a large handful of popcorn and shoved it into his mouth.

"Ugh, you are such a guy," I told him moodily.

"Whatdoyoumean," he grumbled, his mouth still full of popcorn.

I felt my face instantly flush.

"Um, well, here I am telling you how I feel, and all you can think about is food!"

Surprised by my outburst, Aidan quickly swallowed. "Hey, what's the matter?" he asked, moving closer and taking me into his arms. "I thought we were having fun?"

"I'm sorry," I sighed, my head melting into his chest. "I don't know why I said it like that."

Why did I have to get so upset?

"So then what's wrong?" Aidan asked again, his hand lightly stroking my hair.

"I don't know," I frowned. "I guess...I just have a hard time letting go and having fun. I don't have much experience with it...and there's just so much that I want to know."

"Well then," Aidan said, tilting my chin up so that I could see his face, "let's not waste any more time."

You would have thought that after all the years I'd spent wondering who I was, my mind would have been consumed with questions; wanting nothing else but to find out the truth about my past; to know all the answers, but with our warm bodies just slightly touching, and Aidan's perfect smooth lips only inches from mine, there wasn't anything else in that moment that I cared about. All I could see...all I could feel...and all I could want...was him.

A sly smile spread across my face. "Maybe we could waste one more minute."

"Are you sure?" he asked, leaning closer and hugging me tighter.

"Most definitely," I assured him, and before I could even take another breath, Aidan eagerly closed the small distance between us.

I would never get used to it. That strange, glorious, lightheaded feeling that overtook me every time our lips mingled. It was so confusing. I thought I might faint from the dizziness, but the blood pumping rapidly through my veins made me feel like I could run a marathon. It was so invigorating.

So then why did my knees wobble with uncertainty as his hands caressed my neck?

Afraid of collapsing, I leaned my hips against the counter for support, but he only pressed his body closer, making me tremble even more with instability. His hands continued to roam my body, progressing down my back to my waist, and my hands groped his shoulders for support.

"Aidan, wait," I gasped as his hand began to travel down my leg, and thankfully, he did. His hand immediately ceased its exploration, and his frenzied eyes, which were fixed passionately on my face, began to calm.

"I'm sorry, Selkie," he said breathlessly. "That was too far."

"Yeah, just a little," I said modestly.

"I'm sorry," he repeated, this time disappointment flooding his face.

"Hey, you don't have to apologize," I said, stroking his cheek. "You didn't do anything wrong."

"I just...I don't want you to think that I was planning that or anything. I really didn't mean for it to go that far."

"It's alright. I understand."

"It's just so hard," he said, stepping away from me. "You make me so crazy!"

"Well, I would be lying if I said you didn't make me crazy too."

"Really? You're not just saying that to make me feel better?"

"Are you kidding? Of course not! You make me feel amazing. I love kissing you, but I'm just not ready to..." I turned my face away. "I'm not ready for...well you know."

"I do know," he said, taking a step forward. "And I would

never make you do anything you didn't want to do."

"I believe you."

"Do you?" he asked, taking my hand.

"Hey, when I asked you to stop...you did, even though I know it was hard for you."

"It was very hard for me, actually."

"Okay...but you did it, right?  So then there's nothing you need to worry about."

"So you're not mad at me?"

"Hey, you saw me earlier, remember?  If I was mad at you, I think you'd know it!"

"That's very true," he grinned.  "So I guess I'm off the hook."

"Well, not quite," I said, pulling him towards the living room.  "Don't forget you've still got a lot of explaining to do."

"Oh right," Aidan smirked. "I don't know how that could have slipped my mind?"

"Well, I might have had something to do with it," I said with a shrug. "But that's not really important right now, is it?"

"No, I guess you're right," he laughed, and then flopping onto the couch and pulling me down next to him, he asked, "So where were we?"

"You were about to explain how I managed to show up here in Belfast?"

"Oh, right. Well...you flew on an airplane."

"I think that's obvious," I said, nudging him playfully with my elbow. "But why here, why Maine?"

"When your parents died, it was discovered that you had no living relatives in Northern Ireland. They had either all died or had moved away. The only person that they could locate was your father's aunt, your great aunt."

"What was her name?"

"Um, Trudy I think. Yeah, Trudy Doyle."

"And she lived here in Belfast?"

"For a time. After her husband died in the late 80's she moved here to get away from all the fighting that was happening in Ireland."

"Fighting? You mean like the bomb that killed my parents?"

"Yeah, and there were a lot more terrible things that happened; that are still happening."

"So she moved here to Belfast to get away from all of that,

and then I flew here to live with her. But then, where is she? Why am I not with her?"

"Well, this is the part that really sucks. You did live with her, for about two weeks, until she had a heart attack and died. She was an older woman, and she had been in poor health for a long time."

"And she was my only family."

"Exactly, and since you had no other family in Ireland, you couldn't go back there, and you didn't have any family here, so you had no place to go. The state took you into their custody after Trudy's death, and well...you know the rest."

"So, what? Am I like doomed to never have a family or something," I asked, a sudden rush of depression swarming over me. "I mean, how can one person have such terrible luck?"

"I don't know, Selkie. It's really messed up, and I can't even imagine what it would feel like to not have a family."

"It really sucks! That's how it feels...and it makes me mad, because I've always tried to be a good person, you know. I've never really complained or blamed anyone else for my crappy life. But I feel so angry sometimes, like I don't deserve what's happened to me...and I can't help but think that I got gypped."

"I can totally understand why you would feel that way...but what about all the amazing things you do have? I mean, shouldn't they count for something?"

"Like what?"

"Well, *me* for one thing..."

"Oh I'm sorry, I didn't mean..."

"No, it's alright. I get it. You're upset, and I don't blame you, but I just can't let you look at your life and see pointlessness. I know it hasn't all been incredible, but you have me, and you have Tabitha..."

"And I don't know what I would do without you two, but is that all that I get?"

"What about your gift?"

"What about my gift, Aidan? Sure, it's amazing, and it makes me feel good, but really at the end of the day, it's only nice pictures of flowers and sunsets. The fact that they can come to life is, well, almost unbelievable...but is it enough?" I grabbed my notebook and opened to the flowers that I had drawn earlier that morning. "They're beautiful," I said, my finger gliding slowly over one of the many perfect pedals on the page, "but can those few bright, happy moments make up for all the loss that I feel? Could it ever take the place of my family?"

"Honestly, no. I don't think that your gift could ever give you the family that you want, but I do think that it can give you something just as good. There's a reason you are why you are,

Selkie. God gave you a special talent; a purpose for your life, and that's not something you should take lightly."

"But what can my pictures really do in the long run, Aidan? Rainbows. Flowers. Snowstorms. I mean, besides making me feel good, what are they worth?"

"You're a Lightscaper, Selkie. Your drawings bring a little bit of God's light and love into this world, and that by itself is an amazing responsibility."

"But there's more, isn't there?" I said, leaning forward and gazing intently at him. "You keep hinting at something, but you never come out and say it. Why?"

"Because it's complicated..."

"Isn't everything with you, with all of this?"

"Well, yes, and for good reason."

"Let me guess," I said, crossing my arms. "It's dangerous."

"Only if it's used incorrectly."

"And it's possible that I could make a mistake, do something I'm not supposed to do?"

"Well, yes. You're only human, Selkie. We all make mistakes."

"But what are you really worried about here, that

something bad might happen to me, or that I might mess up something if I do it wrong?"

"Honestly?"

I nodded my head.

"Well, both have crossed my mind several times! Of course I always think about your safety, but this isn't like drawing some snow and then erasing it if you don't like it. Whatever you drew would be permanent. You couldn't change it, or reverse it, and there's a lot more at stake than just a few flowers."

"So then I guess you should make sure to explain it really well to me before I try it," I said strongly. "That way I won't make a big mess of it or anything."

Aidan released a sigh. "You're not going to let this go, are you?"

I shook my head, determined.

"That's what I thought," he said, and then taking my notebook, he flipped to the picture of him standing outside my window. "What were you feeling when you drew this picture?"

"I think that would be obvious," I said with a smirk.

"Come on, this is serious, Selkie. I want you to tell me exactly what you were thinking when you drew me."

"Okay," I said, taken aback by his severity. "I was thinking about how much I missed you, and how much I wanted to see you."

"Is that all?"

"Um...well I was upset. I didn't want to be alone..."

"So you imagined that I was there with you?"

"Yes."

"And then I was."

"Yes...but that was just a coincidence."

"Was it, Selkie? What about that day in the park, after a whole week of not seeing me, do you remember what you drew?"

"Well, I drew you..."

"And what happened?"

"You showed up," I said slowly, my head swimming with confusion.

"Do you notice a pattern forming? Those times that you wanted to see me...you drew me, and then...there I was. You see, it's never been a coincidence, Selkie. It's always been you."

My heart fluttered with panic. "So you're saying that I have the ability to control where you go, just by drawing it?"

"No, Selkie," he said, calmly taking my hand, "It's much more complicated than that. I'm pretty sure you have the ability to control anyone just by drawing them."

I took a deep breath, but the air never reached my lungs.

"You have the power to manipulate where they go, and what they do, just by placing your pencil on the page."

"You're kidding, right?" I asked, my voice weak with disbelief.

"No, Selkie. I'm not."

There was no controlling it now. My frantic heart was only a few seconds away from pounding right out of my chest. I tried to take deep breaths to calm myself, but my body wouldn't respond.

"So then, your serious?" I asked, my head reeling.

"Yes, Selkie. I'm completely serious."

"Well...then...crap," I said, completely dismayed, before my head went fuzzy, and the whole world went black.

# Chapter 28

**"Selkie, can you hear me?" asked a soft, familiar voice within the darkness.**

"Yes...I can hear you," I answered, my eyes fluttering open to find Aidan's concerned face only inches from my own. "What happened?"

"You fainted," he said softly, caressing my cheek, "and you're lucky I have fast reflexes, or you might have hit your head."

"Why does it feel like I did?" I asked, sitting up and massaging my throbbing temples.

Aidan, who was crouched on one knee beside the couch, moved to sit next to me.

"I think you got a little overwhelmed," he said, wrapping his arms protectively around my body and pulling me to his chest. "I knew this was a bad idea. I shouldn't have said anything."

"No, Aidan," I said, quickly pushing his arms off and scooting away from his tempting embrace, "you were right to tell me. I can't believe that I actually fainted, because that's super embarrassing, and like you said, I must have been overwhelmed, but as you can see I'm perfectly fine now so..."

"Selkie, please! Let's not do this. Just a second ago you were so upset your whole body shut down. Who knows what could happen next time. It's just not worth getting hurt over."

"But technically I didn't really get hurt," I countered, reaching for my sketchbook and opening to a blank page, "and besides you were here to catch me, so it's no big deal!"

"Come on, Selkie," Aidan begged, his hand outstretched to take the notebook. "Don't be ridiculous."

I hugged the notebook to my chest and scooted farther down the couch. "I'm not being ridiculous, Aidan. Okay, so I freaked out a little when you told me I could control people's actions like a master Jedi or something, but I'm stronger than you think I am, and I won't do that again. So please, just forget about what happened and let's continue."

"Ugh," Aidan groaned, his head in his hands. "Why do you always have to be so stubborn? Why can't we just forget about all of this?"

I could see that my willful approach wasn't helping things. I would have to find another way to convince him.

"I know this is hard for you," I said delicately. "But could you just try for a second to imagine how I feel?"

Aidan hesitantly lifted his head.

"I have always been a nobody, Aidan; a girl with no

past…and no future.  I didn't have anything to call my own, or anyone to call my family.  But then you came along and showed me a life, a world that I never could have dreamed up.  A life where I was special, important even, and now that I've found where I belong, I can't just go back to being who I used to be, not after all that you've told me.  I need to know who I really am, and everything that I can do.  No matter how overwhelming it might be."

Aidan released a frustrated sigh.  "I know how much this means to you, Selkie.  I'm not an idiot.  I can see how happy it makes you…but it scares me.  I know I have all the answers you're looking for, but if something ever happened to you, because of what I know…I could never forgive myself."

I reached my hand out and placed it on his shoulder, "Aidan, I…"

"No, please," he said brusquely, "let me finish."

Hurt by his dismissal, I slid my hand off his shoulder, having every intention of distancing myself even further from him, but he quickly grabbed my hand, and placed it between his own.

"In this whole world nothing matters more to me than you do, Selkie, and I will do whatever I have to do to make sure that you're safe," he stated confidently, almost as if he was trying to convince himself rather than me, and then taking a deep breath, he lowered his gaze to our hands resting atop his knee and smiled.

"But if I love you," he said softly, turning to face me, our hands still mingling, "I can't ignore what you need, just because it terrifies me to think that you could get hurt. I have to be able to be both protector, and boyfriend now. Which is why," he said apprehensively, "I've decided to stop fighting you about all of this, for good, and start helping you. But..." he added, before I could get too excited, "I do have one request."

"Anything," I said, holding back a smile.

"I know how you can manipulate people, and thanks to the few times you drew me, I know what it feels like for them when you do it. But what I don't know is what might happen to you once you discover it for yourself. There are always consequences for the things that we do, Selkie, and only God knows what that means for you and your gift. So, I want you to promise me that you will never use this part of your gift unless I'm with you."

I waited for him to continue, but he didn't.

"Wait, that's it? That's all you want?"

"Yes," he said, a small smile forming on his lips.

"Well that should be easy enough, I think."

"So then you promise?"

"Yeah, sure."

"I'd like you to say it, Selkie. If you don't mind?"

"Oh, sorry, of course I don't mind," I said, squeezing his hand. "I forgot how important promises are to you. So, let's see, I promise to never draw people unless you're with me. How's that?"

"Perfect," he said, leaning in and giving me a quick peck on the cheek. "Now, let's begin."

"Um...could you hold that thought for like five seconds," I asked, suddenly standing up.

"What's the matter?" he asked, worry flooding his face.

"Um...nothing's the matter," I said, a little abashed. "I just really have to pee."

"Of course you do," Aidan smirked.

"And what is that supposed to mean?" I asked, my hands sliding to my hips, ready for a challenge.

"Nothing," he said quickly, his arms raised in surrender. "You're just always full of surprises, that's all. Now stop trying to pick a fight with me and use the bathroom already."

"Hey, don't tell me what to do," I teased, and then sticking my tongue out at him I quickly retreated down the hallway to the bathroom.

I guess I should have seen it coming, what with my achy body and erratic mood swings all day, but somehow, I'd completely missed all the signs. I had been so consumed with Aidan and everything else, that I hadn't been smart enough to put two and two together, and it wasn't until it was staring me right in the face that it all made sense; the reason for all the fights, and all the tears; the culprit behind all the bickering and irritability. It was the bane of every girl's existence, "that" time of the month, and it was just another thing to add to the growing list of stuff I needed to worry about.

Once I had "fixed" the situation, and sulked for a few moments, I rummaged through the medicine cabinet for some Midol to help with the stabbing pain that was now assaulting my abdomen, and then washed my hands and left the bathroom. I headed straight for the kitchen, ignoring Aidan's curious gaze as it followed my every move, and then poured myself a glass of water, and swallowed the two small blue pills in a single gulp.

"Don't ask," I told Aidan as I returned to the couch, and then seeing his anxious face, I added, "You wouldn't want to know anyway. Its, you know, girl stuff."

"Ah," he said, nodding his head. "Enough said."

"I thought so."

"So do you feel well enough to do this, or should we..."

"Oh, no! We are not going to put this off any longer. Don't

worry about me. I'm totally fine," and then grabbing my notebook and pencil, I said, "let's do this!"

"Before you get too excited, we need to start with the basics. Objects and movement. Anything that already exists in the real world you can move and manipulate. Like this remote for example," he said, grabbing it off the coffee table. "Why don't you try drawing it in a different room of the apartment?"

Without hesitation I went right to work, quickly sketching the small black remote with its dozen or so buttons on top of Tabitha's red and white striped comforter.

"Okay, now what?" I asked, once I had completed the picture and was satisfied with the outcome.

Aidan, with the remote still in hand, smiled, "Just like with the flowers, close your eyes and imagine."

He had barely finished his sentence before I eagerly squeezed my eyes shut and created the picture once again inside my head.

"Alright, you can open your eyes now," Aidan prompted.

"But how is that possible?" I asked, opening my eyes, immediately searching the room for the remote, but finding nothing. "I only had my eyes closed for a second."

"That's all it takes. It's pretty much instantaneous, but don't take my word for it, go check it out."

I ran to Tabitha's room, giddy with anticipation, and opened the door to find the remote right where I had sketched it.

"This is crazy," I yelled to Aidan as I grabbed the remote and inspected it. "It traveled through space in like, warp speed, and it still looks exactly the same."

I turned around to find Aidan standing in the doorway.

"I know, it's pretty cool, huh?"

"Pretty cool? This is awesome," I said, unable to control my enthusiasm.

"And you feel okay? I mean you don't feel weird or anything?"

"Yeah, I feel great! Now, come on," I said, grabbing his hand and pulling him back to the couch. "I want to try it again."

For the next hour, I happily filled the pages of my sketchbook with objects from the apartment like toothbrushes, magazines, shoes, and even small furniture; sketching them in the most random of places, only to track them down and send them back to where they belonged.

At first, as I scampered through the apartment playing my strange game of hide and seek, Aidan watched with amusement, laughing now and again at my ridiculous childlike behavior, and even joining in to help think up creative spaces to place the items. After a while, however, his mood began to change from one of cheerfulness, to one of uneasiness and distress.

"Are you sure you're feeling okay?" he asked me for the twentieth time.

"Yes.  I'm fine, Aidan.  Now stop worrying about me and have some fun."

"But it's just that you've been using your gift a lot today," he persisted, "and I don't want you to push it.  I told you, I don't know what can happen if you overuse it."

"Well, like I said before, I feel absolutely fine."

"And you would honestly tell me if you felt differently?"

"Of course I would, but I really don't think that's how it works.  If anything, I feel stronger after doing all of this.  So what do you say we move on to step two?"

"I don't think that's a good idea," he said, opening the fridge and grabbing an apple from the bottom drawer.  "You've already done so much already.  Don't you think you've had enough for one day?"

"I told you, I feel fine.  Now come on, you know how impatient I am!"

"Okay, fine," he sighed, giving in. "But only for a few more minutes, and then I think you need to rest."

"Deal!  So what's next?" I asked, flipping to a clean page,

my hand poised to draw.

"Well, it's obvious that you've conquered objects and movement, so the next step is people and movement."

"But I've already done that, right?  I mean, I've already drawn you and it worked.  So why not give me something harder?"

"Impatient much?"

"No, I just mean that I already know that I can do that, so why not teach me something I don't know?"

"Because the next step is a lot more complicated than the others...and I don't think we should skip anything."

"Okay, fine," I said, plopping my sketchbook on the counter, "we won't skip any steps," and then leaning over the page I started a new sketch.

I was so eager to move on to my next challenge that I was a little sloppy with some of my lines, but when I closed my eyes and heard the apple fall to the floor, I knew that it had worked.  I quickly spun around to the place where Aidan had been standing only seconds before but found nothing but empty space.  I smiled.

Then came the knock on the door.

I bent down and retrieved the half-eaten apple from the floor.

"Who is it?"

"Selkie," Aidan's voice boomed from the other side of the door.

"Um...I'm sorry. Who's there?"

"Yes, ha, ha. You proved your point," Aidan's muffled voice rang out. "Now will you let me in?"

"The doors open," I called out. "Come on in!"

"You think you're pretty funny, don't you?" Aidan said as he closed the door behind him, the slightest hint of a smile on his lips.

"Actually, I think I'm *really* funny."

"But look what you did to my apple," he frowned, taking the bruised fruit from my hands.

"Well, you gave me no choice, and besides I didn't have enough time to draw it in."

"Oh, really," he said, dropping the apple on the counter and moving closer. "You had enough time to draw my entire body, and not this tiny apple?"

"Well, that's for me to know, I guess."

"That's true," he said, wrapping his arms around me and nuzzling his head into my hair. "But what would the artist do without her muse and all the knowledge he possesses?"

"That's a good point," I said, relaxing into his embrace. "I don't know what I'd do without you."

"I'm pretty sure you wouldn't be able to do this," he said, leaning in to kiss my nose, "and definitely not this," he added with a grin as he lowered his sweet lips to mine.

"Are you trying to distract me?" I asked, our lips barely parted.

"Yes, of course" he whispered, his lips traveling leisurely across my cheek to nibble at my ear.

"I can't believe I'm actually saying this, but could you stop?"

Aidan pulled away slowly, his face full of disappointment. "Do I have to?"

"Yes," I said firmly, surprised by my own strength. "But only until you've taught me step three."

"And then we can pick up where we left off?" he asked, his eyes flashing with longing.

"We can do whatever you want," I said, sliding my hands up his chest and resting them around his neck.

"Well in that case," he said, picking up my sketchbook and handing it to me, "I think this would be the perfect time to teach you step three."

# Chapter 29

**"Let's for a moment think of life as a giant chess board," Aidan began seriously.** "When you draw objects and move them from place to place, it's just like if you picked up a pawn and, without thinking, placed it on a different spot on the board."

"Like when I drew the remote and stuff."

"Exactly, and the same thing works with people. You can easily move them around from place to place, just like a pawn. Like when you moved me to the park and outside your door."

"And I can do this with everyone?"

"I'm pretty sure you can," Aidan said, squaring his shoulders, "but before you get too excited about that, you need to understand what it is you're really doing. When you move a pawn, or a remote," he said, picking it up off the table, "they have no feelings or thoughts about what you've done. They go where you put them, and they'll stay there until you move them, or draw them somewhere else...but humans, unlike chess pieces and other inanimate objects, have the ability to think and move for themselves, and messing with a person's freewill can be very dangerous."

"How is that, exactly?"

"Let's go back to the chess game. What happens after I move my pawn?"

"Well, I guess it would be my turn to move and try to block you or take your pawn."

"Yep, and after you move?"

"Then it would be your turn again."

"So then do you see what I'm getting at?" Aidan asked enthusiastically.

"Umm…no, not really," I frowned.

He briefly smiled at me and then tried again. "Everything in life, just like in chess, has a chain of events, Selkie. We move along in life, waiting for someone or something to get in our way, and we change our course accordingly."

"Like the day we met," I said, excitedly, finally beginning to understand. "I went to the park, expecting a normal day, but then you hit me with the Frisbee and my whole life changed."

"Exactly. So when you draw people, you're potentially changing the sequence of their entire life."

"You mean I can change the future?" I asked, my eyes bugging out. "Wow, that's big!"

"Tremendously big, actually, but you also have to take into consideration what they might encounter on the way."

"What do you mean?" I asked, my mind working hard to keep up.

"When you move people, like drawing me standing outside your door, it might have seemed to you like I just disappeared into thin air and then manifested on the other side of the door, but it doesn't work that way."

I scrunched my face in confusion.

"You have to remember the sequence, Selkie. When I "disappeared" I actually walked over to the door, opened it, and then walked outside."

"But how is that possible? It would have taken you too long."

"It happens very quickly for you, but for me, everything slows down, and I can see where I'm supposed to go, where you've drawn me, and I can also see how I'm supposed to get there. It's like a...universal connect the dots."

"So you still have to go through all the motions."

"Yes. Sadly, it's not as magical for me as it is for you. I still have to move down the chain before I can get to my destination."

"And what if your chain took you near other people?"

"Then I would have to deal with them before I could continue on, and that's where it gets tricky. You can only see the beginning and the end, where I start and where I finish. I can see that, plus the journey I have to take, but neither of us can control the pawns outside of our game. There's no telling whom I might meet, and how they might affect my path. All we definitely know is that I have to eventually end up at the place where you've drawn me."

"So then anything can happen to you in between, and I would have no control over it."

"That's right. Your gift has its limits, Selkie, and it's important that you never forget that. Life will always have a way of surprising you. You can't always be in control, and you can't always know what's going to happen."

"So then what's the point?"

"What do you mean?"

"Why was I given this gift, Aidan? I mean I can understand the whole landscape thing, making flowers bloom and what not, but why people? I don't understand what I'm supposed to do with it."

"I'm sorry, Selkie," Aidan said, resting his hand on my leg, "that's one thing I can't help you with. I don't have a clue what you're supposed to do with this part of your gift, but since it's from God I can only imagine you're supposed to do good with it."

"What, like drawing Tabitha winning the lottery?" I asked sarcastically.

"Maybe, who knows? It might take you some time to figure it all out, but I know you'll find a way to use it to help people and make the world a better place."

"What makes you so sure?" I asked him timidly, looking away.

"Because you've got a good heart," he said, scooting closer and wrapping his arm around me. "And I know you'll figure it out and do the right thing."

"You have a lot of faith in me," I said, laying my head on his chest. "I just hope I don't let you down."

He didn't say anything else, but just squeezed me closer to his chest. So close in fact that I was able to feel through his shirt the many layers of bandages that covered his healing wound.

An amazing thought suddenly occurred to me, and I sat up. "Aidan, if I can affect the future and change a person's path, do you think I could speed up the healing process?"

"I...don't think I follow you," he said, pulling away so that he could look at me.

"Okay, just think about it. I can control a person's body and decide where I want it to go in the future, and their body listens and goes where I want it. You say that you have to go through all the steps, but for me, in "real" time, it happens very quickly. So here's what I'm getting at. The other day at work there was this poor plant that was in the break room, and it was all pathetic and dying. I felt so bad for it that I drew a picture of the plant the way it used to look, all blooming and healthy, you know, and then...it was."

"But that's a plant, what does that have to do with a person?" he asked, clearly stumped.

"Well, don't you see? It should work the same way. I should be able to control a person's entire body, draw what I want it to be like in the future, like with the plant, and it should instantly be."

"I don't know, Selkie," Aidan said, obviously uncomfortable with the way the conversation was going. "Healing people, miracles, isn't that stuff better left to..."

"God," I interrupted, raising my eyebrow. "Who do you think gave me this power, Aidan? I know this sounds crazy...but it feels right to me."

"And you don't think you might be pushing your limits here?"

"No, I don't. I can't explain it, but I know that this is part of it all," and then grabbing my pencil, I said, "and now I'm going to show you."

I vigorously began to sketch; terrified about what might occur once I was finished, but incredibly hopeful that I was doing the right thing. Though my mind was whirling with doubt, all my instincts were yelling at me to continue, to keep going until the picture was complete. I barely breathed the whole time, too concerned with making the picture perfect to worry about anything else, and with my stomach tied up in knots, I sketched the final line and then closed my eyes.

I thought he might have made a sound, or maybe even squeezed my hand, but the whole room around me was still and silent. I slowly opened my eyes, a little nervous of what awaited me, and found Aidan standing by the window with his back to me, looking out on the late afternoon sky.

"Aidan...are you alright?" I whispered, afraid to break the eerie silence.

He slowly turned to look at me, and I saw his eyes were rimmed with tears.

"Oh my God," I cried, quickly standing up, but before I could take one step toward him, my stomach lurched and my head swam with dizziness. Unable to steady my legs, I fell back onto the couch, and then he was there.

Fighting the urge to throw up, I swallowed, and said, "I did it wrong, didn't I?"

"Selkie, are you okay? What's the matter?"

"No, don't worry about me," I said, pushing his hands away. "I only care about you.  What did I mess up?"

His hands were on my face, wiping away the tears I hadn't noticed were falling from my eyes. "You didn't do anything wrong.  Look," he said, pulling up his shirt to reveal his smooth, gorgeous, and unharmed chest.

My hands moved instantly to his beautiful skin, roaming across the healed area that only seconds ago had been coarse and battered.

"It worked," I said, smiling through the tears.

"It worked," he beamed back at me.

"Then why...why were you crying?"

"It's hard to explain," he said, tucking my hair behind my ears.  "I wasn't expecting it, I guess.  I thought you were going to fix your ankle, or something...but then you closed your eyes, and the whole world slowed down, and I knew...I knew that you had chosen me...and I was happy."

"Did it hurt?" I asked him, wiping away the rest of my tears.

"It hurt at first, but then this amazing warm, comforting feeling came over me, almost as if I could feel the light flowing through my body.  I've never felt anything like it...and then...I was better.  Just like you thought."

"And so you were crying…because you were happy?"

"Yes, Selkie," he said, lightly rubbing my arm. "You've made me very happy. Now tell me honestly, how do you feel?"

"I'm not sure," I said, taking a deep breath. "I think that took a lot more out of me than the other stuff. I'm a little dizzy, and I think if I stood up I would probably get sick."

"Then why don't you just lie down and rest for a while."

"That's sounds like a good idea," I said as another wave of nausea flooded over me. "But what will you do?"

"I'll just stay here and watch over you," he said, as I lay down, my head resting in his lap. "It's kind of what I'm good at, remember?"

"Oh, yeah. That's true," I said, closing my eyes, "I'll just rest for a few minutes, at least until my head stops spinning, and then we can do something fun."

"Okay, but you just rest now," Aidan said quietly, stroking my hair. "Take your time, and I'll be here when you wake up."

"You promise?" I asked as the darkness closed in.

"I promise," he said, and then leaning down to whisper in my ear, he added, "And you know me, I hate to break a promise."

# Chapter 30

**With legs flailing and arms wildly thrashing about, I plummeted into the startling black abyss.** A rush of cold air slashed across my bare skin, cutting in deep, as I swiftly spiraled downward into the terrifying unknown. My trembling hands searched frantically within the vacant space for something, anything to hold on to, but it was no use. I was falling too fast. I couldn't see anything below me, but I knew there was something down there, waiting for me. Afraid of what I would encounter, I relentlessly clawed at the air, again and again, but it was hopeless. Nothing could keep me from dropping. So I continued my frightening plunge into darkness with only one thought in my mind. How long would I fall before I reached the bottom?

My body shook with fear and I jolted awake.

Instantly aware that my head still lay safely across Aidan's lap, I kept my eyes closed, not wanting to concern him with more nightmares, and breathed in deeply.

"So what exactly are you doing here with Selkie?" Tabitha whispered harshly.

"I'm not sure I know what you mean," Aidan replied politely.

"Oh come off it," she spat. "You know what I mean. Why

did you leave, and why the hell are you back?"

"Well, I don't know if that's really any of your business," Aidan said, his temper rising.

"Well you know what, Aidan, if that's really your name, I think it is my business. Because Selkie is my best friend, and that means that it's my responsibility to take care of her."

"Can't she take care of herself?" he asked curtly.

"You really have no idea, do you?" Tabitha chided. "Our Selkie here has always lived in a dream world, where she thinks that something or someone is going to come and sweep her off her feet and take her away from all of this; as if she could escape from this crappy life of ours, and not be an orphan loser anymore. But I know different, okay? I know this is it for her, for us. I've seen what life has to offer...nothing!"

I cringed a little at Tabitha's words, but kept my eyes closed, pretending to be asleep. I wanted to hear what she had to say. Aidan was no dummy though. He knew that I was awake and listening. I could tell by the way he began to trace small circles along my lower back to comfort me. He knew me so well.

"I'm sorry to say this, but it seems like you have a very sad outlook when it comes to life," Aidan commented.

"And what do you know about it? Yeah, it might be sad, but at least I'm realistic. Selkie on the other hand is nothing like me. She hasn't had to deal with a lot of the crap I've had to, and I want to keep it that way. So I don't want you coming into her life just to screw it all up."

"I'm not sure what Selkie's told you…"

"Oh please! So now you're gonna play the good guy act? First you show up and make her all woozy. Then you disappear and go, God knows where, breaking her heart, and messing her up and everything, just to come back and sweep her off her feet again. I mean, what's up with that? And how long do you plan to stay this time? Until you have another place to stay? Or until you get tired of her and move on to someone else?"

"Hold it right there," Aidan said firmly.

I held my breath as Tabitha fell silent.

"I don't care what you think of me, or if you approve of my actions," Aidan said, his hand holding steadily to my waist. "All I care about is Selkie. She knows the reason why I wasn't around, she understands, and that's really all that matters. You have absolutely no clue about who I am, and for that matter, I don't think you have a clue about who Selkie is. She is a strong, amazing person, who looks at the world differently than others, but that doesn't mean that she doesn't deserve your respect and love. She doesn't need your pity, or your mothering. She can take care of herself…"

"Yes I can," I said, sitting up, officially ending the dispute.

"I can take care of myself, but I don't think that's really important at this moment."

"I'm sorry," Aidan said, his eyes apologetic. "I didn't mean to…"

"Shhh, it's okay," I said, placing my finger over his mouth. "You don't need to do that, but you do need to apologize to Tabitha, and *you*," I said, pointing a finger at Tabitha, "what were you thinking, attacking him like that?"

"What? I was doing it for you!"

"Harassing my boyfriend is not your responsibility, Tabs. I mean seriously! You don't know anything about him!"

"And you do?"

"Oh no! We are not having this conversation again. So both of you just need to apologize and get over it…now!"

"I'm sorry, Tabitha," Aidan said immediately, "I was out of line."

"Damn right you were!"

"Tabitha!"

"What, Selkie? He was rude!"

"And you were a jerk, so what? Now freakin' apologize!"

"Okay. Geez. I'm sorry."

"Well, I think that's the best you're going to get from her," I said, turning to Aidan with a shrug. "Now let's just forget about all of that and eat. I'm starved!"

"You should be," Aidan said. "You've been asleep for hours."

"Really? What time is it?"

"It's almost nine."

"Oh my gosh, why didn't you wake me up? We were supposed to do something fun?"

"You needed to rest," he said gently, brushing my tangled hair from my face.

"Shoot, I was the one who worked all day," Tabitha interrupted loudly. "What do you need to be tired about?"

"Okay, what's the deal, Tabs?" I asked, giving her my "what the hell's the matter with you" look. "Why are you in such a bad mood?"

"It's nothing," she said dismissively. "Let's just eat already."

Dinner was definitely tense.

Though they had both apologized, I don't think either of them had actually forgiven the other for what had been said. Aidan stayed close beside me for the rest of the evening, hovering over me like the protector he was, and Tabitha just kept rolling her eyes at him, at me, at the world, until finally she'd had enough of it all and went to bed. I decided that it was probably a good idea for us to go to bed too, seeing that I had to work in the morning, and so as Aidan headed to the bedroom, I made a stop at the bathroom for my nightly routine.

I had finished brushing my teeth and was just about to floss when Aidan appeared in the bathroom mirror.

"Selkie, I need to go check on something outside for a sec, but I'll be right back."

"What do you have to check on?" I asked, pulling out the white, minty strand from the plastic case.

"It's nothing really," he said, avoiding my gaze. "I just want to check around the perimeter, you know, to be safe."

I turned away from his reflection and looked him straight in the eye. "Is something out there, Aidan?"

"It's nothing you need to worry about, okay? You are completely safe in here."

"Then why do you need to go outside?" I asked, a little anxious.

"I told you, I just want to make sure you're..."

Aidan's face suddenly contracted in pain, and he doubled

over, crashing to his knees as he clutched at his stomach.

"Aidan, what's the matter?" I asked, dropping to my knees beside him, but before he could answer me, the demented sound of hissing reached my ears.

"I'm fine," Aidan said, pushing himself off the ground. "They just surprised me that's all. It's the side effect, remember? To help me sense when the Shadows are near. It usually doesn't affect me like this."

"And they're usually not this loud."

"Which can only mean one thing," he said, dragging me out of the bathroom.

Tabitha's door opened then, and she appeared in the hallway looking bleary eyed and really pissed off. "Is that the freakin' snakes again? Why are they so loud?"

"I don't know," I said quickly. "Why don't you just put on your stereo or something?"

"That's a good idea," she said half asleep, "but I wish I had some stinkin' ear plugs. I mean, shit," and then she staggered back into her room and closed the door.

"There must be a lot more out tonight than usual," Aidan said, once we were back in my room. He grabbed his dagger from the side of the bed and began to strap it around his waist.

"No wait, you can't go," I said as I began to tug at his leather strap.

"Selkie, what are you doing?" he asked, carefully removing my struggling hands from his sheath and holding onto my wrists.

"I don't want you to go out there," I said as I continued to struggle.

"But this is what I do, Selkie. This is how I protect you!"

"I don't want you to go," I repeated more loudly.

"But why?" he asked as he sat down on the bed and pulled me down next to him. "What's the matter?"

"I don't want to be alone," I cried out, covering my face with my hands, trying to hide the tears that were flowing down my cheeks.

"Selkie, shhh, don't cry," Aidan comforted, his arms already secured around my body. "They won't hurt you. I won't let them, but I need to go."

"No, please, not when they're singing like that."

"What do you mean?" Aidan asked confused.

"Can't you hear them? Can't you hear what they're saying?"

"I only hear them hissing, Selkie."

"No, no.  They won't stop calling my name.  I can't stand it," I wailed.

"Okay, okay, just calm down, and I'll think of something."

Suddenly above the hissing sound came a loud scratching noise outside my window, and as fast as lightning Aidan was at the window, his dagger in hand.

"Oh God, what is that?" I screeched, scooting farther back on the bed and pulling the covers over me.

"I don't know.  I can't tell from in here.  I need to be out there where they are."

"No, please," I begged.  "I need you."

Aidan kept his dagger at the ready but turned his face to me. "Are you sure that's what you want?  I could easily go out there, and this could all be over."

"But you could get hurt," I whined.

"That's my job, Selkie."

"No, not tonight it isn't.  You're my boyfriend right now, not my protector, and I want you to stay.  I need you to stay."

"Then I will," he said, dropping his dagger, "but I need to call for some backup."

At first, Aidan's conversation with Brendan didn't go so

well, there was a lot of screaming on Brendan's side and a lot of arguing on Aidan's, but as soon as Aidan mentioned the Shadows and the number he had estimated to be outside my apartment, Brendan stopped fighting and came to the rescue. In fact, all three brothers showed up.

"We have to be quiet," Aidan told them as we huddled just inside the front door of the apartment. "Selkie's roommate is close by in the other room."

"Well then why are we meeting in here?" Brendan's deep voice bellowed.

Ewan put his finger to his mouth and made a loud shushing noise.

"Oh, I'm sorry," Brendan whispered, "but this is ridiculous. Let's go outside so that we can actually talk and figure out what's going on."

"That's out of the question," Aidan stated blankly. "Selkie needs to be protected."

"So then let Liam or Ewan stay behind."

"No," I said, a little too loudly. "No offense boys, but I want it to be Aidan."

"And seeing as I'm her protector, I need to make the decisions. Not you Brendan. So let's just shut up and do this."

"Okay, what happened?" Liam chimed in.

"I'm not sure. Everything was fine, we were just going to bed when this strange wave hit me, and then that's when they started up. Selkie said she could understand what they were saying, that they were calling for her."

"Calling for her?" Ewan said, worry clear on his face.

"Calling for her how, exactly?" Brendan asked, somewhat annoyed.

"The same way they always do when I hear them," I answered. "With my name. Always my name. Over and over again. It makes me sick."

"But how can you even understand then?" Liam asked. "We can't even understand them."

"That's what I want to know," Aidan frowned.

"Well enough of this chit chat," Brendan interrupted. "I could care less about all of this. The problem is the Shadows and their somewhat overwhelming numbers. We need to diffuse the situation quickly, and standing around here is not doing anything. So, I'm heading out to deal with this mess, and if Aidan isn't coming then Liam and Ewan will both have to join me." He opened the door and stepped outside. "Oh, and don't worry Aidan, we can handle this. You just stay here and play house with your little girlfriend, while we go out and do all the hard work," and then turning to me with a fake smile, he whispered, "Nighty night," and then stomped down the stairs into the darkness.

"Umm…Sorry Selkie," Liam said with a shrug, and then he ran down the stairs after Brendan.

"What a jerk," Ewan spat. "He can be such an idiot."

"Yeah, well I'm kind of getting used to it by now," I told him.

"Too bad, because I really like it when you give it to him, you know? I think it's funny to see such a small person stand up to him."

"Hey, I'm not that small," I said, punching his shoulder. "I'm almost as tall as you."

"Yeah, but just wait until my next growth spurt," he said, standing up tall. "I'll be taller than Aidan, and then you'll be really short."

"Well, we'll just see about that," I laughed.

"Uh…sorry to interrupt your little reunion here, but Ewan you'd better get out there before Brendan comes back looking for you."

"Oh yeah, right," Ewan said, shuffling through the door. "It was good seeing you again, Selkie. And don't worry about the

Shadows, we'll take care of them for you."

"Do you really think they'll be alright?" I asked, turning to Aidan.

"Of course they'll be fine. You don't need to worry about a thing. They've had just as much training as I have, and there are three of them. Those Shadows don't have a chance."

"But they don't have your abilities, and Ewan, he's still so young."

"What is it with you and Ewan?" Aidan asked as he closed the door and locked it.

"What do you mean?"

"I don't know. You're just different with him, more relaxed or something."

"Oh, I don't know, he's just fun to hang out with. Why? Are you jealous or something?"

"What, of my kid brother? That baby? Of course not."

"Then why did you get so weird when we were talking?"

"I didn't get weird," Aidan said, grabbing my hand and leading me into my bedroom.

"Yes you did! You got really quiet and just stood there staring at us."

"Well maybe that's because I had nothing to say," he said, plopping down on the bed. "I didn't feel like I had anything to add to your conversation."

"That's probably a good thing," I said, leaning my knee against the bed and looking down at him. "Because we were so busy having fun talking to each other, that you probably would have just been a distraction."

"Why you," he said, grabbing my hips and throwing me onto the bed. "You're such a tease."

"No I'm not," I giggled as he loomed over me, threatening to attack. "I was being completely truthful, and there is something else you should know," I said with a sly smile.

"Oh yes, and what's that?"

"I've decided to leave you for your fifteen-year-old brother."

"Is that so," Aidan asked, his eyes ablaze with amusement. "Well I don't think that's going to happen."

"And why not?"

"Because you would have to leave this room to find him, and there is no way I am letting you off of this bed."

"And what if I try to escape?"

"You won't."

"How can you be sure?"

"Because I know that you will be much too busy to be thinking about him or anything else for that matter."

"But I don't even have my sketchbook in here with me to keep me occupied.  What else can I do to keep my mind off of things," I asked, innocently batting my lashes.

"I think I have a few good ideas," he said, lowering his body down beside me and wrapping one leg over one of my own.

"Well in that case," I said, turning my body to face his. "I think I'll stay."

The hissing outside my window continued for quite some time, but I hardly noticed it.  Aidan was a wonderful distraction.

## Chapter 31

**My obnoxious alarm beeped several times before I mustered up enough energy to roll over and turn it off.** After the long, wonderful night I'd had with Aidan, I was tempted to hit the snooze button and delay the day for a few more minutes, but when I realized that Aidan's side of the bed was cold and empty, I turned the alarm off and promptly sat up.

"Don't worry, I'm here," he said, smiling from the doorway. "I made you breakfast, so I hope you're hungry."

"Yeah, I am," I said, rubbing the sleep from my eyes and crawling out of bed. "Have you been up long?"

"Just a few hours," he said, walking over to hug me. "Brendan woke me up when they left to go home, and I just decided to stay awake."

"How did it go last night?" I asked, looking up at him.

"Good. It took some time, but they destroyed a few and scared the rest of them off."

"And nobody got hurt?"

"Just a couple cuts and bruises," he said with a shrug. "No biggie."

"So then it's over?"

"For now," he nodded. "But something big is coming. I can feel it in my gut. The Shadows are taking more risks and building their numbers. They're definitely planning something."

"Yeah, something for me," I said softly, lowering my gaze.

"Hey," Aidan said, pulling me to his chest and wrapping his arms around me. "I've got this. Nothing bad is going to happen to you."

Feeling a little discouraged, I murmured into his shoulder, "I wouldn't make promises you can't keep."

"So what, you're doubting me now?" Aidan asked, grabbing my shoulders and forcing me to look into his eyes.

"It's not you," I said quickly, raising my hand to his stubbly cheek. "I can feel it too. Something is definitely changing. First the nightmares. Now the Shadows. I'm really scared about what might be coming, and I just don't think that I'm ready for it."

"You'll be fine," Aidan said in his reassuring tone. "I just need you to trust me."

"I do."

"Then there's nothing to worry about, alright? Now come on, your breakfast is getting cold."

Aidan was, surprisingly, a very good cook. Sometime

between his combat lessons, and his *History of Selkie* classes, he managed to perfect the technique of making the most delicious ham and cheese omelets I had ever tasted. Still feeling drained from healing his chest, and hoping to regain some strength, I easily devoured two servings of eggs, a piece of peanut butter toast, and half a carton of orange juice.

When I had eaten my fill, and Aidan had stopped making fun of me for my serious appetite, I took a quick shower, threw my hair up into a high ponytail, and then put on my uniform. Once I was completely ready, Aidan showed me how to wrap my ankle properly, so standing on it all day wouldn't cause me too much pain, and then I took the last five minutes I had to spare before leaving for work to check on Tabitha.

I had to knock three times before she opened the door, and even then she just walked away, turning her back on me to scrounge in her closet, determined to pay me no attention.

"Tabs, can I talk to you for a sec?"

"We're gonna be late, Selkie," she said, her head still shoved inside the closet.

"It will only take a second," I said, sitting on her bed, refusing to leave.

"Fine." She stood up, having successfully retrieved her favorite pair of orange converse from the mess she called a closet, and glared at me. "But you only have three minutes. So you better talk fast."

"I just wanted to see if you were okay."

"What do you mean?" she asked, sitting down to lace up her shoes.

"Well, you just seemed a little upset last night, and I wanted to know what was up."

"It's nothing," she said firmly, turning back to the closet to grab her gray and purple hoodie.

"That's what you said last night too, but something is obviously bothering you.  I mean the way you attacked Aidan…"

"It has nothing to do with you and your perfect little boy toy," she spat.

"See, you did it again, what the hell is going on?  Why do you have to be so mean?"

"Because I'm jealous, Selkie," she said, spinning around to confront me.  "Is that what you wanted to hear?"

"Jealous…of me?" I asked perplexed.  "Why?  I thought you were seeing Gabe."

"He dumped me, alright?"

"What?  I can't believe this.  Why didn't you tell me before?"

"Because first you were asleep and then Aidan was with you. Anyway, it doesn't really matter."

"Of course it does, Tabs," I said, standing up. "Oh, I can't wait to get to work and give that jerk a piece of my mind."

"No, you can't do that, Selkie," she said, tears brimming in her eyes. "He's not a jerk. He was actually really nice about it. He told me that he thought I was awesome and everything, but that he was into somebody else, and he didn't want to lead me on when he knew nothing was going to come of it."

Oh crap!

"And did he tell you who this other girl was?" I asked guarded, knowing perfectly well who he was "into".

"No, he just said that he couldn't stop thinking about her, and that it wasn't fair for me to be with him when he was thinking about someone else."

He couldn't stop thinking about me? Double crap!

"But like I said," she continued, zipping up her hoodie, "he was really nice about it, and honestly, I wish he had been more of a jerk, 'cause at least then I could hate him."

"Well, that was still a pretty jerky thing to do, Tabs," I said, placing my hand on her shoulder. "You're probably better off hating him."

"No," she said, wiping away her tears, and grabbing her purse. "I'm tired of being angry. I wanna be like you for a change. I wanna be happy."

Having known Tabitha to be somewhat of a cynic, and observing firsthand her many failed attempts to lighten up her outlook on life, I certainly doubted this newfound quest for happiness, but when she genuinely smiled at Aidan and asked if he was walking to work with us, I began to hope that this time it would stick.

With nothing but the sound of squawking seagulls to impede us, we walked down the road together in a pleasant, undemanding silence. As we reached the water's edge, the sound of lapping water reached my ears, and I breathed in the cool, crisp air of the early morning. The three of us continued past the harbor, and as I looked up at the golden tinged sky, delighting in the beauty that surrounded me, my heart was moved by the splendor of it all, and I sent up a quiet thanks to the one who had most magnificently created it. Just then, a patch of sun struck my face, and I smiled.

"So I guess this is goodbye," I told Aidan, once we had reached the store. Tabitha had already said her goodbyes, and had headed in to secure our registers, leaving us alone in the parking lot.

"I know it's only a few hours," he said, stroking my cheek, "but now that I've spent so much time with you, it's kind of hard to let you walk away."

"What will you do?" I asked, leaning my face into his palm.

"Oh, I'll be around. Like always. You probably won't be able to see me, but just know I'm always here protecting you."

"Won't you get bored?"

"Are you kidding?" he asked, hugging me close. "I have your beautiful face to keep me occupied."

I blushed.

"Now you better head in," he said, pushing me toward the door. "I don't want to make you late."

The familiar sound of a roaring motorcycle engine stopped me in my tracks, and Aidan quickly spun around to see Gabriel pulling up beside us. Aidan took a step closer to me, wrapping his arm protectively around my waist, and watched as Gabriel turned off the engine and dismounted the dangerous machine.

"Hey, Selkie," Gabriel smiled as he took off his helmet and ran a hand through his ruffled black hair. "I was hoping you were working today. Who's your friend?"

Aidan straightened up. "I'm Selkie's boyfriend. Aidan. And you are?"

"Oh, I'm Selkie's *friend*," Gabriel said, over emphasizing

the last word.

"This is Gabe," I told Aidan quickly. "He just started working here a few days ago."

Gabriel's dark eyes abandoned Aidan's glare, and landed right on my face, forcing me to abruptly look away.

"Well we should probably get to work," Gabe started, stepping forward. "You know how Stephen can get."

I recoiled from Gabriel's advance, and Aidan squeezed me tighter to his side.

"She'll be there in a minute," Aidan said strongly, never taking his eyes off of Gabriel.

"Okey, dokey," Gabriel smiled. "I'll see you in there, Selkie," and then whistling a cheerful tune, he walked away from us and into the store.

"Are you alright?" Aidan asked once Gabriel was gone.

"Yeah, I'm fine. He just sort of gives me the creeps sometimes. The way he looks at me."

"Well, he obviously has a thing for you..."

"Something you don't have to worry about," I interrupted. "He might have a thing for me, but there is nothing between us."

Aidan wrinkled his forehead.

"Hey, I love you, remember? He can stare at me all he wants, it's not going to change anything."

"Are you sure?" he asked, pulling me into his arms.

"I'm positive," I said, kissing him lightly on the lips. "Now, I really need to go before I get into trouble."

"Okay, but just one more thing," Aidan said, and then leaning down he kissed me tenderly, parting my lips with his sweet tongue, and making me all dizzy, before pulling away with a mischievous smile. "Just in case he was watching," he said. "Now go, before I'm tempted to do it again and make you really late."

"Don't forget. I love you," I said, walking away from him.

"I love you too," he said, his eyes sparkling with infatuation. "See you soon."

As the sliding door closed behind me, and separated me from my loving protector, my heart sank with longing. Yielding to my desire, I turned around, hoping to catch one more glimpse of him, but he was already gone. From the corner of my eye, I saw Stephen fast approaching with a look of disapproval on his face, most likely caused by my tardiness, and so without another thought, I pulled my eyes away from the parking lot, and hastily made my way into the store.

"So that's the guy?" Gabriel asked as he hung up a pile of

plastic bags at the end of my register.

"Excuse me?" I said, my back to him, careful to avoid his piercing gaze.

"You know," he said, haughtily, "that guy you were talking about before, the one who's keeping you from taking a ride with me."

"That *guy*," I said, spinning around to face him, "happens to be my boyfriend, and he's not keeping me from doing anything.  I didn't want to ride on your stupid motorcycle because I don't trust you…and how dare you talk to me like this when you just broke up with my best friend."

"Can't we just leave Tabitha out of this?" he asked, lowering his voice and taking a step toward me.

"No, we can certainly not leave her out of this.  The other day you promised me that you would be careful with her, and that is the only reason I agreed to be your friend.  You told me you liked her…"

"Not as much as I like someone else," he interrupted, taking another step closer.

"Oh no," I said, rolling my eyes at him.  "First of all, I have a boyfriend, and second, I would never date anyone that my best friend has already dated…"

"We weren't even really dating.  We were just hanging

out."

"Did she know that?" I asked, placing my hands on my hips. "Because it seemed to me like she thought you guys were dating, but more importantly, I already told you I wasn't interested."

"I don't believe that," he said, taking one more step toward me, and closing the distance between us, his dark eyes smoldering with some kind of emotion I couldn't define.

"Why are you doing this?" I whispered as I cowered against the counter. "Why won't you just listen to what I'm saying? I don't want anything to do with you."

"I don't think you really know what you want, Selkie Reid. I see the way that you look at me when you think I'm not paying attention. I know you're interested. You just haven't figured it out yet," and then backing away, he said, "I'm a patient person, Selkie. I can wait, especially for someone as intriguing as you, and when you're ready to have some fun, and ditch that blonde stiff, you just let me know."

"That's never going to happen," I said, standing up tall.

"What's going on here?" Tabitha asked as she approached the register and handed me my apron. "Are you two fighting already?"

"No, on the contrary," Gabriel smiled innocently at her.

"We're just getting to know each other a little better."

"Alright, well let's just get it all out," she said strongly. "Just because we didn't work out Gabe, doesn't mean we have to hate each other.  I mean we all have to work together and I don't want it to be weird.  So from now on, let's just try and be friends. All of us," she said, eyeing me.

"Well that sounds cool to me," Gabriel said, and then slowly turning to me, he asked, "So what do you think, Selkie? Can we be friends?

Tabitha was too concerned with fixing her problems and moving on to notice the way Gabriel looked at me just then...but for me, there was no denying it.

This was a game for him.  A game he desperately wanted to win...and one that I had no idea how to play.

## Chapter 32

**Pretending to be friends with Gabriel proved much more daunting than I had expected, with his constant gazing eyes looming over my every movement; as if he was a hungry tomcat tracking his next meal, ready to pounce at any sign of weakness.** His smile said it all. He was confident, cocky even, positive that I would eventually surrender to him and his bizarre reality. The only problem with that, however, was that I wasn't weak and helpless like some tiny little mouse. I wasn't his prey to be conquered and devoured. I was strong, determined. I would not be caught.

All day he stalked me, and all day I resisted. Not once faltering as he baited me with his friendly banter, and relentless attention. Even when he cornered me in the break room, insisting that we sit together and get to know each other, for Tabitha's sake, I didn't give in. I just squared my shoulders, looked him straight in the eye, and said, "Not gonna happen," before planting a great big smile on my face and walking out of the break room.

"What are you smiling at?" Tabitha asked as I approached the registers.

"Oh, I just had a nice conversation with Gabe," I lied.

"See, I knew you'd like him if you just gave him a chance.

What were you guys talking about?"

"Oh, nothing really," I shrugged, turning to my register, and then seeing the time on my screen, my smile widened. "Almost time."

"Almost time for what?" Gabe asked, leaning his hands against the counter.

I immediately dropped my grin, and then thinking better of it, I put it back on and turned to face him, "Well, to leave of course. I don't know about you, but I can't wait to get out of here."

"Oh yeah? Got some big plans, or something?" he asked, his eyes filled with honest curiosity.

"Selkie, have big plans? You've got to be joking," Tabitha scoffed. "She never does anything, except draw, but that doesn't count."

"Tabitha," Stephen's high-pitched voice sang, from a few registers over. "Can you come here for a second please?"

"Oh lord, what does he want," she asked, rolling her eyes. "If he wants me to work again tomorrow, he can think again."

Once Tabitha was out of earshot, Gabriel left his station and came to stand in front of me, his elbow leaning against the card slider. "So no big plans?" he asked again.

"No not really," I said, busying myself with organizing my receipts.

"Do you want some?" he asked, his dark eyes flashing.

"No thank you," I answered politely.

"Are you sure? I've got some really awesome hang out spots."

"Wait, was that you I saw hanging around outside the gas station the other day?"

"That's funny," he said, leaning closer. "But honestly, Selkie, I could take you to places you've never been."

"What, like the local biker bar? Please, that is *so* unoriginal. Now why don't you go and try to at least look like you're doing something and leave me alone."

"Okay. Fine, but it's only a matter of time."

"Yeah, and when the time comes, and you get fired, I'll actually be able to get stuff done."

Tabitha returned then, complaining under her breath about Stephen making her work more hours, and as Gabriel quickly retreated back to his side of the register, I mentally noted the score...Selkie 1, Gabriel 0...before returning to my receipts, and closing out my register.

Thirty minutes later, once I had signed out and said

goodbye to Tabitha, who unfortunately had to stay until closing, I headed to the front entrance of the store. Knowing Aidan would be along shortly to walk me home, I went outside to wait for him. As the glass door slid open, I was surprised to see him already waiting for me, and in his little blue car no less.

"How was your day?" he asked, opening my door for me.

"It was okay, I guess. Much better now that you're here."

Aidan flashed me a smile, and then closing my door, he headed around to the driver side and hopped in.

"How did you get your car back?" I asked, putting on my seat belt. "You didn't steal it did you?"

"No of course not. As soon as you left I got a call from Liam. I guess mom convinced dad that it would be safer for both of us if I could drive."

"Oh, well that was nice of her."

"Yeah, she's really great like that. I can't wait for you to meet her."

"Do you think she'll like me?" I asked timidly.

He gently touched my cheek. "Who couldn't like you?"

"Thanks," I said, my skin warm from his touch.

"For what?" he asked, his hands now playing with my hair.

"For being so nice to me."

"No problem," he said with a smile. "Now where to? Do you need to go anywhere before we go home?"

There was no time like the present. He had shown me his entire world, and now it was time I showed him all of mine.

"Yeah, if you wouldn't mind I'd like to drive to the harbor. There's something I need to share with you."

As we drove across town, I could tell Aidan was curious about our little escapade, but he was remarkably patient and didn't ask too many questions. When we reached the harbor, I had him pull off to the side of the road, just passed the entrance, and then instructed him to take off his shoes.

"Is this really necessary?" he asked as he unlaced his boots.

"It is if you don't want your shoes to get soaked. Now stop whining, you're supposed to be the strong one, remember?"

Hand in hand, I led him down to the water's edge, careful not to step on any shells or sharp pebbles on the way, and then guided him over a series of slippery, algae covered rocks to a hidden cove at the base of the cliff.

"What is this place?" he asked as we climbed over a few more rocky obstacles, our hands and feet covered in the cold green slime.

"This is my hiding place. I found it when I was nine, and I come here when I'm upset, or just need to be by myself for a while."

"It's beautiful."

"Yeah, but we're not really even there yet. Just wait."

There were fewer rocks to walk on the further into the cove we traveled, and the frigid water felt like prickly needles against our bare feet, but we journeyed on, and within a few minutes reached the hole in the cliff that had become my refuge.

"So this is it," I said, climbing into the cave, and pulling out a blanket concealed within the inner wall.

With a smile on his face Aidan crawled in after me, his large body just managing to squeeze through the opening, but when his head knocked hard against the stone ceiling he grimaced, and said, "It's very cozy, Selkie."

"Oh sorry, I guess it's not really big enough for two people. I just wanted you to see it."

"No, it's nice," he said, rubbing the top of his head. "I'm glad you brought me."

"I'm glad I did too. I've never shown this to anyone before...I've never wanted to. But everything's different with you, Aidan, and it just felt right to bring you here."

"I know what you mean," he said, grabbing my hand, "and I've got something to share with you too."

"What is it? Another secret?"

"It's better if I just show you," he said, reaching into his pocket and pulling out a small black velvet box. "When Liam dropped off the car I asked him to bring this. Go ahead, open it," he said, handing it to me. "It belongs to you, as does my heart."

With shaking hands I opened the box and was shocked to discover a rather ancient looking gold ring staring up at me. In the center of the ring were two hands clasping a red stone heart, which was adorned with a diamond-encrusted crown.

"It's a claddagh ring," Aidan said, taking the ring from its case. "It's an Irish tradition, and it symbolizes my love and loyalty to you."

"It's beautiful."

"It was my mother's, and she gave it to me in hopes that I would find someone to give it to. Someone that I loved...and someone I wanted to spend the rest of my life with."

"Aidan," I said stunned, "Are you asking me..."

"To marry me," he interrupted, his face full of joy. "I know it sounds crazy, and we don't have to do it today, or next week, or even next year, but I want you, Selkie. Forever and ever, I want to be with you. I've already promised to protect and love you for the rest of my life...and now I officially give you my heart." He reached out and picked up my left hand, gently placing the ring on my finger as he said, "Selkie Reid, I love you more than I can explain, more than seems possible. I want to spend every day with you, and someday, I want you to be my wife. This ring, and my heart are yours if you want them."

"And you're sure about this?" I asked, my heart brimming with elation. "You're not joking?"

"I couldn't be more sure about anything," he said, lowering his soft lips to kiss the precious gift that was now resting on my finger.

With tears in my eyes, I looked down at my hand, and then back to Aidan's glorious face. "This is completely insane, and Tabitha will probably kill me for it, but I love you so much..."

"So then...is that a yes," he asked, cupping my face in his hands. "Please tell me it's a yes."

"It's a yes," I said, smiling through my tears, and then overwhelmed with happiness I flung myself at him and kissed him passionately, without restraint. He kissed me deeply, and the spark in my heart ignited, becoming a wild, uncontrollable flame that flickered with an ever-growing desire.

Many fiery moments passed, and in Aidan's arms I had lost all sense of time and place. All I knew was the touch of his hands, the taste of his skin, the warmth of his love. I didn't care about anything else.

If I had, I might have noticed when the sun began to set, allowing the moon to take its place in the sky.  I might have noticed the way the wind blew harder and the water crashed dangerously against the shore.  I might have even noticed how we were both in serious danger...but like I said...I didn't care about anything else.  I was selfish...foolish...I was in love.

# Chapter 33

One second Aidan's gentle fingers were caressing the delicate skin of my neck, and the next second, with his mouth releasing a terrible groan, his fingers were hastily groping my arms and pulling me further into the cramped cave.

"Oh God, Selkie," he said, scrambling to reach his dagger. "I'm so sorry."

"Aidan, what's the matter?" I asked, reaching for my hoodie that I had previously discarded.

"I'm such an idiot! That's what's the matter! I lost track of the time, and now they're coming. I've got to get you out of here." With his dagger finally free of his sheath, he grabbed my wrist and pulled me out of the cave into the moonlight, and not wanting to waste time trying to navigate the slippery rock path, he began to wade through the frigid water.

"How long do we have?" I asked frightened as I struggled to keep up, the icy water lapping at my knees.

"Not enough," he growled. "They'll be here any second."

With the water now up to our waists, it took even more effort to stay upright, and when my foot struck the side of an obscured rock, I slipped and fell face first into the water.

"We have to move faster," Aidan yelled, once I had resurfaced.

"I'm trying," I cried out, my already injured ankle shaking with weakness. "But I just can't go any faster."

"We don't have any other choice, Selkie. Now please we have to move."

But it was already too late. The mass of Shadows swiftly descended on us like lighting in a thunderstorm, and no matter how fast we pushed our bodies through the water there was no escaping them.

"Stay behind me," Aidan commanded, his dagger shining brightly above our heads, "and when I tell you to run, you run."

"I'm not just going to leave you here," I screamed, cowering behind Aidan as a Shadow rushed at us.

With a deadly blow Aidan struck the Shadow in the chest. "That wasn't a request, Selkie. Now we need to keep moving," he said, parrying another Shadow's attack. "We need to make it to the beach."

As Aidan continued to slash out with his blade against our foe, I squinted through the darkness and found the moon's delicate beams reflecting off the white sand of the beach about twenty feet away. The Shadows were beginning to flank us on both sides, and though he was fighting bravely, Aidan was at a disadvantage. Whereas the Shadows were able to float lithely above the water, we were unfortunately still knee deep in it, and Aidan couldn't move fast enough. Fearing for both of our safety, I placed my hands on either side of his waist, and tugging at his shirt, pulled him toward land.

When my feet hit the grainy earth, I breathed a sigh of release. We had made it...together. We were still surrounded by Shadows, Aidan's radiant dagger working fiercely to keep them at a distance, but all we had to do was make it up the hill to the car and everything would be fine.

"Ssseeeelkie," a Shadow crooned from above.

I looked up just in time to find two slithering hands reaching for me. I screamed as its icy fingers grasped my shoulders and attempted to pull me up off the ground. Aidan spun around and with great precision sliced right through the Shadow's arms. For a brief moment it cringed away from the light, which was just enough time for Aidan to reach into his pocket and throw me his keys.

"Run," he yelled as he pushed me in the direction of the hill.

"I can't," I said, desperately clinging to his arm. "Not without you."

"I'll be fine," he said, spinning around to deflect another Shadow's advance. "I'm not the one who matters here."

"You matter to me," I cried out. "I can't..."

"You can, and you will," he said, prying my fingers from his forearm, and shoving me away. "I can't keep this up much longer."

"All the more reason for me to stay."

"They feed off your energy, Selkie. The longer you stay, the harder it will be for me," and then, for the first time since I had met him, Aidan's face was full of panic. "If you love me, Selkie, then you'll listen to me."

Well how could I argue with that?

With tears streaming down my face, I turned my back on him and staggered up the hill away from danger. Several of the Shadows attempted to follow me, but Aidan blocked their path, swinging his blazing weapon back and forth to distract them. When I reached the car safely, I turned around to catch one more glance of my gallant protector, and that's when the Shadows encircled him.

"Aidan, watch out," I screamed, my hand hesitating on the car door.

"Selkie, get out of here," Aidan commanded, lunging forward to sink his dagger deep into the belly of a Shadow. The Shadow floated backwards with a horrible screech, and at the same time the circle of darkness closed in tighter on Aidan.

I took a step away from the car, not knowing what I could do, but desperate to find some way to help. Though Aidan was in the heat of battle, he noticed my timid advance.

"Don't you take another step," he yelled, ducking as a Shadow swung at his head. "If you do, we'll both be dead."

Aidan continued to strike out ferociously with his glowing blade, but overpowered by the large throng, he failed to observe the one Shadow that managed to break free of the circle and begin its charge up the hill toward me. Paralyzed with fear, I could only watch as Aidan noticed his mistake, and endeavored to rush after the clever Shadow, his face wincing with pain as dozens of icy appendages blocked his way to me.

"Selkie! Run," he screamed as his body became ensnared in a mass of black, his head the only part of his body still visible.

"I can't," I cried out, as the Shadow continued to advance. "I love you."

Still struggling against the vicious horde, Aidan's mouth opened to speak, but before he could say one word, the Shadows completely overcame him, and his head disappeared within the hovering darkness.

From the corner of my eye, I saw the Shadow's snaking body reach the top of the hill, and towering over me with its hand outstretched toward my throat, it loudly crooned my haunted melody, "Ssseeeelkie. Ssseeeelkie."

With shaking limbs I pressed my back against the car, wishing more than anything that I had run when I'd had the chance, and waited breathlessly for the Shadow's chilling touch.

Just then, an enormous flame, like the eruption of a volcano, broke through the huddled circle that had engulfed Aidan, and all the Shadows went flying backwards away from the light. Aidan stood there, bruised and beaten...but strong, and with a flick of his wrist his dagger flew through the air, up the hill, to the center of the Shadow's back. A great golden light burst through the monster's chest, igniting an intense fire that quickly spread through the Shadow's entire body, and devoured every last speck of its devilish black frame.

"It isn't over," Aidan said weakly as the mass of Shadows crept slowly back into my vision. "Get in the car and go, now!"

This time I wouldn't hesitate. With my hands still trembling, I fumbled to find the right key to jam into the lock and then threw myself into the driver seat. Fastening my seat belt, I put the car in drive and slammed my foot against the pedal. The tires squealed loudly against the pavement, and then I was flying forward into the night.

Bleary with tears I drove along the coast, my hands curled tightly around the steering wheel, determined to get as much distance between the Shadows and me as I could. Aidan had thought that my leaving would give him the advantage he needed to defeat the Shadows, and I believed that he knew what he was doing. After all, he was my protector, and he knew more about these things than I did. He seemed certain that running away was my only option, and so I did it, because I trusted him.

I mean it's not like I chose to leave him alone with those monsters. He had made it perfectly clear that he didn't want me to stay, and no matter what I said there was no convincing him.

So then why did I feel so guilty?

Maybe I could have put up more of a fight, or done something to help, but the way he looked at me, his face pale and stricken with fear, made it impossible to refuse him. I knew it looked bad. Once again I had chosen to run away from my problems instead of facing them, leaving someone else to clean up the mess, but that was what Aidan had wanted. What else could I have done?

As the car's beams scanned the empty road in front of me, my eyes frantically scanned the water's edge for any sign of Aidan. Suddenly, a strong gust of wind struck the left side of the car, surprising me, and I swerved off the road, hitting a small patch of gravel that made the tires spin. Not knowing what else to do, I slammed on the breaks, and after a few scary moments the car came to a complete stop.

With shaky fingers I turned off the car and threw the keys into the passenger seat, unwilling to drive any farther, and laid my head against the wheel. Giving in to all the fears and doubts that were raging inside of my head, I began to sob uncontrollably, and not having Aidan there to comfort me, I turned to the only other person who I thought might listen.

"God," I whispered, feeling a little weird talking out loud to someone I couldn't see. "I don't know how to do this, and I don't even know if you're listening, but I need your help. If there was ever a time that I was hoping for you to be real, it would be now. I know Aidan believes in you, and every so often I feel like you're with me, protecting me and stuff, and so I'm asking that if you really are there, and you really care about me, that you'll help Aidan. Be *his* protector and get him out of this mess." I lifted my head and looked up at the hazy sky. "I don't want to make any promises to you that I can't keep, but I'll do whatever I can to spread your light, and make this world a better place, but please, please just help him."

At the exact moment that I finished my prayer, all the clouds in the sky parted to reveal a dazzling white moon, surrounded by a billion sparkling stars. Amongst the mass of fiery lights I found the Big Dipper, and with my finger against the windshield I traced the pattern, connecting each star to one another to form the famous constellation.

It's like a universal connect the dots!

Aidan's words from the previous day rang loudly in my head, and I knew I had received my answer. Why hadn't I thought of it before? I had been stupid to think that I was useless in the fight against the Shadows.  Aidan wasn't the only person with God-given abilities after all.  I was a Lightscaper.  I could change the outcome of future events, make sure that Aidan succeeded, and all I needed was a nudge of heavenly inspiration to do it.  Whispering a quick "thank you" toward the sky, I leaned over the seat and found my bag that contained my sketchbook and pencil.

Not knowing how much precious time I had already wasted, I immediately got to work creating my next picture. Unable to control every single detail, I had to concentrate on the most important things.  So I drew the only two things that mattered.

*　　*　　*

The car had barely come to a complete stop outside the harbor, before I was opening the door and running down the hill. When my bare feet hit the water, I cringed from the cold temperature, but desperate to see Aidan I kept moving deeper and deeper into the freezing water until it was up to my waist. Using my arms to propel me forward, I hastily splashed my way across the cove to my hiding place.

It was very dark, the sun still hours away from rising, but I could see well enough to know that all the Shadows were gone. At least one of the things I had drawn had come to fruition, and I was instantly relieved.  Grabbing on to the stony cliff I pulled myself out of the water, and carefully tiptoed across the wet rock to the cave's entrance where Aidan sat silently, his head in his hands.

"Hey, are you alright?" I asked, wrapping my arm around him. "You're not hurt, are you?"

"No, you made sure of that," he said, his voice strangely distant.

"Okay...so then...what's the matter?"

"I told you not to draw without me," he said, looking up, his eyes harsh.

"I was just trying to help."

"I didn't need your help," he said, squirming away from me.

"Well how was I supposed to know that?"

"It doesn't even matter. You promised to never do that stuff without me, and you just went ahead and did it anyway."

"Because I thought you were in danger," I said defensively. "I might not have as much experience with this stuff as you do, but there were tons of Shadows here, too many for you to fight on your own. Yeah I broke a promise, but you were in trouble, and I just saved your life."

"That's not your responsibility," he said, crawling out of the cave. "I am perfectly capable of taking care of myself. I had it covered."

"It didn't look that way to me," I said, crawling after him. "Why are you being like this? Why can't you just be happy that we're both okay?"

"Because it should have been me," he shouted, turning away. "I should have been enough."

"Aidan...what are you talking about?"

"I couldn't do it, Selkie," he said much quieter, his voice shaking with emotion. "I couldn't protect you."

"What do you mean? I'm here, safe in one piece."

"You shouldn't have been here at all. I was irresponsible, and it almost got us both killed."

"But we're both fine..."

"Because of you," he said, spinning around. "It had nothing to do with me. You were right. I was overwhelmed, and if it wasn't for you, I'd be dead."

"So I did help," I said, walking over to him. "Then why are you so mad?"

"Because I'm the protector, Selkie. I shouldn't need anyone's help."

"Is that what's bothering you? You're upset because you

couldn't do it all by yourself?"

"It's not just that," he said, crossing his arms. "I'm the one who's supposed to be taking care of you, not the other way around."

"But if I can help you, what's the big deal? Just because I'm a girl…"

"It's not because you're a girl," he said, rolling his eyes. "I'm not being sexist. We have plenty of protectors that are girls."

"So then what are you saying?" I asked, timidly reaching out to grab his hand.

He took it willingly, and squeezing it tightly, he released a sigh. "I was too busy pleasing myself to notice it was getting dark outside. I was distracted," he said, lifting his other hand to stroke my face, "and that made you vulnerable. Don't get me wrong, I was grateful when you helped me win tonight, but I can't rely on you to save me when times get tough. I should have been ready for them, but I just couldn't hack it."

"And you think it's because you were with me?"

Aidan dropped his hand. "I *know* it's because I was with you."

"So what? That's it," I said, throwing up my arms in frustration. "You make one mistake, and now you don't want to be with me?"

"It's not what I want," he said, grabbing my arms and pulling me to his chest. "But your safety comes first, and I can't protect you like this."

A thought suddenly occurred to me, and I pushed myself away from him. "You can if I help," I said excitedly.

"No Selkie, I don't think so. It doesn't work that way."

"Why not?"

"Because it doesn't."

"That's not an answer."

"Okay, fine, because you can't just follow me around and draw me out of fights."

"Well, of course not every fight. Just the ones that are really tricky."

"Selkie, this is ridiculous."

"No it's not! I mean just think about it. You wouldn't have to worry so much. All you would have to do is protect me until I could finish the picture."

"What, I'm supposed to let you sit around doodling, while Shadows try to attack you?"

"Try is the important word in that sentence," I said,

moving closer. "I trust you. You wouldn't let them touch me."

"I don't know…"

"Oh come on, it's a great idea," I said, grabbing his hand again. "You still get to do all the protecting, but you won't have to worry so much about me getting hurt, or you for that matter. Plus, I'd be able to use my gift, and I wouldn't be breaking our promise, because I'd be with you, and most importantly we could be together. I mean…don't you want that?"

"Of course I do, but…"

"No, uh uh," I said, plugging my ears with my fingers. "I don't want to hear any more of your excuses. This will work. I know it."

"You're never going to give up, are you?"

"I'm never going to give up on you," I said, leaning forward and kissing his cheek. "So…what do you say?"

"I say that you're crazy, and I love you for it, and I'll admit…it's an intriguing concept."

"So then, you'll try?"

"If it means staying with you, I'll try anything once, but just to be sure," he said, retrieving his phone and hitting number one on his speed dial, "I think we need to have a little chat with Jeremiah."

## Chapter 34

**It was a little after midnight when Aidan and I arrived, drenched and thoroughly exhausted, at the church's secret side entrance.** Ewan was waiting at the door to meet us, and after hugging us both tightly, and checking Aidan's body for any wounds that might need immediate medical attention, he led us through the church's empty upper levels to the hidden passage beneath the floor.

As the glowing door slid open, a waft of hot air generated by dozens of raging torches along the rock-strewn hallway, assailed my cold skin. As we walked down the path, my hand snug within Aidan's grasp, I couldn't help but think that the extra torches, which were not lit the evening of my break in, were alight this evening, especially for me.

After winding our way through the underground haven for a number of minutes, we arrived at a fork in the passageway, and then taking a left, we wandered down the hall for several more paces, before approaching a set of large wooden doors adorned with some sort of ancient writing.

"It's Irish," Aidan said, noticing my interest in the unique carvings, "and it reads 'solas an domhan,' which means 'the light of the world'."

"I wish I could read it like you do," I told him, squeezing his hand.

"Something else I can teach you then," he said, smiling down at me. "Now, are you ready?"

"For what?" I asked with a shrug. "You haven't really told me what we're doing here."

"We're going to speak with Jeremiah, he's the leader of our clan, and I think he'll be able to help us out, but first I want you to meet my family."

"Oh, I wish I had a change of clothes," I said, looking down at my disheveled appearance. "I don't want your parents to think I always look like this."

"Don't worry about that," he said, tucking a loose hair behind my ear. "You always look beautiful to me."

"Aidan, don't you think you're forgetting something?" Ewan piped in, his face concerned.

"I'm getting to it," Aidan said, eyeing his brother.

"Getting to what?" I asked.

"Alright, I don't want you to freak out, but when I said I wanted you to meet my family, I didn't just mean my parents."

"Then what exactly did you mean?"

"What Aidan is trying to say," Ewan interjected, "is that we consider everyone in the clan as being a part of our family, and almost all of them are right behind this door waiting to get a glimpse of you."

On the drive over, I had assumed that since Shadows only attacked after the sun went down that the Sanctuary would be vacant, with all the protectors out on duty and the wards using the time to sleep...but apparently that wasn't the case on this particular evening.

"You mean the entire clan is in there?" I asked terrified as I attempted to smooth out all the wrinkles from my shirt.

"Well not the entire clan, exactly," Aidan said, trying to appease me. "Some of them had to go out on watch."

"And mom and dad are in a meeting with a few of the other elders, so you won't have to worry about seeing them right away either," Ewan commented.

"But most of the clan is in there waiting for me, and I have to go in there looking like this?"

"It's really not that big of a deal," Aidan said, leaning down to kiss my forehead. "They're going to love you," and then grasping the doors large golden handles, he added, "Now come on, there's no time like the present."

The medieval-esque room we entered, with its vaulted

beamed ceilings and gray stone floor, was abuzz with activity. Sitting around one long wooden table, conversing loudly in both Irish and English, were twenty or so men and women of Aidan's clan. Across the room by the roaring fireplace stood several small children, each with a tiny rock in hand, taking turns playing, what looked like, an intense game of hopscotch, and sitting in a circle in the opposite corner, were a small group of teenagers that were laughing loudly together as they took funny pictures of each other with their cell phones.

It appeared that everyone was so caught up in their games and conversations that they hadn't realized we had joined the gathering, and so the three of us stood their together, unnoticed for several moments, until Aidan finally spoke, "Good evening," his voice rang through the chamber, "can I have everyone's attention."

The room fell instantly silent, and every head turned in our direction as Aidan spoke, but no one was looking at him, they were all looking at me...and their unfriendly eyes spoke volumes.

"I know that there have been a lot of rumors and stories going around about me lately, some of them true and some of them not so true...and I wanted to set the record straight."

"Whataya think ya doing, bringing her here like this?" spat a short, gray haired man, with an Irish accent as thick as his beard. "Don't ya have any respect, boy?"

"I didn't come back to fight with you, Peter," Aidan said.

"Then what did you come back for?" asked a blonde woman standing at one end of the table.

"I came to talk to Jeremiah, and to introduce Selkie to you all," Aidan said, straightening his shoulders the same way he did every time he was preparing for a fight.

I squeezed his hand tighter.

"Well wasn't that nice of ya," spoke a tall man from the center of the table. "It's quite a grand meetin', isn't it?"

Aidan opened his mouth to protest but was distracted when a pretty young woman with curly brown hair and bright green eyes stood up. She gave Aidan a quick glance before walking away from the table and addressing the crowd. "Alright that's enough," she said, raising her perfect manicured hands. "Why don't you all just mind your own business and leave Aidan alone."

"So now Elena's joinin' with him too?" growled Peter.

"I'm not joining with anyone," Elena disputed, walking over to us. "But Aidan's our family, no matter what, and we don't treat our family like this."

"Thanks Lena," Aidan smiled. "But you don't need to stick up for me. I think I can take care of Peter."

"Didn't look like it from where I was sitting," she said, her friendly eyes glowing with amusement. "Now introduce me to your friend before they all start a riot."

"Oh yeah, sorry," Aidan said, stumbling over his words. "Elena...this is Selkie."

"It's nice to meet you, Elena," I said with a smile, as I reached out to shake her hand.

"Call me Lena," she said, taking my hand and shaking it firmly. "Everyone else does. Now, was that so hard," she said, turning back to speak to the rest of them. "It's not like she's a Shadow or something."

"That'll be quite enough from ya, Ms. Lena," spoke a tall, heavyset man from across the room.

Elena dropped her smile immediately, respectfully bowing her head to the man as he approached her, and then quickly returned to her seat without another look in my direction.

"And I think it's best if we all got on with whatever it is we're supposed to be doin'," the burly man, with a strong Irish lilt, continued. "Don't tell me we've all got nothin' to do!"

"No Jeremiah," said the crowd in unison, and without another word, everyone sprang into life, and putting away their games and dirty looks for another time they exited the room, leaving Aidan and I alone with the rather imposing Jeremiah.

"Ah, so this is the wee lass that's been causin' all the trouble," Jeremiah said as he offered his hand to me.

"This is Selkie Reid, sir," Aidan told him.

"And so it is, but can't the little darlin' speak for herself?"

"Yes she can," I said, eyeing Aidan as I took Jeremiah's hand. "And excuse me sir, but if you don't mind, I'd appreciate it if you didn't call me little."

"Well, there now, so she can speak for herself, and with quite a strong tongue too. No wonder ya stirred up such a mess."

"I didn't mean to mess up anything," I said, lowering my eyes to stare at my feet.

"Aye lass, I'm sure ya didn't mean to do anythin', but ya did it all the same."

"It wasn't her fault, sir," Aidan said, coming to my rescue. "It was mine."

"It was your fault, now was it?"

"Yes sir. I made contact with Selkie, even though I knew that I wasn't supposed to. She knew nothing about us or who I was. So you see...it's not fair that she gets blamed for everything."

"So you're sayin' she had no choice in the matter?"

"Yes sir."

"No, that's not true," I said defiantly, raising my eyes to Jeremiah's face. "I had every choice in the matter. It was just as much my decision to see Aidan as it was for him to see me. He's just trying to protect me."

"Selkie, please," Aidan said, grabbing my arm.

"No Aidan. Stop trying to take it all on yourself. We're a couple. We do things together."

"Well what a grand pair we have here," Jeremiah said with a smile. "Both of ya fightin' over whose fault it is for fallin' in love."

"I'm sorry, sir," Aidan said quickly.

"Oh don't be apologizin' to me, Aidan. I know all about what fallin' in love can do to a man. It makes us do crazy things."

"Yes sir, it does," Aidan said, wrapping his arm around my waist. "And that's what we came to talk to you about. We need your help."

"Well I don't know if I'm the one ya should be askin' for help, but I don't want to spoil your speech. So go on and tell me what it is ya want."

"There are actually two things I wanted to ask you."

"Now why doesn't that surprise me," Jeremiah said with a crooked grin. "We best be sittin' down then, I suppose."

With large, heavy strides Jeremiah led us over to the table, gesturing for us to sit down on a nearby bench, while he walked around to the opposite side and chose a bench directly across from us.

"So, what'll it be, Aidan?" Jeremiah asked as he leaned forward and placed his elbows on the aged wood.

"First, I'm a little concerned about the amount of Shadow activity Selkie's been experiencing the last few weeks."

"And how's that?"

"Well, every day the amount of Shadows around her is growing. I know they're drawn to her the more she uses her gift, and she's been using it more frequently lately..."

"'Cuz you've been showin' her a thing or two, have ya?"

"Well, yes sir, I have..."

"Which was totally my fault...again," I said quickly, before Aidan could apologize. "I made him show me, sir, even though he didn't want to."

"Go on," Jeremiah told Aidan, completely ignoring my outburst.

"I've never seen or heard about so many Shadows being

together all at once, especially not with just one Lightscaper around. They track her every movement from sundown to sun up, and even when she doesn't draw they stalk her. They're extremely determined, sir."

"Not to mention creepy," I whispered, more to myself than anyone else.

"Oh, and that's another thing," Aidan said, nodding at me. "Selkie says she can hear them talking to her. Have you ever heard of a Lightscaper being able to understand them before?"

Jeremiah, who had been focusing intently on Aidan for the entire conversation, turned his piercing blue eyes on me. "When they speak, whatta they say to ya?"

"Well they're not very creative, they only ever say my name, but it's enough to freak me out."

"And ya say they watch her, even if she hasn't drawn anythin'," Jeremiah asked, turning his full attention back on Aidan.

"Every night for the last few weeks."

"So what's come up then?" Jeremiah asked, scratching his chin. "What's got them all in a tizzy?"

"I thought you'd be able to tell me," Aidan said, thwarted.

"Well to be honest with ya, laddie, I haven't the darndest

idea," Jeremiah said with a chuckle. "The Shadows have always been a nasty sort, and devilishly clever of course. Always pickin' up new ways to trip us up, and I can't say that this is any different. All ya can do is keep a good eye out, I suppose."

"And that's it?" Aidan asked, his shoulders drooping in disappointment.

"Well now," Jeremiah said, reaching over the table to clasp Aidan's shoulder, "It's better than nothin',"

Knowing I wouldn't get another opportunity, I took a deep breath, and asked, "What about me?"

"Well what about ya?" Jeremiah inquired as he cocked his head to the side and fixed his eyes on my face.

"Selkie, maybe this isn't a good time," Aidan whispered, placing a hand on my arm to silence me.

"When would be a good time?" I asked him through my teeth.

"I don't know. Some other time, when we've been able to talk about it first."

"But I thought this is why we came...to ask him," I said, pointing my finger towards Jeremiah, who sat silently watching our guarded exchange with fascination. "You said you'd ask him."

"I know I did, but..."

"Oh come now, laddie," Jeremiah interjected with a smile. "You'd better just be out with it. I haven't got all night, and I don't see ya changin' her mind anytime soon."

"Yes, sir," Aidan said, bowing his head slightly. "I'm sorry to bother you about this, but...well...Selkie's had an idea."

"It's not an idea," I spoke up quickly. "It's a plan. One that I know will work because I've already done it."

"And what's this plan ya have, lassie?"

"I want to use my powers as a Lightscaper to control the outcome of Aidan's battles."

"How do ya mean, exactly?" Jeremiah asked, puzzled.

"Well, if I draw him defeating the Shadows, then he will," I said, turning to smile at Aidan. "I can control where and how in the future Aidan ends up, and he won't be able to lose."

With a hesitant smile on his face, Aidan squeezed my hand under the table, and then turning to Jeremiah, he asked, "So what do you think, sir? Can it work?"

"What you're talkin' about," Jeremiah said slowly, his wide eyes staring unblinkingly at my face, "has never been done in the history of man. No Lightscaper has ever been able to change the course of human events."

"But Selkie can, sir. I've seen it. I've experienced it!"

"It's impossible," Jeremiah murmured incredulously. "If Selkie can do what ya sayin', that would mean that..." Jeremiah's eyes got wider still, and a look of shock washed across his features. "I'm sorry," he said suddenly, standing up. "I must leave ya for now. I must talk with the Council, immediately."

"Sir, what's happening? What's wrong?"

"Nothin' as of yet," Jeremiah answered, his eyes distant. "But you best be stayin' here tonight in any case," and then turning away from us, he hurried across the room to one of the many wooden doors that lined the chamber's walls.

"Sir, is this really necessary?" Aidan called out, a slight tinge of panic in his voice.

"It's extremely necessary, laddie," Jeremiah said, his hand poised on the handle of the door. "'Cuz if Selkie can do what ya say she can, well then you don't want to be goin' out in the darkness all alone...Now, go and get some rest," he said kindly as he opened the door and stepped into the hallway, "You're goin' to need it."

## Chapter 35

**"What was that all about?" I asked Aidan as we left the chamber and made our way down the hallway.**

"I have no idea," Aidan replied, puzzled. "I've never seen Jeremiah act like that. Usually he's the one we all turn to for answers."

"So what do we do now?"

"Well first, I want to get you settled in," he said as we approached a door at the end of the hallway. "This is your room for tonight."

Opening the door, Aidan walked into the small room, turning the light switch on as he went, and then gestured to a cot in the corner. "It's not much," he said, going to sit down on the makeshift bed, "but you'll be safe here."

"Where are you going to sleep?" I asked, sitting down beside him.

"In my old room, I guess."

"Is it far from here?

"Just a couple hallways down," he shrugged.

"Do you think you could sleep in here with me?" I asked,

taking his arm.

"I don't think that would be such a good idea," he said, shaking his head. "The clan has strict rules about men and woman sleeping in the same room together. You have to be married to do that, and since we're already on thin ice, it's probably best if we don't break that rule too. But don't worry, Selkie. You don't need to be scared," he said, wrapping his arm around me. "No one will bother you here. Just try to sleep, and I'll be here when you wake up."

"You promise?"

"I promise," he said, leaning over and lightly kissing my lips. "Now I'm going to go find out exactly what's going on, and then get some sleep myself."

"Would you do me a favor?"

"You name it."

"Would you come and kiss me goodnight before you go to bed?"

"How about I kiss you now," he said, placing his hands on the side of my face, "and then again right before I go to bed. Would that be alright?"

"That would be perfect."

Gently tilting my head to one side, Aidan pulled me close,

and touching his sweet lips to mine, he kissed me passionately, our mouths moving together in perfect harmony, until a light knock at the door forced us to pull away.

"Who is it?" Aidan asked as we both slid away from each other.

"It's me, Ewan.  Can I come in?"

"Come on in, Ewan," Aidan said, standing up, and walking to the door.

"Hey guys," Ewan greeted cheerfully as he pushed the door open and entered the room, and then eyeing my flushed cheeks and swollen lips, he said, "I wasn't interrupting anything, was I? 'Cuz I could always come back later."

"No need," Aidan said, running a hand through his cropped hair.  "I was just getting ready to leave."

"Oh, good," Ewan smiled.  "I came to find you because the Council is having a meeting right now, and I thought you would want to be there when they got out."

"Yeah, Jeremiah left us in a hurry.  Does anyone know what they're talking about?"

"Same rumors as usual.  You'd think after all the meetings they've had about you and Selkie that they'd have nothing else to talk about.  What happened when you guys met with Jeremiah, anyway?"

"Let's just say I might have given him and the Council some new stuff to chat about, and I doubt they'll be finished with the session until morning."

"Well, then you might as well get some sleep," Ewan said, walking to the door. "Oh and I almost forgot," he said, spinning around. "Mom and dad were hoping you'd come by and see them. They're waiting outside the hall until the Council releases."

"Why don't we just walk over together," Aidan said, stepping towards his brother. "And don't worry, Selkie," he added, turning his head to me. "I haven't forgotten my promise. I'll stop by to say goodnight on the way back to my room."

"I'll be right here," I said, pulling my legs up on the bed, and wrapping my arms around them. "But don't take too long."

"I'll be back before you know it," he said, smiling at me, and then following Ewan into the hallway he turned back once more to give me a quick wink, and then shut the door behind him.

Already regretting my decision to stay put, I ran across the room to the door, hoping to convince Aidan to take me with him, but when I heard the lock bolt from the outside I knew my attempt was futile.

I was stuck.

Untying my muddy shoes and placing them under the bed, I gazed uncomfortably around at my sleeping arrangements. I had always been terrible with new places, never feeling secure enough to relax or lower my guard, and sleeping in a strange room, no matter how tired I felt, was consistently the hardest part to overcome. Aidan had promised that I would be safe within the Sanctuary, but the bright yellow walls that surrounded me felt more like a prison than a refuge, and no amount of deep breaths could appease the peculiar sensation of suffocation that had overtaken me.

So what was I supposed to do now?

Even though the soft white pillow at the foot of the bed looked very inviting, and my eyes were heavy with sleep, I couldn't bring myself to let go and lie down. Aidan had made it impossible for me to leave, and my mind had made it impossible for me to sleep. So there was only one other option I had left.

I moved across the room to a small white dresser, the only other object in the room besides my cot and began to rummage through the drawers. I was eager to find something within it to keep me occupied until Aidan returned, but when my investigation only turned up extra pillows and linens, I sulked back across the room to my cot.

There were no burning torches in this room to keep me warm, and my clothes, which were still uncomfortably damp, clung to my skin, leaving me chilled. Giving in, I peeled back the light blue blanket and white sheet on the bed, and was just about to get under the covers when I heard the lock unlatch and the door swing open.

"Well that didn't take you very long," I said, turning around to greet my visitor.

"I didn't know you were expecting me?" Brendan said with a cocky sneer as he walked into the room and closed the door behind him.

"What are you doing here?" I asked confused. "Where's Aidan?"

"He's having a little chat with our parents," he said, taking a step forward. "I was surprised to see that you weren't with him...and I thought this would be a great time for us to catch up. You know, just the two of us. So tell me. What did Jeremiah say? Did he give you his blessing?"

"I don't think that's any of your business," I said, crossing my arms in defiance.

"Oh, but you see," he said, moving even closer, "that's where you're wrong. All of this is my business, Selkie...because this Sanctuary is my business. It's not just you and Aidan's lives that are involved in all of this," he said, his voice rising. "And I am just so sick and tired of you getting in my way."

"Me? Getting in your way? I think it's the other way around."

"You think you're so special, don't you?" he said, eyeing me with curiosity.

"Excuse me?"

"You heard me," he said as he closed the distance between us. "You think that just because you want something, that you're entitled to it; that if you whine and beg enough you'll get whatever, or whomever you want. Well I'm sorry to tell you this," he said, reaching out and grabbing my arm roughly, "but it's never that simple. If you want something bad enough," he added, shoving me backwards into the wall, "you have to fight for it."

"Brendan, what are you doing?" I screeched as he grabbed both my wrists and pressed them hard against the wall above my head. I struggled to get away, but he was too strong.

"What's the matter, Selkie?" he spit, thrusting his body forward so that our hips were touching. "I thought you liked to fight."

He tightened his grasp around my wrists.

"Stop it, Brendan," I said, still struggling to get free. "You're hurting me!

"Always thinking of yourself, aren't you?"

"Please, Brendan. Don't do this!"

"Oh, not so tough anymore, are you?" he said as he clasped both of my wrists in his left hand, leaving his other hand free to greedily caress my cheek.

"Aidan will be back any minute," I threatened, not knowing what else to do.

"Ah, Aidan! My silly little romantic brother," he crooned, moving his hand down my neck to my chest, "I just can't seem to figure him out these days." Then running his hand down the side of my leg, he added, "and I can't help but wonder what it is he sees in you, why he's so passionate about you."

With my hands still forced above my head, he gave me an evil smirk as he pressed his whole body against me and then lowered his dry lips to my mouth. Unable to push him away I just closed my lips as tightly as I could and waited for him to finish.

When he finally pulled away his face looked amused. "Just like I thought," he said, looking me up and down. "You're anything but special."

"I never said I was," I spat at him through clenched teeth.

"If I want your opinion, I'll ask for it," he growled, wrapping his hand around my throat and pulling me into another one of his disgusting kisses.

"Don't struggle," he ordered, trying to part my lips with his tongue. "I want to see everything that Aidan is getting."

I tried to pull away, but every time I fought him his hand squeezed tighter around my neck. Unable to breathe, I gasped for air, and he took that opportunity to get what he wanted.

With tears running down my face, I looked to the door for some kind of rescue, and that's when Aidan broke through the door and lunged for his brother.

"What the hell do you think you're doing?" Aidan yelled, grabbing Brendan's shoulders and pulling him off of me.

"Aidan," I screamed as I pulled my wrists free and stumbled onto the bed away from the ensuing fight.

"Selkie, get out of the way," Aidan roared, his eyes gleaming with fury, and then shoving his brother hard against the wall, he punched Brendan firmly in the stomach, sending him toppling to the ground with a loud groan.

"Get up," Aidan shouted, pulling Brendan back up to his feet. "Get up and fight."

"What, are you going to break my nose again?" Brendan laughed, holding his gut. "Go right ahead, but that's not going to take back the fact that your girlfriend's a slut!"

"What did you just say?" Aidan asked, clenching his fists.

"I said your girlfriend was asking for it...and I just gave her what she wanted."

"I told you that if you ever hurt Selkie again that you'd regret it, Brendan," Aidan said, his face burning with rage. "And now I'm going to make good on that promise."

"Aidan stop," I yelled, grabbing his arm and pulling him away from Brendan. "It's not worth it."

"It'll be worth it for me," he said, leering viciously at Brendan.

"He's your brother."

"And he just attacked you, Selkie. Why are you standing up for him?"

"I'm not standing up for him! I just can't let you do this."

"So you just want me to let this go?"

"No, of course not," I said with tears in my eyes. "I hate him for what he's done to me, and he deserves everything that's coming to him, but if you do this, your family will never be the same. I've already messed everything else up, I can't destroy your family too."

"She's got a point, Aidan," Brendan nodded.

"You shut up," Aidan spat, raising his fist. "I'm not done with you yet."

"Yes you are," I said, grabbing his hand and forcing him to unclench his fingers. "You're here," I added, placing his warm hand against my cheek. "That's all that I need."

"Are you sure this is what you really want?" Aidan asked discontented.

"I'm sure this is what will be the best thing for us in the long run."

"Selkie, that's just not good enough for me."

"Well it's good enough for me," Brendan said cheerfully as he pushed past Aidan and headed to the door.

"Hold on a second," Aidan commanded, grabbing Brendan's arm and spinning him around. "Just because Selkie isn't going to do anything about this, doesn't mean that I'm not going to. As soon as the Council releases I'm reporting you to Jeremiah. Let's see how long you keep your ward status after this."

"So you honestly think Jeremiah is going to side with a traitor like you?" Brendan scoffed. "He'll never believe anything you have to say. Not after everything you've done. I'm the one who follows all the rules, who does what he's supposed to do, remember? Anything you say I'll deny, and when you get kicked out for good, I'll be the true protector of this family."

"That's impossible. You don't have the gene. The Council

would never allow that."

"Well they said they'd never allow a relationship between a Lightscaper and a protector either, but look where we are," he said, opening the door and stepping out into the hallway. "It seems the times are finally changing little bro, and as soon as the Council agrees with me that you're a danger to the clan, I'll have the birthright for myself."

"That will never happen," Aidan said, squaring his shoulders. "I won't let it."

"Don't get in my way, Aidan," Brendan warned, his eyes black with hate. "'Cuz if you do," he continued, tilting his head in my direction, "you'll lose something much more important to you than your protector status."

## Chapter 36

**"Are you sure you're alright?" Aidan asked for the third time as he examined the fresh bruises on my wrists.**

"I told you, he didn't do that much damage. He just scared me more than anything."

"God, I could kill him for what he did," Aidan snarled quietly.

"Don't say things like that," I frowned, scooting closer to him on the cot. "You could never really hurt your own brother."

"Then why does it feel like I could easily do it...right this second?"

"Because you're angry."

"Which I have every right to be, and so do you! How can you act like this is no big deal?"

"Because it isn't," I shrugged.

"But how can you say that, if I hadn't come back to check on you, he could have..."

"Forget about what could have happened," I interrupted, taking his hand. "You stopped him. That's what matters. Except for a few bruises that will heal, and a great desire to wash my mouth out, I'm okay."

Aidan crumpled his face in thought. "I just don't get it. It's like I don't even know him anymore. I never would have imagined he was capable of doing something like this."

"People do crazy things when they're desperate."

"That's another thing. He thinks by pushing me out he'll get to become a Protector, but there is no way that would ever happen. He doesn't have what it takes. He would only be a liability."

"Then we just have to make sure that he doesn't get what he wants."

"And how do we do that?"

"I'm not sure, but I do know that I'll think better once I get some sleep."

"That's probably a good idea," Aidan agreed, taking off his shoes and shoving them under the bed.

"Wait! What are you doing?"

"Going to sleep," he said, pushing me over and tucking his legs under the blanket. "What does it look like I'm doing?"

"But I thought you said we weren't allowed to sleep in the same room?"

"To hell with what we're allowed to do. There is no way I am leaving you alone in this place for one second, and as soon as we talk to Jeremiah I'm getting you out of here."

"And what about you?" I asked coyly, sliding my legs beneath the covers and cuddling up beside him.

"What about me?"

"Are you going to be getting out of here, too?"

"I go wherever you go," he whispered into my ear. "Forever."

"I was hoping you would say that."

\*   \*   \*

The next morning came far too early.

Ewan arrived to wake us just after seven. With more energy than I would prefer for that time of the morning, he informed us that the Council had finally adjourned, and that Jeremiah was waiting for us. Groggy with sleep, Aidan and I quickly scrambled to put on our shoes and fix our haggard appearances, before following Ewan out of the room and down the hall to the Chamber.

Clinging to their last flickering flames, the torches along the hallway made our path eerily dark. No longer feeling at ease with the darkness, after seeing what could be lurking within it, I squeezed Aidan's hand for support.

"You're okay," he whispered, clutching my hand tighter. "We're almost there."

Though I could barely see a foot in front of me, Aidan knew exactly where he was going, and he carefully guided me through the gloomy passage without incident. When we arrived at the door, Ewan pulled it open and gestured for us to enter.

"This is as far as I can go," he said, clasping his hand on Aidan's shoulder. "Good luck."

"Thanks," Aidan said, smiling warmly at him, "but I'm hoping we won't need it."

Jeremiah stood with his hands clasped behind his back in front of the fireplace, staring motionlessly into the blazing flames. At the sound of the door closing behind us, he slowly lifted his head before turning around to address us.

"Ah, so it's time then, is it?" he asked, rubbing his tired eyes.

"You asked to see us," Aidan answered, squeezing my hand as he pulled me forward.

"And so I did, laddie," Jeremiah nodded, walking to the table. "But why don't we sit down for a spell. It's been quite the long evenin'."

We quickly did as he requested.

"Excuse me sir," Aidan began once we were seated, "but before you start, there is something very important that I need to tell you."

"Well I'm afraid whatever ya need to tell me, laddie, will just have to wait for the time bein'."

"But sir..."

"No Aidan," Jeremiah said, raising his hand to silence him. "What I have to tell ya can't wait. So don't go on interruptin' me."

"Yes sir," Aidan surrendered instantly. "It won't happen again."

"There now," Jeremiah said, rubbing at his eyes again. "If only what I had to tell ya was as easy as that. But I'm afraid it's not easy at all."

"What is it, sir?" Aidan asked, leaning forward.

Jeremiah considered Aidan's question for a moment and then crinkling the skin between his eyes, he sighed, "The Council has come to a decision."

"A decision about what?" Aidan asked slowly.

"Before I be tellin' ya anymore, Aidan, I need ya to know that this is the Council's final decision on the matter."

Aidan sat up straight, squaring his shoulders. Preparing for a fight. I pressed the side of my body closer to him and braced myself for what could only be bad news.

"What have they decided?" Aidan asked again, this time his voice hard, expectant.

Jeremiah looked down at his hands. "I think ya know what it is I'm goin' to tell ya."

"I'd still rather hear it for myself."

Jeremiah nodded. "We've been silent on this matter for far too long now, laddie. And after what ya told us about Selkie, the troubles you've been havin', we just couldn't go on ignorin' it."

"You'll have to be more specific, "Aidan said guarded. "What can't you ignore anymore, sir?"

"It's come to our attention that what Selkie can do, changin' the future and all of that, has never been recorded in our books. There's somethin' special goin' on with her…somethin' that could change everythin'…for all of us. We don't know what she's capable of, but we know she must be protected."

"And you think that I can't do that?"

"We know you can't, laddie," Jeremiah said, standing up. "Not when all ya're thinkin' about is her."

"But that doesn't make any sense," Aidan said, jumping out of his seat. "Selkie's my life. All I think about is keeping her safe."

"Don't try and fool me, boy," Jeremiah said, crossing his arms over his chest. "I was young and in love once too. I know ya can't think of just her safety all the time."

"So then what are you getting at exactly?" Aidan asked, his voice rising. "Are you saying you're not going to let me be Selkie's protector anymore?"

"But you can't do that," I squealed, tightening my hand around Aidan's arm. "I don't want anyone else but him."

"It doesn't matter what ya want, Lassie," Jeremiah shrugged. "Ya're not even supposed to know we exist, and ya certainly don't have any say in the matter. Aidan's the only one who has a choice."

"Wait! What do you mean I have a choice?"

"It's simple, really. The Council has agreed that ya're Selkie's rightful protector, and ya should be the one out there keepin' her safe against the Shadows."

"But..."

"But ya should know better than any of us, that a protector can't have any distractions. Ya're goin' to have to choose, laddie. Either ya take the path that's been planned for ya and protect Selkie from afar…or ya go with her now and be done with it."

"And what if I don't want to choose?" Aidan challenged. "What if I wanted to keep things the way they were?"

"Then ya'd be more foolish than I thought," Jeremiah said, shaking his head. "There's no goin' back now, Aidan. Ya've made ya choices, and now ya've got to live with them. So what will it be?" Jeremiah said, walking around the table and standing in front of us. "Who do ya choose?"

"It's not like that," Aidan said, looking down at me, his eyes tortured. "I can't…"

"Come now, Aidan. We've given ya plenty enough time to sort it out."

"Please," Aidan begged, turning to look at Jeremiah. "Don't make me do this."

The desperate and hopeless look on Aidan's face at that moment shattered my heart into a million pieces. Loosening my grip on his arm, I slowly stepped away from him, cringing slightly at the pain from the broken shards of my heart that now stabbed at my chest.

"You don't have to do this," I whispered, unable to raise my voice any louder.

"Selkie, what's the matter?" Aidan asked, immediately reaching out for me.

I stepped farther away from him.

"I can't let you do this," I said tearfully, backing away. "So you don't have to choose."

"Selkie, wait," Aidan said, grabbing my arm and pulling me to him.

I would have resisted...but I didn't want to.

Clinging to him with all my might, I released the flood of tears that had risen within me and sobbed uncontrollably into his chest.

"I can't let you throw your whole life away," I cried.

"Shh," he comforted, kissing my forehead. "You still don't get it. You're my entire life. I would never leave you."

"But your family, the clan, you can't just walk away."

"I was really hoping I wouldn't have to," he said, turning his head to glare at Jeremiah. "But do you think I could ever be happy here without you?"

He placed his hand beneath my chin, lifting my head up, and gazed lovingly into my eyes. "I love you, Selkie Reid...and I will always choose you. No matter what."

"Well ya've made ya're decision," Jeremiah said, walking toward us. "I hope ya don't live to regret it."

"Never," Aidan whispered with a smile.

"Alright then," Jeremiah huffed, extending his hand. "From now on ya live life like one of them," he said, gesturing to me. "Ya could no longer join us here at the Sanctuary, and ya must hand in your dagger immediately."

Aidan's body jerked at Jeremiah's request. "But without my dagger, how am I supposed to protect Selkie from the Shadows."

"I told ya, laddie. She is in great need of a protector who will commit themselves to her safety, and only that. She will be reassigned as soon as possible."

"But you said it yourself, I am her rightful protector."

"A true protector cares nothin' about himself, but only for his duty. Ya've made ya're choice, laddie," he said, extending his hand once again. "Now let's get on with it."

"Aidan don't..."

"No, it's alright, Selkie," Aidan said, un-strapping his sheath from his waist. "If this is what I have to do to keep you, then it's worth it," and then carefully handing the dagger to Jeremiah, he said, "I hope the Council realizes what they're doing."

Jeremiah smiled as he took the weapon and placed it under his arm. "We have always done what's best for the Lightscapers, laddie, and nothin' today has changed that. Now, ya best be off," he said hastily, pushing us in the direction of the door. "There's much to be done, and I don't want to keep the Council waitin'."

## Epilogue

**The sun was shining brightly the day we left.** I remember because as Aidan and I exited the dark interior of the Sanctuary and stepped out into the real world, the sun's iridescent beams struck our faces, instantly warming us.

"What a beautiful morning," I said, squeezing Aidan's hand. "I don't think I could have drawn a better one."

"You forget how talented you are," Aidan said kindly as we walked down the front steps of the church, but I could hear the distance in his voice.

I stopped walking.

"Aidan, are you sure you can do this?" I asked, turning to face him. "Are you sure this is what will make you happy?"

"That's kind of a ridiculous question," Aidan said with a smirk.

"Because we could still go back, you know. I'm pretty sure Jeremiah wouldn't mind."

"But I would mind," Aidan said, raising his hand up and resting it on the side of my face. "I would mind it very much."

"Please, don't do that," I said, removing his hand.

"Don't do what?"

"Don't pretend like everything is okay when it isn't. Like it's not tearing you up inside to have to leave this place."

Aidan sighed, releasing the tension he had thought he was hiding from me, and then glancing back at the church, he asked, "How did you know?"

"This is your home, Aidan."

"It was my home," he said, turning to look at me, "but it can't be that anymore."

"It can if you still want it to be," I said, hating myself for admitting it.

"But that's just it." He shook his head. "I don't want to be anywhere unless you can be there too."

"But it's not fair. I hate that you have to sacrifice everything for me, and I can't give you anything in return."

"You already give me everything I need, Selkie."

"For now," I shrugged.

"For always," he corrected, and then with a smile that made my heart stutter, he leaned down, wrapping his arms around me, and softly pressed his lips to mine.

I didn't know what the day would bring, or what future

plans the Shadows had for me, but at that moment, within Aidan's strong arms and surrounded by the sun's protective rays, I honestly didn't care.

"So where to now?" Aidan asked happily as we walked out of the churchyard and onto the street.

"I was thinking we could go home," I said, fighting back a yawn. "I hardly slept a wink last night, and I could definitely use a few more hours of sleep. Unless you had something else in mind, that is?"

"You're the only thing on my mind, as always," Aidan said, taking my hand and pulling me close. "And it just so happens that I enjoy watching you sleep just as much as I enjoy watching you when you're awake."

"And you're sure you won't be bored?"

"Nothing about my life with you is ever boring, Selkie," Aidan smiled. "Trust me."

"I always have…" I said, leaning in close to rest my head against my protector's chest, "…and I always will."

End of Book One

60289791R00225